GOOD
GUYS

MINDY
MISENER

GOOD GUYS

A NOVEL

MELVILLE HOUSE
BROOKLYN • LONDON

Good Guys

First Melville House Printing: August 2026
Distributed by Penguin Random House LLC, 1745 Broadway
New York, NY 10019 USA.
www.penguinrandomhouse.com

Melville House Publishing
46 John Street
Brooklyn, NY 11201
and
Melville House UK
Suite 2000
16/18 Woodford Road
London E7 0HA

mhpbooks.com
@melvillehouse

ISBN: 978-1-68589-265-4
ISBN: 978-1-68589-266-1(eBook)

Library of Congress Control Number: 2026939621

Designed by Beste M. Doğan

Printed in the United States of America
1st Printing

A catalog record for this book is available from the Library of Congress

For LFM

Let any one of you who is without sin
be the first to throw a stone at her.
John 8:7 (NIV)

PART ONE

CHAPTER ONE

JO

Three times in my life I've called my sister for help.

The first, I was at a motel almost an hour from Curtisville. Any closer, Gary said, and he might be recognized. Minutes earlier he'd left with his fake ID.

When Georgie heard my voice, she laughed. "Get a ride from your boyfriend," she said. There was a plasticky clatter as she hung up.

I had been here before, waiting for Gary to return with a grocery bag hanging from his fingertips and a smirk that left me sure there was some joke to all of this. He could have almost any girl he wanted, so why me? I asked once if it was because I was from the church where his dad was the pastor. He looked genuinely surprised. "You think I care what my parents want?"

I guessed I did. Gary lived like everything was either already funny or would be soon. But I had believed there was a sincere, vulnerable part of him somewhere beneath his swagger, his machine-gun laugh. I hadn't found it yet, though. I was starting to realize I never would.

Why, then, was I here? The last two times he'd checked us into this motel, I'd ignored the question until he came back, then drowned it in screwdrivers until I was indifferent to what happened next and incapable of remembering most of it anyway.

I turned on the TV, but the attempt to distract myself made me feel worse. I rechecked the curtains to make sure not even a sliver of the room would be visible from the outside. I felt both alone and watched. I was definitely starting to feel sick. If the world were good and fair, someone would come for me now. But I hadn't seen my mom since I was eight. Dad was in the hospital for another back surgery, and Georgie, apparently, hated me. Her reasons were obvious. I was absent right when Dad needed us, I was having sex with Gary, and I was too much like Mom, unsatisfied and ambitious and trying to escape.

The lock beeped and Gary came in. His keys crashed onto a side table, and he began emptying the bag. Vodka, orange juice, cups, chips, condoms. The orange juice was for me, because shots made me puke. The chips, presumably, were for him, later.

"Can you take me home?" I asked. "I don't feel good."

"You were fine ten minutes ago." He shrugged off his jacket, tossed it toward me. If he had been anyone else, I would see the fact that it landed on my head as a mistake. But he was too good a shot for that. He snickered while I snatched it off. "I already paid for the room," he added. Already he was mixing me a drink, then holding it out with a flourish.

I didn't take it. "I don't want to do this anymore," I said.

"It's a little late to start caring about purity."

"I don't care about that," I said, which was true in a way, even if I also felt a bodily regret I couldn't shake.

"What's the problem, then?" He wore a pale blue polo shirt. His short, light brown hair was spiked with gel. I used to find him so attractive it was hard to meet his eyes.

"I just think I should go home." I tried to sound bored, but my voice was tight with panic.

"Then call someone." He gestured at the phone. "I'm staying here."

There was no one I could call. I didn't have friends who were old enough to drive because I wasn't old enough to drive. Georgie, my only hope, had refused.

Even if I could find a ride, there would be the question of what I was doing at a motel an hour from Curtisville, with Gary's Grand Am parked conspicuously outside.

"Come on, Jo. Let's watch something and relax." He meant this as an opportunity. We could pretend the whole exchange didn't happen. We could pretend I wasn't trying to say no. "Come on," he repeated. "Sit down." He patted the bed next to him. I sat. "Drink," he said. I drank. "There you go," he said, like he knew I was catching on. And, finally, I was. Look at me, incapable of getting out of a situation I got into on purpose.

I CALLED GEORGIE FOR THE second time a little over two years later. Hours before, after Dad had gone to bed and my sister had parked herself in front of the TV to "do her homework," I headed for the back door. Our mastiff mix, Hulk, followed me, hoping for a walk. "Go away," I whispered. He turned back toward the living room, but only after a long searching look I tried to tell myself was his normal expression.

It was March. I took Georgie's coat, a huge canvas thing that had once belonged to Dad. It was so heavy I felt like I had a body slung over my shoulders.

I crossed Route 9, skirted a marsh, pushed into forest. Because I'd never worn Georgie's coat before, I'd never figured out that, on me, it was so loose that cold air poured into the collar and cuffs and hem. The busted zipper didn't help.

I had no plan. Maybe I'd stumble on a cabin with smoke

floating from a chimney. Maybe I'd get picked up by someone going to Boston or New York. Maybe I'd die of hypothermia. Maybe the search dogs would find me in a stiff curl at the base of a tree, wrapped in this jacket too big and too broken to save me.

I combed through this scenario, from the panicked search to the wrenching discovery, until the idea was no longer interesting. I didn't actually want to die. But now I was lost.

My sense of time eroded until I could no longer be sure it was passing. I crossed my arms to keep the front of the jacket closed. Each time my foot broke the surface of the stiff old snow, my arms flung out for balance, then folded back to my chest. I must have looked like a bird who kept changing her mind about flight. When a milkiness crept into the edges of my vision, I thought I might be losing it. But it was morning, or almost morning, and I was at an intersection I vaguely recognized. Across from me was a gas station. Its neon sign blinked the letters O P E N. I was so numb I might as well have been learning the word.

Bells on a strip of leather slapped the glass door as I entered. I asked the man behind the counter for a phone. My lips were distant, unresponsive. But he understood.

"Pay phone's outside," he said, nodding toward the door I'd just come through. I could barely see his eyes under the curlicued brim of his Red Sox hat. Still, it was obvious what he thought of my ugly jacket and slurred speech.

"I don't have any money," I managed. He sighed and heaved an old desk phone onto the counter. I picked up the receiver, grimed by a decade's worth of strange ears and mouths and hands. I couldn't call Dad, who'd be upset in a way that was worse than mad. Georgie had recently gotten a cell phone, though, which I considered a waste of money. Who needed to talk to Georgie so urgently they couldn't just call our landline?

Me, apparently. I'd even bothered to learn the number, which I now dialed.

"It's me," I told her.

"Where are you?"

"Cumberland Farms."

"Which one?"

"The one in Gray."

"There are two in Gray." Georgie had always been better at landmarks and directions than I was. I was good at reading a map, but she was good at knowing things without one.

"The one on 202," the man said. I didn't know he could hear her. I wanted to move away, but the phone's snarled cord was a short leash.

"Who's that?" Georgie asked.

"I borrowed his phone."

"What is going on?" I heard a rare note of anxiety in her voice. You could tell Georgie's whole life as a history of not getting worked up. Not about almost failing out of tenth grade, not about Dad's gigantic medical bills, not about Mom leaving us again. Georgie had barely lifted her face from her Game Boy when Mom bent to kiss her goodbye.

Now she asked, incredulously, "Are you drunk?"

"Come get me. Please." I was trying not to cry.

"Stay right there," she said, and hung up.

The man returned the phone to its hidden shelf. "You need anything? Coffee? A muffin?" His voice had softened a little.

"No thanks."

"It's on the house, hun." The way he said *hun* turned my insides. When he started around the counter, I headed for the door.

"Hold your horses," he said, lifting a paper cup from a stack and filling it with hot water from a red-handled spigot. "Water's free." He left the steaming cup in front of the coffee makers and retreated to his stool behind the register, like I was wild.

I sat on a stack of bundled firewood, drank so fast I seared my insides. The wall of refrigerators hummed to fill the silence. The man pretended to have forgotten about me, which I knew was the most decent thing he could think of to do. Eventually he said, "Your ride's here." Outside, Dad's Taurus was lurching to a stop. I hurried out without a thank-you.

As I dropped into the passenger seat, Georgie took me in from top to toes.

"So that's where my jacket went," she said. "I thought you hated it."

"I do hate it."

She gave a little snort, then paused long enough for me to think she was coming to the obvious conclusion, which was that I'd wanted something of hers to take with me. That I'd thought the jacket would protect me, or at least make me feel less alone.

But all she said was "I don't understand what's going on."

"I took a walk." The morning sky was the color of mop-bucket water. I sat back, closed my eyes as we bounced over potholes. It would be nice to keep going like this for a long time, I thought, long enough for Georgie to forget how I'd taken her ugly jacket and walked eight miles in the middle of the night. Or long enough for me to become someone who didn't do this sort of thing in the first place.

"Jo?"

"I got rejected," I told her.

"What? Where?"

"Everywhere." This wasn't entirely true, but it was true enough. As of the day before, four of the six schools I'd applied to had rejected me: Dartmouth, Wellesley, Georgetown, and Tufts. I had gotten into Southern Maine, but I didn't want to go to Southern Maine. I still hadn't heard from Peabody, but it was the most selective of all the schools I'd applied to. I didn't have a chance.

"Seriously?" For the second time that night, she sounded actually upset. Then she said, "I wonder if it has to do with Gary."

I stared at her. "You want to talk about Gary *now*?" The growing light had clarified her features: thick blond lashes, full cheeks, dimpled knob of a chin. My sister's basic physical appeal was always most obvious when I was mad at her.

For a while after I'd called from the motel, Georgie and I didn't talk about Gary. But then I started avoiding him, which meant I quit church for good, which meant Dad got upset, which meant Georgie got upset that I'd upset Dad, who was just home from the hospital again and not doing very well.

Georgie pulled into our driveway and turned off the engine. "I just wanted to see if you wanted to talk about it." Then, defensively: "I'm trying to do the right thing here."

"You called me a whore!"

"No," she said. "I called you a . . . never mind."

My eye roll was so big it took my head with it.

"It was a bad time, with how Dad was and everything. I didn't like what was going on with you and Gary."

She'd come home one afternoon when Gary and I were there.

Dad was at one of his thousand physical therapy appointments, or maybe getting another scan. Georgie was supposed to be at practice. She didn't care that she sat the bench. Her relationship with basketball looked a lot like her relationship with church: She was somehow very committed while never expecting more than the minimum from herself. Anyway, she'd forgotten her shoes, and drove home for them. I didn't know until Gary came back from the bathroom and said, "Uh, your sister's here." I heard the front door slam. In the silence that followed I wanted to laugh, which made me realize I was actually kind of scared.

Gary started taking me to the motel after that.

"What are you trying to say?" I asked Georgie.

"Just that—that night you called me—I wasn't thinking, and I—"

"Whatever. It doesn't matter."

"Okay." I wasn't sure she believed me. I wasn't sure if I wanted her to.

I had worried at first that Georgie would tell. She was a good Christian girl. She volunteered for the church nursery and brought the old folks' cars around on icy days. She was friendly with guys, including Gary, but not *too* friendly. She attended the Bible study that Gary's younger sister, Tara, had started at our high school.

But a week passed, then another. And I remembered how, of all the instructions in the Bible, *do not judge* seemed the most important to her. Not, it seemed, because of what Jesus said about the measure you use being the one used against you, but because Georgie didn't like to have to make a final decision on anything. "What do I know?" she would ask, about things she should definitely know about.

I said, "All I care about now is getting into college, and getting away from *this*." I gestured at the car, the house with its broken porch and sagging gutters, the matted snow of our lawn, dotted with dark knots of dog droppings.

Georgie was included in my gesture. She had to know that.

"I'm going to make it up to you," Georgie said, in her stout way that promised failure. I snorted to remind both of us that I was the only one good for my promises. I was the one who planned and executed. You didn't need to know us for ten minutes before you understood: I was going to make something of myself, and Georgie was not.

But still, Georgie had something I didn't, something I had long struggled to name. Maybe it was confidence. Not in herself, exactly, but in her life.

"Jo?"

I thought of the time I had a splinter buried in my palm. Dad broke off the only available edge when he tried to get it out, and I couldn't dig into my own skin without feeling woozy. Georgie came along with tweezers and a damp cloth. "Don't close your eyes," she told me. "You have to expect the feeling. But squint so you don't see too much." Her grip was too strong to yank away from, her hands warm and firm. Somehow it was comforting to know I couldn't escape her even if I wanted to. I was still bracing for the pain when she exclaimed "Got it!" and dropped my hand.

What did I need from her now? *Don't let go*, I thought, but it was a wish too private to say. Besides, all she offered was help. Help was temporary. Holding on was forever.

"Jo?"

"Stop saying my name," I said.

"I'll figure something out."

"If you say so," I said.

Inside, I took the hottest shower I could stand, dressed in the thickest sweats I owned, and climbed into bed with a hot-water bottle. Georgie and I shared a wall thin enough for me to hear her sigh, betraying a weariness I didn't usually associate with her. The sound made me realize she really did want to help. And maybe she could. I could ask her to change her mind about college. Maybe we could start together at Southern Maine. We could room together. I could help her with her classes and we could take turns doing laundry. Sure, we would drive each other nuts sometimes, but we would make it work.

I promised myself I would talk to her in the morning.

THE THIRD TIME I CALLED—that's a longer story.

CHAPTER TWO

GEORGIE

It's not fair what happened to Jo, not fair that she's got a record now—not the criminal kind, but the internet kind, which in some ways is worse. None of the articles mention me, and they should, though Jo wouldn't want me to say that. She wants to think she had a clear good choice and a clear bad one, and made the bad one. I don't think it was so straightforward, but, as Jo would say, of course I would say that.

I still find myself going over the whole thing, as if I could figure out exactly how much I'm responsible for. Does it count for anything that I was usually trying to do the right thing? And how far back would I have to go to understand it all anyway? Maybe I would need to start with that forty-pound box of napkins falling off a shelf at the mill warehouse. Or before that, with Mom drifting away from us but pretending she wasn't. Or twelve years before that, the day Dad got sized up by his high school track coach and sent straight over to the shot put. A volunteer assistant coach named Mark Clemmens—who was also a seminary student—was waiting for the throwers to assemble. Somewhere nearby, a short, bony miler named Dawn Wallerford—my mother—was doing laps.

But some stories are too long, or too full of gaps, to tell. So I probably have to start more recently, with what I remember clearly. Like how, a little over a year ago, I learned that Gary Clemmens was dead.

• • •

I HAD BEEN WORKING AT Pine Creek Senior Living Center for a month. The decor was fusty and the whole place smelled like a combination of antiseptic, roast beef, and air freshener. Less obvious was the smell of bodies, but it was there, damp and human like laundry forgotten in the washer. But I liked the job. I hadn't felt this useful for years.

I was going to fetch Nancy for dinner. She was new, so one of the intake staff had put a sign on her door: HELLO MY NAMES NANCY. The missing apostrophe made me think of Jo, who was starting her junior year at Peabody College. The last time I'd seen her, she mentioned wanting to start a blog where she posted examples of bad grammar. To show my support I emailed her to report the sign taped to the window of Betty's Variety, where she used to work—COME GET YOU'RE PIZZA!!!

Ugh wow, she wrote back, but she didn't mention the blog. She didn't come home for the summer, either. I knew she was relieved to be away from me and Dad and our crummy house and our same old problems, but her absence still stung. Her first year at college, she'd invited me to visit a few times, but I knew I'd only embarrass her in front of all her smart new friends, so I didn't go, and then she stopped bringing it up.

"Sounds like a dead-end job to me," Jo had said when I told her about my new position at Pine Creek. We talked about once a week. I knew she was mostly calling to keep tabs on me and Dad. She wanted to make sure we weren't screwing anything up faster than she could fix it.

Jo still refused to get a cell phone—which, if you asked me, was overly frugal for someone with a full ride to a fancy college—so if I wanted to talk to her I had to call her dorm. I always hoped she wasn't there, so I could imagine her having lunch on a lawn, or laughing with a study group. But most of the time she picked up, leaving me with the knowledge that she was alone in her room again.

I wanted my sister to take my new job seriously. I was good at it—getting bodies into and out of wheelchairs, wiping, washing, raising my voice to be heard. Rita told me once that I had the gift of tenderness. Rita was my boss. I was sort of scared of her and sort of wanted to be her friend. "I'm just trying not to hurt anybody," I said. "That's more than most people can say," she replied. Then she said, "Oh, you're not *that* great."

To Jo, I said, "Obviously it's a dead-end job."

"Hilarious," she said. Then: "Wait a minute. What about your classes?"

I had so far avoided mentioning the fact that I'd dropped out of my community college classes for the semester, just in time for a refund. She groaned. Jo wanted me to go to nursing school like I'd always talked about, but I was starting to understand that I had only talked about it because Jo thought I should have a plan.

"I thought you'd be happy for me," I said, because Jo hadn't thought much of my previous job, taking orders at the Yarmouth Dunkin' Donuts.

"I'll try," she said.

"What's up with you?" I asked. Jo tended to find herself a more uplifting topic than me. "How's that writing class?" There was a big-name writer at Peabody that semester. Something like a hundred students had tried to get into his class, but he took only twenty. Jo had been chosen, of course.

"Investigative journalism," Jo corrected. Then she said, "It's fine."

"You'd be a great journalist."

She laughed, sounding half annoyed and half pleased. "You say that about everything I try."

Did I? But this felt true. Jo was smart and persistent. Sure, she could be high-strung, but she also had a spine of steel. And she was a really good writer.

"Honestly," she admitted, "I'd love to do that sort of thing for a living."

"Do it!" I exclaimed, but she sighed. "What?" I asked.

"It's not that easy," she said.

It seemed to me like the more time she spent at that elite college, the less sure she was of herself. Obviously there was no point in saying so.

When the old people at Pine Creek asked about my family, I always talked about Jo. She was the only one whose story didn't get me a pitying look. She was sixteen months younger, I'd say, but she was born older. This always got a laugh. I'd talk about how she skipped a couple grades, how we graduated high school together, how now she had a scholarship to a top college in Massachusetts—Peabody, yeah, all girls. If the person I was talking to hadn't nodded off yet, I'd start in on differences—she was little, I was big; she had gold-brown eyes and dark, fine hair, and I had blue eyes and *this* mess. Often I'd get interrupted at this point—*You have great hair!* This was true. I had a lot of it, at least. It was thick and wavy and streaked with blond. I kept it long even though it made my neck ache and took twelve hours to air-dry.

One resident, Paul, said, "I bet some young man is going to appreciate that hair very much." I felt myself flush, and he chuckled.

"Or maybe he already does?"

"No comment," I said. "Isn't it time for bridge club?"

NANCY'S DOOR WAS CRACKED a few inches. I knocked, called, "Hello, Nancy?" and waited. Most of the staff swooped right in, businesslike in a way that said there was nothing to be ashamed of. Rita called me Miss Manners for waiting, but I wasn't trying to be polite. I only wanted to avoid walking in on anything I didn't know how to handle. I had enough experience in that department already.

"Nancy? Dinnertime." I nudged the door, which swung silently open. Nancy was sitting up in bed, fully dressed and fully asleep. A copy of the *Portland Press Herald* was at her side. As I approached the bed, my gaze landed on a front-page headline: *Curtisville Man Dies in Iraq*. Beneath that was a picture of Gary.

My hand was over my mouth, but I didn't remember putting it there. I leaned closer to read.

> On Tuesday, Garrett Clemmens of Curtisville was killed outside of Baghdad when a roadside bomb struck his armored vehicle. Three other Americans were wounded in the attack.
>
> Specialist Clemmens—or Gary, as he was commonly known—was a familiar figure in Curtisville, where he excelled in high school athletics. An All-State basketball player for three years, Clemmens led Curtisville to the Class B State Championship game in 2003, when he scored a championship game record of 32 points despite spraining an ankle in the second half, and in 2004, when he broke his own record, scored 32 points, and made the

> Curtisville Cougars basketball team state champions for the first time in school history. He went on to play for the University of Maine–Orono, where he averaged 9 points per game over two seasons before enlisting in the Army. His father, Mark Clemmens, is the pastor at Word of Life church in—

"Isn't that a tragedy?" Nancy asked. Then she said, "I didn't mean to scare you."

"Yes—no—sorry." I tapped the picture. "I knew him." Each of my heartbeats was chased by a ringing emptiness. *Oh God*, I thought, but it didn't feel like a prayer.

"Honey." Nancy sounded distraught. Being at Pine Creek had taught me that there were two types of old people—the ones who were sorry about every unfortunate thing that found you and the ones who thought it was best you got used to having your back against a wall. Nancy was the nicer type.

"We grew up in the same church," I said. "His dad's the pastor. Word of Life, in Curtisville." I was saying things that were right there in the article. But I wanted to prove to Nancy how much this mattered, even though I couldn't tell her the real reasons why. "I know his sister," I concluded. When did Tara learn? Why hadn't she called?

"Honey," Nancy said again, with even more feeling this time. She paused, searching for inspiration on what to do or say next. Then she started gathering up the newspaper. "Here. Take this." She was flapping it at me so desperately I obeyed, tucking the folded paper under my arm before I helped her into her wheelchair. As we glided out the door and down the wide hallway, Nancy told me about guys she'd known who died in "the war"—I wasn't sure which one—a classmate, her cousin's fiancé, a boy who took her to a movie. I steered the wheelchair around the nose of a vacuum, then around good old Marlene, who at ninety-four years old insisted on using her walker to get herself to dinner three inches at a time. Did age grind down every tragedy to a story so short you could tell it on the trip between a mechanized bed and a plate of diced steak? If so, was that good or bad?

Nancy was patting my hand. "Georgie. Stop."

I stopped. Rita was approaching.

"Georgie got terrible news," Nancy told her. "Her friend died in Iraq."

"Not really my—" I started, at the same moment that Rita said, "Is that so?"

Rita had a pixie cut and chandelier earrings that swayed while she stared at me. No one messed with her. Just the week before, she'd told Edward's son he was being selfish for promising his father he'd bring him home. Then, softening, she told him she knew it was hard, and patted his back while he sobbed into his hands. I wanted to be like her—so sure of how she responded to a situation that it was bound to turn out right.

"Show her the article," Nancy ordered me.

I held out the paper. Rita looked without touching, like she was at a museum. She asked, "Do you need to go home?"

"I'm fine," I said.

"If you need to leave, you should leave." She nudged me aside. "I'll take it from here," she said. Over her shoulder she added, "I'm sorry about your friend." At least I thought those were her words, because she was walking away from me, and the vacuum was coming closer.

• • •

FOR A WHILE I SAT in the Taurus with the door open and one foot on the patched-up asphalt. In front of me was a maple whose yellow leaves glowed in the sunlight. The bright weather felt tacky, like a floral dress at a funeral. Somehow I knew it wasn't a boom, not if you were right close to it. I imagined it more like a snap, a ripping of air, and that was the last you knew of it, if you were lucky. And if you weren't lucky—oh, God. Oh, Jesus.

They still weren't prayers.

I tried Tara's cell, hung up when I got her voicemail. She was probably with her parents, but even with this news I couldn't bring myself to call them. They knew about Tara but not about *us*, and it remained my position that we should keep things quiet a little while longer. "It's only been a few months," I told her, whenever she asked how much longer I was going to say *a little while longer.*

"You don't believe this is wrong, do you?" Tara had asked me, a note of challenge in her voice. "Of course not," I said. When we first got together, I'd wondered if some feeling of shame or guilt would creep in, but it never did.

So it wasn't dating a girl that gave me pause, it was the girl I was dating. Most of the time, there was no problem. But periodically she would ask me a question like, "What do you think you really owe another human being?" or "Do you think *all* suffering can lead someone closer to God?" Partly it was her asking *me* these questions that was ridiculous, but partly it was that she gave voice to them at all. Her questions were unanswerable, so what was the point in asking them?

The last time I'd seen her, I'd found her going through things her parents had asked her to pick up from their house. Among them was an old journal. At first we'd laughed at her preoccupations with her grades and her carefully printed prayers for her future husband, but then she came across an entry in which she'd written, *The absolute love of Jesus is all I want to know and share in this life.* At this she went silent, clamped her lips between her teeth. Her chin wrinkled as she fought tears. After she won the struggle, she looked at me. "I don't know how to graft that kind of faith onto my life now."

I patted her awkwardly. "You're doing great."

"Am I?" She started gathering the items spread around us—cross-country trophies, projects in three-ring binders, a couple Beanie Babies—and returned them to the plastic box along with the journal. "I know you don't like to talk about this stuff," she said, pushing on the lid until it snapped into place.

"It's fine," I said, and we both pretended to believe me.

We didn't talk for a few days after that, and then she'd called to see if I wanted to visit that weekend. I said okay, but in a way that made her ask, "Are you sure that works for you?"

"I think so," I said.

She was silent.

"Really," I said. I added, weakly, "Rita might need a shift covered."

Tara said, a little icily, "Then why don't you let me know what works for you."

Now it was Thursday, and I was calling only because her brother died. I was surprised she hadn't called me herself with the news, but I couldn't blame her, either.

I'd promised myself I would never do this again—bail on someone exactly when they needed me. But it seemed like I already had.

JO

CHAPTER THREE

It started with an email from my sister. I'd spent the whole evening at my desk, working on a PoliSci paper on destabilization in Latin America. Now I felt like a toothpick had been hammered into my neck. Also, I had to pee. Girls from my hall were in the common room watching that night's episode of *America's Next Top Model.* One of them lifted her chin at me as I went by. I'd been invited to watch with them. But I no longer thought that a few communal hangouts at the beginning of the school year would make us all great friends. I didn't have time for great friends anyway. I lifted my chin back without breaking stride.

A cardstock sign taped to the bathroom door had an arrow that could be turned to point to one of four quadrants: SHOWERING, HAIR/MAKEUP, PEEING, POOP ALERT. The arrow had been on POOP ALERT since the first week of classes. I didn't like going in with that sign on the door, but if I changed it people would know it was bothering me. In college certain things weren't supposed to bother you, like poop jokes and a lack of parallel structure on a handmade bathroom sign.

Back at my desk, I remembered that Georgie had emailed me a few hours ago, subject line empty. My sister was an unpredictable emailer. I'd get nothing for a week or two, then a string of jokey messages that read like tone in search of content. The body of this email said only *maybe you already saw this on facebook, but if not then fyi.* She'd pasted a long, blue hyperlink to the *Portland Press Herald.*

I hadn't seen "this" on Facebook. I used to log on daily to study my classmates' clothing and party habits with clinical curiosity, but it was depressing to realize that I knew the names of dozens of girls who had no idea who I was. I didn't use it much anymore, which made me more productive, if not actually happier.

I clicked the link and waited for the page to load. Twenty seconds later, I was still waiting. It was possible my laptop had frozen again. I bought it before my sophomore year of college. I'd spent the summer at home, working at Betty's. My earnings were supposed to go toward tuition, but I couldn't resist buying myself this one thing. It was the cheapest model at Best Buy *and* it was on sale.

Dad and Georgie went around saying I had a full ride. I couldn't bear to correct them even though my scholarship covered only about a quarter of my costs. I'd applied for the Presidential Scholarship, which covered everything, but I'd been awarded the Maud T. Browning Scholarship, which covered a lot less and came with a required tea hour with Maud's aging son, Edgar, twice a year.

Honestly, though, I would've enrolled without a scholarship, maybe even if they'd charged me double. Peabody College! People I'd heard of had gone here, even if two of them were the wives of presidents. There was a January term where you did an independent project in a small group or one-on-one with a professor. There was an alumni club somewhere in New York City. The money would have to sort itself out.

And it did, a little bit. I got a Pell and another small grant. I got a subsidized loan and some award money from my high school. I got a campus job. Still, I was on track to owe seventy-eight thousand dollars when I left Peabody with a BA in Comparative Studies. Though I could parrot a definition of Comparative Studies, I still didn't get what it was. It was my major because I hadn't been able to commit to anything else. English had too many novels. Political Science had too much politics. History had too many primary sources. And so on.

I didn't exactly regret coming to Peabody. It was just a lot of money to owe for a major so broad it was kind of about nothing. I told myself it could be worse. In one of the FAFSA information sessions I'd attended in high school, a guy asked, "Eighty-four thousand dollars, a hundred and three, what's the difference?" When I told him the difference was nineteen thousand dollars, he said, "That's literally not what I'm saying." But it *literally* was.

Each time I had tea with Edgar, he quizzed me on my major and career interests. "Wonderful, *wonderful*!" he exclaimed each time I admitted I wanted to be a writer. Then he'd ask, "And have you considered teaching?" I didn't want to grade papers for the next five decades. To satisfy him, I would say, "A little." It was the same conversation every year. Whenever I reminded him that I was from Maine, he described the gables on his house in Bar Harbor. "It's a wonderful state, *wonderful*," he'd say. "What a lucky place for you to grow up."

But people who loved Maine that much were first of all rich and, second, didn't actually live in Maine, not year-round. I thought Maine was fine, but not that great. Most of its famous coast made me feel like I'd hit the ragged edge of a torn page. There should be more here, I'd think, but there wasn't, just sun-shriveled seaweed clotting fractured boulders. The Atlantic was blackish on cloudy days and murky green on bright ones. Winter was slick with snow, spring was slick with mud, and summer was slick with humidity.

Fall was nice, though.

I lifted my laptop to cool my thighs. I didn't have a computer my first year at Peabody because, as brochures and tour guides and admissions officers all assured me, I didn't need one. Besides the library computers, I'd have access to the lab in Jarrett, which was open twenty-four hours a day. Freshman year I practically lived in Jarrett's windowless lab, where I sat on an expensive office chair whose armrests had ten settings, none of which I found comfortable. Jarrett was stifling when it was cold out and freezing when it was hot. The lab had a strict no-food policy, but drinks in covered containers were allowed, so I sipped chocolate milk spiked with instant coffee to keep me going on long days. Meanwhile, everywhere else on campus, girls were peeling open sleek laptops, using squares of satin to wipe invisible dust off glossy screens.

I didn't actually think my low-end laptop would put me on equal footing with my classmates. Within hours of arriving on campus, I realized that most of my Peabody "peers" weren't peers at all, and not only because I was sixteen for the first full month of college. These girls took summer trips to Europe, had endless conversations about who'd gone to which prep school. When I looked up some of those schools, I realized how many of them had basically gone to college already. Their high schools had gorgeously landscaped campuses, glassy labs and fitness centers, teachers with PhDs. No wonder these girls applied terms like *dialectic* and *teleology* as confidently as the tinted glosses they smoothed onto their lips.

I knew more or less what those words meant, but I couldn't bring myself to use them for the same reason I didn't wear tinted gloss. I was sure the shade would be wrong in a way that was obvious to everyone but me.

At first I'd hoped four years would be enough time to gain the self-confidence of a true Peabody Pea. But as I passed the halfway mark to graduation, I had to admit that I wasn't changing fast enough. Now, as my junior year began, I was realizing that upon my graduation I was still going to be me, just with a degree and a pile of debt.

Anyway, my laptop worked well for about four months. Now, besides getting hot enough to fry an egg, it had two keys coming loose and a battery that drained so fast I could practically hear the trickle. The week before, it had died during my fifty-minute Jane Austen lecture. After class, when I went to my famous journalist professor's office hours, he had to move three stacks of books and a chair so I could access an outlet. Then we had to wait awkwardly for the machine to juice up, during which time the professor, who insisted we call him Seamus, asked me twice what my major was.

THE PAGE FINALLY LOADED. My eyes fell on the headline, then the picture of Gary. I startled like an animal. Now I was on my feet without knowing where I might go. On the wall in front of me was a framed poster print of a Winslow Homer seascape I got at a tag sale my first semester at Peabody. I liked Frida Kahlo's strange and bloody double self-portrait best, but I didn't know if I could stand to look at it for the next four years. And what if Georgie saw it? Would she get that, when I looked at it, I thought about us?

The seascape was covered in a sheet of cheap plastic that reflected a fun-house version of myself. My neck was too long, my head too big. I looked too alone. And all Georgie had to offer was *fyi*. *Fyi* would be appropriate if I had planned a picnic and Georgie saw rain in the forecast. *Fyi* suggested I knew what to do with this information.

Why did it seem that Georgie knew what to do with this information but wasn't telling? She had always taken things in stride. Like the second time Mom left us. We were still living in Michigan, though Dad was starting to talk about following Pastor Mark, who'd moved to Maine that year. It had been a weird few months. We were in the middle of the country, halfway between Mom and Mark. Dad's parents lived nearby, but they'd never forgiven Dad for marrying Mom and giving up his athletic scholarship to Ohio State, so we barely saw them. Mom's first trip to LA was supposed to be a few weeks. Then she extended it to a few months. She'd phone us once or twice a week. She tended to forget about the time difference, though, and would call after our bedtime. Then she would remember about the time difference and say she couldn't talk long because we needed to sleep.

Mom had moved to LA to "explore" her writing. Dad said she needed to get it out of her system. I knew they were saying almost the same thing, but with important differences.

When Mom came back to Michigan, it was, supposedly, to stay. And for a while it seemed she would. She took me and Georgie for ice creams, signed our permission slips, made rice pilaf from a box, stir-fried chicken strips with salt and pepper.

But then, a few days after Christmas, Mom announced that she needed to go back to follow up on some contacts. She said she'd be gone a week, maybe two. As she packed, I followed her from room to room, but nimbly, because she hated it when I got underfoot. I thought I was playing it cool. Watching her refill a travel-size bottle of lotion, though, I started to lose it. I fought the feeling, knowing how Mom hated displays of emotion. I went to look for Georgie, found her in our shared room. She was sitting in bed with her Game Boy, an empty Freezer Pop sleeve hanging from her mouth like a wilted party favor.

"Georgie," I said.

"One more level," she mumbled.

You could tell Georgie the world was ending and she'd say *one more level.*

Moments later, the game emitted a sad little song. Georgie gave a resigned sigh, then looked at me. "What's up?"

"I don't want her to leave again," I managed.

Georgie scooted over, patted her unmade bed. We sat there for a minute, shoulders touching. She knocked my knee lightly with hers. I knocked hers back with mine. This had become our way of saying hi without saying anything. Just sitting next to her, I absorbed a bit of her calm.

"It sucks," she concluded, as if we'd had a conversation.

"Yeah," I said.

"I guess I think . . ." she started. She looked into the middle distance of our small room, shook her head. "Never mind. I don't know."

I thought about pressing her, but I knew it wouldn't do any good. As I leaned against her, watching her avatar leap to collect coins, I told myself she would be enough for me.

• • •

FOR A LONG TIME I didn't sleep; then I was waking up. Sunlight punctured the tree branches outside my dorm room window. When I remembered the news, time tightened around me, like Gary was about to knock on the door.

But he wasn't here. He wasn't anywhere.

Part of me had spent the last few years hoping I would never see or talk to him again. But another part of me had been working up to some sort of encounter. Not a confrontation, exactly, but a chance for me to show him that I was fine, better than fine, that I was *great*. I wanted to simultaneously impress and ignore him. I wanted to be so upbeat about my bright future, and so politely interested in his dull one, that he couldn't help feeling small and irrelevant.

I dumped a packet of instant oatmeal into a bowl, shook powdered coffee into a mug, started my electric kettle. The kettle I kept on my desk, but the rest of the food stash was under the bed. A printed tablecloth hung over my discount pantry. I didn't want anyone to know that I ate sixteen meals a week at this desk. That I was on the five-meals-a-week plan not because I could comfortably afford those meals but because I craved complicated dishes someone else prepared. And because I was tired of eating alone.

I had two new emails: the college's morning newsletter (*Good Morning, Peas! 9/27/2007 Events & More!*) and a message from Seamus (*reading for today*). The next one down was Georgie's. I hadn't replied yet. I had nothing to say.

Seamus's email, sent to the whole class, said, *change of plans—read the NYer ice cream truck mafia piece instead of the McPhee. thanks, s.*

This was the second time Seamus had made a last-minute

change to the reading. He himself had told us he'd never taught a college class before. But we all knew of his bestselling book, *Jericho*, about a megachurch pastor who'd embezzled church funds while carrying on three affairs at once. I wanted to read it, but it was on hold at the Peabody library until April.

Seamus's disorganization could be annoying, but today I didn't mind. Having an urgent task helped pull my thoughts away from Gary. It helped that the ice cream truck mafia piece was good.

So far, students mostly liked Seamus. He had messy brown hair, dark eyes, and a wiry build. He mentioned his famous writer friends by first name only ("Dave" and "Jon" and "the other Dave") but still managed to be irreverent about his own success. He assigned interesting readings and was convincing when he lectured on the structure or approach of a piece of writing, even if he tended to treat his interpretation of an essay as the only objectively true one.

Despite his popularity, though, the mood in the room was stiff when he set his coffee and notebook on the table in front. "I hope you all got my email," he said.

Lily Neils, whose unofficially assigned seat was in front of mine, and whose hair fell in a dark gleaming sheet down her back, raised a six-dollar gel pen.

"Seamus?" she asked, because he was staring into his notebook.

He looked up. "Yeah."

"So, a lot of us didn't have a chance to do the reading?"

"You didn't do the reading?"

"The schedule was changed pretty last minute?"

Seamus tipped his head. He looked like a cat deciding whether to toy or pounce. "I sent that message before I went to bed."

"You sent it at eleven." Lily's tone was flat now.

"And now it's nine-thirty. You had over ten hours."

The room had frozen.

"No offense," Lily said, "but I was asleep when you sent it, and I have class all morning."

Seamus smiled. "I assure you that your sleep habits do not offend me." Then, "So your schedule is totally packed between, say, seven a.m. and this moment? Not even a spare half hour in there somewhere to skim the article? What about over breakfast? Or did you choose to linger over oatmeal with some friends? Maybe in Sayles Hall, by the big windows."

Lily didn't have a response to this.

"It's not a fair question," he told us, "because I did see Lily there, with two other people from this class. To be clear, I'm not upset with Lily for pressing me about the reading. I know she's not the only one who feels this way. So thank you, Lily, for speaking for the class." He gave her a nod that suggested a bow, then asked, "Did *anyone* here read the essay?" He looked around. "One person," he said, "but she doesn't want to draw attention to herself, so I won't do that either." My heart seized. Had he seen the finger I lifted a few inches off the table? Had he *not* seen it? I didn't know which was worse.

"Class dismissed," he said.

"Seriously?" Lily blurted.

No one was moving. Seamus inhaled, held the breath. Whatever he was about to say was clearly what he'd wanted to tell us all along. "If you want to be a journalist," he said, "you have to know the job will make demands—unreasonable ones. One last-minute call or one tricky source or one opportunity will scramble everything on your to-do list for the day. And then you'll have to ask yourself, *Where's my commitment? Is it to getting a cavity filled or telling a story the world needs to hear?*" He picked up his coffee and notebook. "I'll be in my office. I invite the person who did the reading to come by this afternoon. The rest of you, see you Monday."

As soon as he was gone, the room filled with shocked murmurs. One girl said to another, "If my mom finds out about this, she will call the dean."

I couldn't be seen going to his office, not right away. It wasn't like I had real friends at Peabody, but I didn't want anyone to hate me, either. I ate lunch in my room, reported for my shift at the library circulation desk at one-thirty. The person who was supposed to come in after me called in sick, so I offered to cover. I wasn't supposed to work more than ten hours a week, but I'd figured out that no one was keeping track, so I took as many extra shifts as I could. The job was slow and easy. Most of the time, it was like being paid to do homework anyway.

Today, though, I could bring myself to study for only minutes at a time. I kept scouring the internet for articles about Gary. I refreshed his Facebook page, watching the condolences roll in. *RIP*, wrote classmates and basketball players. His coach wrote a paragraph that read like an audition to speak at his funeral. People from church wrote prayers: *Dear Jesus, thank you for the life of this heroic young man. Take care of him in heaven and be with his family now.*

I kept closing the browser, promising myself I was done. Then I would look again.

I could email Seamus with an excuse, but he had an unnerving habit of responding to emails right away, and I didn't want to get sucked into a back-and-forth. So after I got off work I wrote a note explaining that I'd been busy and would come by another time. I was wedging the folded sheet of paper under his office door when I wondered if he'd think I lied about having done the reading. I decided to add some thoughts on the article. But the paper stuck when I tried to pull it out again. I yanked and something, someone, yanked back. I was getting to my feet when Seamus opened the door. He wore an unzipped, nubby old fleece over the same wrinkled button-up he'd been wearing in class.

"Nice to see you, Josephina," he said, then stood back to make room for me. "Come on in."

"You can call me Jo," I reminded him.

"Right. You have quite a name, don't you?" He consulted his roster. "Josephina Amelia Madeline Prescott."

"Lots of people have long names," I said.

He shrugged, like the question still stood.

"My mom named us," I said, to fill the silence. "Both my sister and me." He smiled, and I blurted an irritated "What?"

"I thought you were going to say 'and I.'"

"*I* was not a subject in that sentence."

"I know." Another smile.

"So do I." I couldn't believe I was talking to him this way, but I was annoyed, and also maybe emboldened by how Lily talked to him earlier. Plus, my thoughts kept getting dragged back to Gary, to the explosion still echoing in my brain.

"What's your sister's name?"

"Why do you ask?"

"Just wondering." That shrug again. I figured this was his snoopy journalist side at work, but I couldn't help wanting to tell him.

"Georgiana Eleanor Harriet Prescott. She goes by Georgie."

"Georgie and Jo," he said.

"Our Dad gave us those nicknames. Mom hated them."

"Why?"

"I don't know," I said, though I did. Georgie and I weren't supposed to be like other people. Our names were a sign of Mom's conviction that we were special. The fact that I'd believed Mom accounted for why I was standing right here.

"Well, I think 'Jo' is nice. It's easy, at least. Try having people call you *See*-mus."

I laughed, even though, when I first saw it in print, that's how I thought it was pronounced, too.

"Did your mom get over the nicknames?" he asked.

"I don't know. I don't see her anymore." He raised his eyebrows, so I said, "She moved to LA to write for television."

"How'd that work out?"

"Did you ever see the show *Good Guys*?" I asked.

He frowned. "No, but I'm not a TV person."

"It got canceled anyway. Its first episode aired the week after 9/11."

He puffed out his cheeks. "Tough break."

"Yeah, it was too bad." The truth was I didn't know how I felt about the show. On one hand I didn't want Mom to succeed without us, and on the other I didn't want her to be a failure. The results, which hung somewhere in between, satisfied neither of my preferences. I watched the show when it aired. I remembered thinking it was okay, at least, but that they were too aggressive with the laugh tracks. At the end, Mom's name appeared briefly. A few weeks later, the show disappeared. As far as I knew, she hadn't done any more work in Hollywood. Her IMDb page had only the *Good Guys* credit. I still checked once in a while.

"And now you want to be a writer, too," he said. Then, "That's what you wrote in your application for this class."

The course had been wildly overenrolled, so everyone had to write a letter saying why we should be let in.

"It would be nice," I said. "But nobody makes a living as a writer."

"Your mom did."

"Not for long," I said.

"Oh. Well, I do."

"*Almost* nobody, then."

Instead of responding, he leaned back in his chair, dropping his head into the cradle of his interlaced fingers. His elbows stuck out like giant ears. "So what do you want to talk about?" he asked.

"I thought you wanted to talk about the reading," I said.

"What do you want to say about it?"

"I barely had time to do it."

"You mean your reading quality was poor?"

"No. You can ask me anything about it," I said. I thought of my PoliSci paper on destabilization. This was what talking with Seamus felt like. He was putting his own interests in control of the conversation. I said, "I don't think it's fair to change the reading last minute."

"I'm just messing with them," he said.

I felt my expression go blank. Maybe someone's mom *should* report him to the dean.

"Not for no reason," he went on, impatiently. "I'm not doing it for fun. Your classmates are smart. But effective teaching requires disruption. Some students will respond well. Many won't, and that's okay with me. You can really only teach the students who are ready to learn." I made a noise between a snort and a cough, and he said, "No?"

"That's what I was taught in church. 'A soul has to be ready for God to accept God.'"

"They might not be wrong about that. So are you ready?"

"For God?" My voice was high and tight. "I don't—"

"No, Jo. To *learn*."

BACK IN MY DORM, I called Georgie. I'd wanted her to figure out that she owed me a lot more than an *fyi* email. I'd wanted an apology. That wasn't how Georgie worked, though. You kind of had to spell things out for her.

When she picked up, she was grim. "Hey," she said, and then, "Horrible, huh?" And I realized she had been waiting all along for my call.

"Yeah," I said. "It's crazy."

"Crazy," she repeated, then asked, "You doing okay?"

"I'm fine." Too late I saw that my instinctive answer made it hard for me to transition into what I'd meant to tell her, which was, *you can't just send me an email like that.* Then again, I didn't actually want to admit that I wasn't fine. Not even to Georgie.

She said, "You should see the front of the high school. There's a huge pile of stuffed animals and flowers."

"I didn't want him to die," I said.

"I didn't think you did," she said, quickly.

"But . . ." I said. I didn't usually think out loud. Speaking honestly without being sure what I would say made me shaky. "I figured I would encounter him again. I just thought I would be more in charge when I did."

I could feel Georgie turning this over in her slow way. She took her time with things she really wanted to understand. But I didn't want her to understand this anyway. Changing courses, I said, "The dining hall closes soon, so I have to go." Then, remembering myself, I asked, "Are *you* doing okay?"

"Oh. Yeah." She sounded a little distant, like maybe this wasn't the question that mattered. I guessed she was thinking about how Dad was doing with the news of Gary's death. I didn't have the energy to worry about that. I cared about Dad, but I tried to keep my worries big picture. Overall health. Overall financial outlook. The smaller stuff, like Dad's mood swings, his fretting over his faith and ours, and the state of the house were all things I was trying to let go of. The irony of being desperate for everyone around him to be saved was, as I saw it, that it kind of put him beyond saving.

"Call me if you need me," I concluded.

"You too," she said.

TEN MINUTES LATER I LOADED a plate with tortellini and roasted squash. I took a blondie from the dessert table, filled a soap-stained glass with chocolate milk. I was seriously behind on my homework now. I intended to sit down with *Northanger Abbey* and not stand up until I was done with the reading for the next day. I pinned the novel open beneath the edge of my tray and began: *No one who had ever seen Catherine Morland in her* *infancy would have supposed her born a heroine. Her situation in life, the character of her father and mother, her own person and disposition, were all equally against her—*

I was thinking I was going to like this novel when a voice cut in: "Can we sit here?"

Lily Neils stood over me, flanked by Morgan Metzger and Susan from my hall. Lily had broad, high cheeks and the kind of skin that made me wonder whether she had very good genes, very good makeup, or both. Morgan's fair skin was smattered with freckles and she had a frank stare. Susan had a long face, well-glossed lips, and gold studs in her ears. Her tote bag had a silk scarf tied to one of its leather handles.

"Sure." I slipped the book into the backpack at my feet, and the girls set down their trays. Morgan had pasta like I did. Lily and Susan had salads. Susan even had her own spray-on dressing, which she used to mist her vegetables. When she placed the bottle back on the tray, I saw that it advertised ten calories per serving.

I offered, as a nervous opener, "I thought it was pretty ridiculous that Seamus expected everyone to have done the reading."

"Seamus is—" Lily started, then finished the sentence with an exasperated sigh.

"I still think he's hot," Susan said, stabbing her greens.

Lily turned to me. "Did you end up going to his office?" Then: "We know you're the one who did the reading." She was smiling. The fact that I couldn't detect any resentment only made me more worried about how well she might be hiding it.

"I told him I thought it wasn't fair," I said.

"Thanks," said Lily. "Though I doubt it will do us much good."

Morgan studied me, then announced, "Well, *I* think Jo is hiding something."

For a disorienting moment I thought she knew about Gary. About how, even though he was dead, he kept blowing up in my mind.

"I-I—" I stammered. "What do you mean?"

"Three things," Morgan said, putting down her fork so she could assign her points to fingers. "First, I'm not interested in Seamus like that—"

"Because you're, like, gay?" Susan interjected.

I hoped no one could tell this was news to me. I knew a lot of my classmates were lesbians or bisexual, but I was still embarrassingly bad at knowing who was what without being told.

"—but I am curious about him," Morgan finished, ignoring Susan. "Second, he always calls on you in class."

"I do the reading," I said defensively. I was relieved, though, that we were talking about Seamus and not Gary.

"Finally," Morgan went on, pressing down a ring finger to make her third point, "he throws this whole weird fit today and cancels class so he can talk with you one-on-one. We just want to know what's going on."

"Easy, Morgan," said Lily. "This isn't an interrogation."

Morgan surprised me by laughing. "Sorry," she told me. "My parents are prosecutors." Then she said, "We're not mad about it. It's journalism class, you know? Like Seamus says, the story is usually right under your nose."

"Also," said Susan, "it's been way too long since we had a student-faculty romance."

"I'm seriously not—" I said.

"I'm *jealous*," Susan said, as if this clarification made it better.

"We are *not* suggesting that," said Lily, widening her eyes at Susan.

I wanted to make an excuse and leave, but the dining hall didn't allow anyone to carry food out, and this was one of my five square meals a week. I was sick of generic-brand cereal, bruised apples, and bargain bagels I had to chew fifty times a bite. Everyone else complained about the dining hall food, but I couldn't help looking forward to filling a tray with flavors and textures that were, to me, good.

My thoughts seemed to have drawn Susan's attention to my tray. "I mean this as a compliment, but how do you eat like that and stay so skinny?"

"Susan, that is so rude!" Lily exclaimed.

I didn't know what to say. I didn't want to admit anything about how I ate, how tightly it was connected to money, to the pantry hidden beneath my bed, the groceries I smuggled into my dorm in my backpack. I didn't want to tell them that I wasn't even hungry tonight, that my appetite had evaporated after I learned about Gary. I had bought this meal, though, so I intended to sit here until the food was gone.

"I think we have managed to offend the person we wanted to join for dinner," Lily announced. "Jo, I apologize. Do you want us to leave?"

"No," I said, which wasn't true.

"Why don't *you* ask *us* questions," Lily said. "You be in charge of conversation now."

I appreciated the offer. I had a hundred questions. How did airline miles work? When your uncle got you an internship in DC, what did you do there? What shade of lip gloss should I wear?

"Jo doesn't have questions," Morgan said. "She's got everything figured out."

"I don't," I protested. No matter how hard I worked, my Peabody grade average sat at a steady A minus. I didn't know what I was doing when I graduated. I didn't have an uncle with connections in DC. The impressive person I was supposed to turn into at Peabody had not materialized. Too late I was realizing that being *impressive* was not a real goal. You had to know what you were trying to do. And I still hadn't figured that out. It was clear, now, that I would graduate without distinction, then go face the world alone.

"Okay," Lily said gently, as if awarding me a point. Then she said, "The thing is, Jo, everyone kind of thinks you do."

GEORGIE

CHAPTER FOUR

The morning of Gary's memorial was so foggy I could taste water in the air. Dad and I meant to get to the high school early, but we got slowed down by lost keys and anxieties about what to wear. By the time we arrived, the high school was parked up. The side streets were lined with cars. Even the unofficial spots near the soccer field were taken. Finally I found an illegal space between dumpsters. It was going to be tight.

"I'll let you out," I said. A benefit of driving the old Taurus wagon was that I could exit, if awkwardly, through the hatchback. While I was easing the nose of the car into the spot, I looked at Dad in the rearview. He was frowning at the asphalt. He'd thought Jo would change her mind and come home. "She's really busy," I'd told him. "Not too busy for this," he'd said quietly. He rarely expressed disappointment in us, and I was left with a guilty twist in my gut.

Dad and I were glazed with mist by the time we got to the high school's double doors. There was going to be a small military funeral, family only, in two days. But Mark and Miriam wanted to do something more public, too. The high school gym was the only place in Curtisville big enough for everyone who wanted to come. And you had to admit it was a good place to remember Gary.

The gym was packed. Both sets of bleachers were pulled all the way out and the floor was lined with folding chairs. Dad pointed to a spot near the top of the bleachers, and I followed him as he climbed faster than he should. At one point he had to grab a rail to keep steady. I ignored this like I knew he'd want me to.

After we sat, I scanned the crowd. Everyone was here—teachers, classmates, coaches. People from church who looked out of place in the gym. People who looked familiar, though I couldn't place them. And even people I didn't think I'd ever seen.

The last time the town came together like this was after the state championship when Gary was a senior. It was past midnight when the yellow bus bringing the team back from the Augusta Civic Center pulled into the high school lot. About two hundred of us were waiting with homemade signs and a sound system. A couple fire trucks were there, too—this was town tradition for state champions. Men were drinking in plain sight, and a cop whose son barely got off the bench all season was going around making anxious jokes about being off duty. When Gary stepped off the bus, there was a roar. Horns blared, the firemen flashed their lights and whooped their sirens. Everyone wanted a piece of him—handshakes, claps on the back, headlocks and noogies from half-drunk dads. I stood off to the side with my friends until I felt a tap on my shoulder. I turned to find Gary smiling down at me.

"Where's your sister?" he asked. He had to lean in so I could hear him over the music, and I could smell alcohol on his breath. I knew Gary had been in trouble once or twice for drinking beer, but this was something stronger.

"At home," I shouted back.

"Tell her I wanted to see her here." Typically Gary was a tease. Even if he refused to crack a smile, his eyes would seem to ask if you got the joke. Now his attitude wavered between grim and pleading, neither of which I wanted to contend with.

"Yeah, okay." I tried to turn away.

"No." He had my arm. "Tell her I want to talk. Okay? Tell her I said that."

Of course I didn't tell her. I didn't even want to think about what Gary had to say to my sister, and no doubt she didn't want to hear it anyway.

A cellist was playing under one of the baskets, exactly where Gary drew dozens of charges. He was quick for a tall guy, would get his feet planted and his hands up a split second before a dribbler smashed into him, at which point he'd fold, then pop up grinning when the whistle blew.

I realized it was what I'd been expecting since I learned he died—that he'd come back again right when we thought he was down for good, stroll in with that smile on his face. *Suckers.*

Dad's breathing was shallow. The bleachers were bad for his back. He had a pad he was supposed to sit on, but he never used it. He didn't want to need anything special.

For a couple years after the accident, he had been okay. Some days were bad, but he could look forward to another good one eventually. In the last year, though, things had gotten worse. It took a while to see the change. Now, the change required effort *not* to see. Dad took an OxyContin every twelve hours, and he spent the final stretch before his next pill white in the face, looking frantically at the clock. Still, he didn't budge from the prescribed schedule. Dad knew about people getting hooked, and he was clear on one thing—he wasn't an addict. He was too strong a person, he said, to go down that route. And I believed him.

The cello stopped and the Clemmens family—what was left of it—came in. It was suddenly so quiet we could hear their footsteps.

Pastor Mark walked quickly, leaving too much space between him and Miriam, who followed in a navy dress, pale hands twitching, eyes small and naked without her usual makeup. Tara came last, in a boxy black dress that stopped just below her knees. Her short hair was tied into a stubby ponytail that looked like a paintbrush. I wanted her to search the crowd for me, but she didn't turn her head.

The basketball coach welcomed everyone. Then Mark stood, spread a Bible across the podium. While he stared into its pages, the microphone picked up the edges of his breathing.

"I'm going to start with a reading from Matthew, chapter ten. 'There is nothing concealed that will not be disclosed, or hidden that will not be made known. What I tell you in the dark, speak in the daylight; what is whispered in your ear, proclaim from the roofs.'" He cleared his throat. The reading seemed to have strengthened him. "There is nothing concealed," he repeated, "that will not be disclosed." I know this is not what you'd expect me to read to you, but this passage has been on my mind since Gary died. I've spent a lot of time thinking about why."

Even I, whose attention was usually wandering at best, found it easy to follow Mark. He compelled you. His messages were straightforward but not so simple that you could anticipate what he would say next. Listening to him now, I found that I missed the familiarity of his voice, his logic, even if I didn't agree with everything he said. I'd stopped attending church in the last few months. I used my weekend shifts—which I volunteered for—as an excuse. I'd thought Dad would mind, the way he minded when Jo had quit church in high school, but he barely noticed. In fact, even he was missing church sometimes. This, more than anything, was a sign of how badly he was doing.

"Gary was devoted," Mark was saying. "To his teammates, his family, his country. And he sacrificed for it. He spent hours in this gym, perfecting a three-point shot that would net his team a state championship. No pun intended."

He grinned bravely, and I heard a woman near me whisper, "I have no idea how he's holding up."

"And I don't know how much unauthorized time he spent in the weight room," Mark continued. Broader laughter now. Gary was notorious for skipping lunch to lift weights, which you weren't supposed to do unsupervised. But like a lot of things Gary did, no one could stop him without looking unreasonable.

"When he first wrote to us from boot camp, he talked about noticing the guys who struggled to keep up. He knew they weren't ready. That's what I'm trying to tell you—that Gary was ready. That he'd been getting ready for a long time to make the sacrifice that mattered. To give his all for what mattered most to him—his God, his country, his friends. I could tell you so much about Gary—how he wouldn't let me put training wheels on his bike, how he insisted on T-shirts two sizes too big because he thought that would make him grow into them faster. How proud I was—I am—of him—"

Finally he had to stop. The room filled with short, hard sniffs, like a hundred valves opening and closing. Dad had tear tracks on both cheeks. My head was bowed by the gravity of the moment but my thoughts were on Jo, on how she would hate listening to this. Had she forgiven me? Sometimes, when she was mad at me, I'd plead, "Tell me what you're really thinking," because I couldn't stand what was buried. I needed to hear it, no matter the cost. But then she'd say, "I *am* telling you what I'm thinking!" I never knew what to make of that.

Tara was twisting a tissue in her lap. I wondered whether she'd worn the dress willingly. Even in high school she didn't wear dresses or skirts. Back then it had seemed like a modesty thing. Apparently even *she* had thought it was a modesty thing. We used to sit together in Mr. Gromberg's chemistry lab on Wednesdays. Tara had started a Bible study and Mr. Gromberg, who went to Word of Life, had offered his classroom for us to meet in. For each meeting, Tara would pick a passage from the Bible, which we would read together. Then she would ask me questions and pretend my stupid answers were interesting. "I didn't think your answers were stupid," she'd told me recently, though I didn't believe her.

Tara and I had compared notes on our Bible study days to see if either of us had felt any sparks, but both of us admitted we hadn't. We were just two teenagers, each there for our own reasons—Tara out of obligation, me because Christianity was a nice ambiguity-free zone in my life, and because Dad wanted me to go. In fact, Tara had embarrassed me back then, too. In high school I moved easily among social groups. Maybe I *was* a Christian, but I was the nonjudgmental type, content to keep quiet about my faith with people who weren't interested. Tara was the opposite. She had her Christianity on a high beam setting, so that even I had to wince away from it sometimes.

But it wasn't just her faith that had made me uneasy. She was so earnest about everything. Once, during a church party at her house, I found her dabbing egg salad onto saltine crackers, then shaking dried herbs on top. "Want one?" she asked me brightly. I shook my head. I liked egg salad just fine. It was Tara's carefulness I didn't want to taste.

She skipped her senior year of high school to go on a mission trip to Ecuador. Then I barely saw her until April 2007—four months before Gary died—when she walked into the Dunkin' Donuts where I was working. I was hunched behind a display of insulated cups, eating a day-old muffin. After wiping my mouth and taking my place behind the register, I needed a moment to go from thinking that here was a person who looked like Tara Clemmens to here *was* Tara Clemmens, smiling at me with recognition. Her hands were in her pockets, her elbows relaxed. Her hair was shorter, and now ended in a blunt cut two inches above her shoulders. The gold bead of a nose piercing caught the light. Her jeans had holes that looked earned, not bought. Something in her smile suggested she was as capable of a good joke as she was of keeping it to herself.

People who get makeovers have this wide-eyed look, like they're rattling around in a shell too big for them. But Tara didn't look like that. She seemed to fill herself to the brim. More than that—she seemed to overflow.

"How—?" I started, then switched gears. "Where—?" And then, forcing myself to make sense, "When'd you get back?"

"A couple weeks ago. I'm living on Bear Pond." Maybe she thought I couldn't place it, because she added, "Up by Bridgton."

But I knew where Bear Pond was. I was still trying to square my memory of Tara with the person standing in front of me.

"How long has it been?" she asked. "Three years?" Then she said, "I guess I saw you at the party before Gary deployed."

I remembered seeing her there. She'd hung around the edges, looking out of place. I'd chalked it up to her having been abroad for so long. Like maybe she'd forgotten how to live in the United States.

My manager stuck his head out of the office to say that if I had time to talk to a friend, I had time to clean behind the coolers. I liked that he assumed I was friends with Tara.

"I get off work in twenty minutes," I told her.

"I can wait twenty minutes," she said. She ordered a coffee, which she carried out to a beat-up little Subaru. I joined her after my shift, though doing so involved excessive folding of my limbs. On the windshield, flecks of rain gathered into drops that inched and ran. She told me she was a caretaker for the nicer homes on Bear Pond. "It's something to do while I figure other things out," she said, then asked about what I was doing. Saving up for nursing school, I said, though it wasn't really true anymore. She said she'd seen an ad for jobs at Pine Creek. "It's not nursing," she said, "but it might give you a similar experience." Then she said, "I'm not trying to tell you what to do."

"I don't mind," I said, and meant it. Her suggestion was nothing like Jo's anxious prodding.

"I should get home," she said. "Do you want to come visit sometime?"

I did, and we agreed on Friday evening. She wrote directions on the back of the receipt I'd given her.

"The last bit is confusing," she warned me.

"I'll be fine," I said.

I wasn't fine. I was mixed up within minutes of leaving the paved road. It was impossible to tell the difference between forks and the long driveways that peeled off. The light was fading and I didn't have cell service. Twice I turned down a road that wasn't even a road, then had to back out when the pine branches started dragging along the sides of the wagon like a creepy car wash. I was almost an hour late when I finally pulled into a gravel drive behind a brown-and-white mobile home. Tara was waiting for me on the porch.

"Told you it was hard to find," she teased, but I knew she'd been worried.

Inside, the place was cramped and outdated—shag carpet everywhere, wallpaper in greens and yellows, furniture older than I was—but it was comfortable, too. I liked that Tara didn't apologize for it. She went to work reheating dinner, and I looked around while trying not to seem like I was snooping. There were two pairs of running shoes and a jacket by the door, a duffel bag in one corner, a set of woven baskets on the floor. On the side table next to the couch was a North American birds guide, a Bible, and an Army portrait of Gary.

I picked up the photo. Without thinking, I blew the dust off, which made Tara look over.

"He sent that to me," she said. "I was like, 'thanks for the glamor shot.'" But she smiled.

"Do you know how he is?"

"We've been in touch. It doesn't amount to much—some emails back and forth is all." She paused. "That doesn't answer your question. I don't think he's great, but he doesn't like to be specific." Another pause. "Mostly I'm glad he's talking to me in a way that doesn't make me feel like I'm a disappointment. Which is more than I can say for my parents."

I nodded like I knew what she meant. I mean, I had a guess. But this was still Tara Clemmens. It seemed impossible that my guess was right. Didn't I want my guess to be right, though? I did. I shook my head a little, like by doing so I could shed the feeling rising in my body.

I picked up her Bible. Bound in soft brown leather, it flopped in my hand like a newly dead thing. I recognized it as the same one she'd brought to church and Bible study in high school. Serious Christians committed not only to one faith but to one Bible, filling the whole thing with underlines and margin notes. Pastor Mark said you knew the strength of a person's faith by the worn look of their Bible. I had wanted to be like that, but I could barely remember to bring my Bible to church on Sundays, let alone read it on all the other days of the week.

When we sat to eat, Tara passed me bowls of food—pasta and ground beef, a salad with croutons—with a kind of grandmotherly urgency. We ate in stiff silence until she said, "So you still go to Word of Life." It was not exactly a question.

"My dad goes. I keep him company." I'd never felt like I needed to defend going to Word of Life. I knew some people didn't like what Pastor Mark preached, but I didn't take it personally. I didn't butt into their lives, did I? So why should they care what I did with mine?

"You don't go," I said, stating the obvious.

Tara gave a little snort. "It's not a theological match anymore."

"Why not?" I asked. "I mean, what do you believe now?"

She cocked her head, wary. "Why do you ask?"

"I'm not trying to save you," I said, and I meant it.

She relaxed. "See?" she said. "That's why I wanted to talk to you. You can believe without looking for a fight. Being Christian didn't make you bitter or afraid." Before I could tell her she was giving me too much credit because I'd never actually been a good Christian, she said, "I don't know what I believe. But I know that I *want* to believe. And that whatever I believe needs to feel like life, not death. Maybe you think that makes me a relativist."

We had all been warned by Mark about the relativists, people who thought everybody could have their own truth. Mark said once you started down that slope, you ended up in a sinkhole of moral compromise. This had made sense for a long time. Didn't there have to be hard-and-fast rules out there, even if I didn't always know what they were?

But I said to Tara, "I don't think you're a relativist."

"Why not?"

"Relativism is supposed to be convenient. It seems like this has been pretty hard for you."

She gave me a long, even look. "Yeah," she said, finally. "It has."

AS I WATCHED TARA FROM my seat in the bleachers, I counted twelve days since I'd last seen her. We'd talked twice on the phone, but they were short conversations because she kept being needed. For now her parents had stopped trying to talk to her about her "choices," which was more or less all they'd tried to talk to her about since she came out to them on a trip home for Thanksgiving two years before. It hadn't gone well, and she'd left early to go back to Indianapolis, where she was living with her then-girlfriend. Apparently Gary was the only one who didn't freak out on her about it.

"I know I shouldn't trust them," she'd told me on the phone, about her parents. "But we need each other right now. It's complicated." I said I missed her. "Yeah, you too," she replied, but too vaguely for comfort.

Mark, Miriam, and Tara were surrounded after the service. All I had time for, when I saw Tara, was a chaste hug. "I'll be home this weekend," she whispered. "Come visit?"

I squeezed her shoulders to say *yes*.

THAT FRIDAY I WENT STRAIGHT from work to Tara's. I felt bad about leaving Dad on his own for the night, but then again, my being around the house helped less than it used to. For a while, we'd had a habit of playing cribbage in the evening to pass the time before his eight o'clock pill, but he'd stopped wanting to do even that. Sometimes I would enter a room and he'd say, "I didn't know you were home." That morning, his expression was empty as I explained I was spending the night with a friend. "Have fun," he'd said.

Tara was out on a run when I arrived. Or that was my guess, because her car was there but her running shoes were gone. I let myself in, sat on the couch, leafed through her copy of *The Progressive Pilgrim*. She'd dog-eared an article titled "God the Mother: On Gender and Parenthood in the Trinity." Two paragraphs in, my mind started wandering. I wanted to care about this kind of thing for Tara's sake, but without her to translate for me, I found it all kind of disorienting. Every perspective sounded convincing to me until I remembered that they couldn't all be equally right. This, I thought, was why it was best to decide what you believed and stick with it no matter what. I wished I was that kind of person. I leaned my head against the back of the couch, closed my eyes until I heard Tara's footsteps on the porch. Even before she came through the door I could hear her breathing noisily. Tara could run six miles and arrive fresh and chatty, so I knew she'd pushed herself. And she tended to push herself when she was upset.

"Hi," she said curtly, wrenching off her shoes. She went straight to the bathroom. The plumbing clunked loudly as the shower came on. Five minutes later she emerged wearing wool socks, jeans, and a sweatshirt. Her hair was turbaned in a red towel and there was a sudsy dab of shampoo on one cheek.

"Want tea?" she asked, clapping a pot on the stove without waiting for an answer. "I want tea."

She had every reason to be mad at me. I should have been there for her in the last few weeks. I should have showed up at her parents' house, or at least had the guts to call and ask for her.

When I joined her in the kitchen, she walked around me twice, like I was a post.

"I'm really sorry," I said.

She stopped so quickly the towel tipped off her head, unfurled. "Sorry? Why?" The thick, warm smell of her shampoo filled the room.

"I didn't really show up for you in the last few weeks. And I was kind of distant before . . . Gary died." It was still weird to say.

"Oh. Thanks." She seemed to only vaguely recognize what I was talking about. She put her head in her hands. "Something bad happened."

"Tell me." My relief that she wasn't mad at me made me clear, purposeful.

"I'm not sure I should tell you." But she spun on her heel, went to a closet in the hall, returned with a digital camera, which she handed to me without a word. The camera's silver paint was scratched, the black wrist cord frayed.

"It came back with Gary's things," she said. She returned to the stove, stared at the pot, which was rumbling softly as the water heated.

"This doesn't have to do with—?" I started, thinking of Jo. Were these nude pictures? Or worse?

"With what?" Now that Tara had decided to show me, she was impatient to get it over with. "Just look."

When I powered the camera on, its little screen showed, first, a grainy square of the floor in front of me. I navigated to the menu, found a grid of three folders titled *idiots*, *hahaha*, and *stuff*.

In the *idiots* folder were 147 pictures of desert, tanks, rooms with plywood walls. Soldiers grinning, soldiers giving and receiving headlocks, soldiers smoking at card tables, soldiers with their middle fingers up. I flipped through twenty pictures, went back to *hahaha*, which had a series of twelve photos documenting a prank in which plastic sheeting was taped around a bottom bunk, trapping someone in. The camera-work wasn't great, and the flash bounced off the plastic and gave everyone devilish red eyes.

Tara approached impatiently, then took the camera from me and navigated to *stuff*. "This one," she said, handing it back.

This folder had photos of a body, definitely not American. It was a boy—maybe a teenager, maybe younger—twisted on the ground. A sick regret pounded through me. On the side of his head, a dark bloody mess. Thicker blood, so dark it was almost black, was pooled under him.

"Oh," I said.

Tara's arms were crossed. She was looking at me like, *So now you know.*

A horrible gravity pulled my gaze back to the dead boy's face.

"Keep going," Tara said. "There's more."

Against my will I clicked the forward button. Next was a series of photos of Ziploc bags lying on rumpled cloth. I zoomed in, then jerked back, as if bitten.

"What is this?" A stupid question. They were body parts. An ear, a thumb, a finger.

I didn't have to go back to the picture of the boy to know who the ear belonged to. I remembered the emptiness on the side of his head.

I'd thought I knew about these wars. Or, I'd thought I knew enough—that 9/11 happened and we had to get even. I'd always been fuzzy about how Iraq was involved. But other people knew, and that had been good enough for me.

The pot boiled over, startling both of us. I moved it to a cool burner, walked Tara to the couch. We sat. The camera in my hand shut off automatically. I set it down as if it were made of porcelain.

"My parents don't know," she said. "They asked me to keep his things for now, until they're 'ready.' Dad gave him that camera before he left. Also, you didn't see it, but—there's a picture of him holding that bag. It's Gary's hand. I'm sure of it." She was looking at her own hands. "The thing is, in the month or two before he died, he was sending me these messages that—I mean, Gary and I were never that close. I thought he was cocky, and he thought I was a square. But over the summer, he started writing me. He didn't say it, but I thought he needed me. He asked me, at one point, if I thought forgiveness was real."

"What did you tell him?" I asked.

"I said yeah. But then he got all jokey again. And sometimes the way he talked made me uncomfortable. Like how he referred to the Iraqis. I figured it was the culture, and a reaction to stress. I know he had a mean streak, even without the war," she said, anticipating my thought exactly. "He seemed particularly bitter. He wasn't even trying to be funny anymore. But you have to understand," she went on, "that he was the only one in the family who wasn't trying to fix me. When I came out to him, he said, 'I wondered.' And then, when I asked him if he thought I was sinning, he laughed." She paused. "I went back and looked at the date of the email about forgiveness. It's the week after the date of some of those photos." She nodded at the camera. "There I was, grieving the brother I thought I had finally connected with. And then this. What am I supposed to do?" Before I could start to formulate a response, she went on. "I know what to do. I have to report it. And it'll be awful—for my parents, for me, for his friends. But it's awful already. That's a real person—he looks like a child—and even if he came out shooting, you think it's cool to take a *photograph* of him? Like he's an animal, or a trophy? You think it's cool to cut him into pieces?" Her fingers had gone clawlike. "You think you'll be forgiven for that, like you always were for everything?"

For a long time we sat without talking. Each time I shifted, the couch springs under me crunched and squealed.

Evening fell in a navy dust. A loon call shivered the air.

"Georgie," Tara said sharply. The whites of her eyes almost glowed in the fading light. "You can't tell anyone about this. I'm going to contact the Army. If that doesn't work, I'll figure something else out. I'll go to the press if I need to. I just can't right now."

"That makes sense," I said, and for the time being it really did. Then I said, "I really care about you. You know?" There was an unusual weight behind my voice. Something about her reaction to the photos drew it out of me. She was fierce and good and beautiful. What else could I want?

She looked right at me, with a calculation that didn't feel clinical. She leaned into me, then, and I kissed her still-damp hair, then held her for a long time.

AT TWO IN THE MORNING I found myself blinking into the dark while I listened to Tara breathe. She didn't wake when I whispered her name, so I eased my arms from around her and slipped out of bed. The clouds had cleared and a half-moon looked at me from over the pond. The cold air lifted heat from my body. I'd thought I knew Gary. I'd thought I had an idea, at least. Not a nice guy, but not, like, evil.

Except he was.

The next thought blanketed me with a dread that felt like panic. It wasn't only that I didn't protect my sister—I didn't protect her from someone who was capable of *this*.

I thought of that night in the car, after I picked her up from the Cumberland Farms in Gray. Jo had laughed when I said I was going to find a way to make things right. She probably thought I'd forgotten my promise. Well, I hadn't. I could show Jo that I was on her side. I remembered the writing class she was in. Couldn't she use this for her project? She'd said she might want to be a journalist. Wouldn't it help her career to impress a famous one?

I didn't want to betray Tara. Then again, in the face of this violence, why should my wants matter? In the cold stillness I closed my eyes, tried to channel Jo's moral clarity—or Tara's, for that matter. What I'd seen was wrong. I understood this profoundly.

No part of me wanted to qualify or hesitate. Which meant something had to be done. Tara wanted to control how and when people learned, but why should she be burdened with deciding? She was trying to do the right thing while also trying to reduce the pain of the situation for herself and her parents. That was understandable, but not necessarily right. Maybe she even needed me, to do for her what she was unwilling to do herself.

My body felt heavy now with a combination of relief and dread. I would, for once in my life, *do* something. I would prove to myself, to Jo, to Tara, to anyone else who cared to look, that I was capable of taking a stand.

About fifty feet offshore was a submerged boulder Tara and I swam out to on summer nights. We'd bring beers in a Styrofoam cooler we anchored with a rope and a rock, then sit together, the water to our shoulders, nursing the beers for hours.

The moon was edging toward the corner of the window. I was thoroughly cold now. But I didn't budge. I felt like I was sitting on one of those rocks, taking smaller and smaller sips of beer, as if by doing so the night could last forever. Because if it did, I could stay right where I was, suspended between commitment and betrayal, between keeping a secret and giving it away.

My investigative project proposal came back with a note from Seamus asking me to see him after class. I covered his scrawl as Lily turned to me. "You coming?" she asked. Lily, Susan, and Morgan were going to Bean There to study. There were three coffee shops near campus, but Bean There was best for studying because they didn't make you leave your table after twenty minutes like Morning Glory, which had big windows and organic everything, and because their chairs were rickety and uncomfortable, unlike the deep couches at Brew Ha Ha, where everyone fell asleep. Also, Morgan claimed she liked her coffee burned.

I'd started going to Bean There with them since they first joined me at dinner. I could justify it because it was cheap: coffee to stay, in a chipped mug I plucked from a wrought iron tree, was a dollar. Refills were fifty cents. The girls really were there to study. Susan gasped with irritation when she couldn't find her mistake on a linear algebra problem and Morgan chewed on her hair while she made flash cards for organic chemistry. Sometimes other girls came up to talk, and there was easy conversation that made me feel, more than anything else had since I'd started college, like I belonged at Peabody.

Turned out you needed friends to make friends, I thought, before realizing it sounded like one of those things that are inherently annoying unless you're the one saying it. Then again, I knew I couldn't call Lily, Susan, or Morgan *friends* without reservations. I worried I was like a pet to them, something small and interesting they'd stop paying attention to after a while. Still, I couldn't help wanting their company. My loneliness had come on so slowly I hadn't realized how strong it was until now. You can't slake a thirst like that with a few sips and then walk away from the fountain.

"Sorry," I told Lily. I didn't want to admit I was going to see Seamus. Morgan still teased me about him, and I didn't want to give her more fodder. I couldn't tell Lily I had work, though, because the lie would be obvious if she stopped by the library. "I told my dad I'd call," I said. "It's been forever since we caught up." This second part, at least, was true.

"Next time," she said, hoisting her backpack onto one shoulder.

Morgan had drifted over. "You're not coming?" she asked. When I shook my head, she said, "Jo, you know we only get anything done because we're too ashamed to distract you." I laughed. Susan was standing by the door, impatient. "You have to come next time. No excuses," she told me. Her seriousness surprised me.

As I watched them file out, I felt a buoyant flicker that, a moment later, registered as happiness.

I FOUND SEAMUS SITTING behind his desk. He had one ankle stacked on the opposite thigh so that his knee pointed at the ceiling in that inflexible way guys have. He was frowning at a large pad. I moved four folders off the chair across from him so I could sit.

He made a note on the pad before dropping it onto his desk. "I want to talk about your topic for the class project. Tell me more about this church."

"I went there growing up," I said. He should know this. It was right there in the proposal. "Something is off about the money. The pastor went around coercing people into contributions they couldn't afford. He wanted to make it, like, a megachurch." Maine was too small for megachurches, but still: Word of Life had become one of the biggest churches in the area.

"*Coercing* as in making threats?"

"Not exactly. He made it all seem very nice."

"What you're describing sounds, simply, like *pressure*."

"Is there a problem with my proposal?" I thought it was a good topic. A popular pastor goes around taking money from people who shouldn't be giving that much, spearheads more projects that bring in more people he can get money from. It wasn't exactly a Ponzi scheme, but it struck me as something in the vicinity.

"It seems a little bit inspired by my book," Seamus said.

"It's different. There's no sex." I wanted to sound edgy, but I flushed and had to look at my lap. "I haven't read your book," I admitted.

"There's no problem with using someone else's work—whether or not you've read it—as inspiration for your own. I'm wondering, though, if there's another way into this topic. Technically, what you have is fine. But I think you've got another story."

"Why do you think that?"

"Because of how angry you are."

His comment knocked me off-balance, and I struggled to regain my mental footing. "My dad should've helped me pay for college. But that money got sucked into building projects." This was true, even if I wasn't mentioning Dad's other money problems, the scam he fell for, his gigantic medical bills, the collection agencies.

"And I'm here and trying not to drown in debt before I even graduate. And all the other girls—" I wasn't making sense anymore.

"I worked in college, too," Seamus said. "And I graduated with a lot of debt. Actually, I'm still paying it back." He gave me a sheepish grin. "I'm not helping, am I."

"I still don't see what's wrong with my proposal," I said.

"It strikes me as a hatchet job, which makes me think you're upset about something other than what you described. So I wanted to talk to you about identifying what—w ait a minute." He riffled in a desk drawer, pulled out a folder of printed pages. "In your application for this class, you wrote about 'having the courage to tell the real story, not the convenient one.'"

"Honestly," I said, "it sounded like something that would help me get into this class."

"Sometimes we're most truthful when we think we're being disingenuous." He didn't look at me as he said this, as if he wanted to give me privacy to consider it on my own. Maybe he was right, but in either case this still sounded like the kind of invented-on-the-spot proverb I'd gotten used to from him. They always sounded good, but I didn't want to confuse sounding good with being right. "I could be wrong," he said. "But just in case, I wanted to bring you here to ask you something. What's the real story here, Jo?"

My eyes zagged away from him. Seamus waited. I thought of Gary dying, his life over before the sound of the explosion faded. Of Gary on the basketball court, always knowing the right place to be.

I thought of him in that hotel room, smiling down at me because he knew I was trapped.

"It seems," Seamus said, "you've thought of something?"

Could I write *that*? I wasn't even done asking myself the question when I had my answer: No. Obviously not.

"I'm sticking with my original plan," I said.

His lips twisted in disappointment, but I could see he'd given up trying to change my mind. He stood as I zipped my backpack, followed me to the door. "I hope you don't mind me pressing you on this," he said. "I suspect you could do something remarkable if you let yourself."

He reached toward me then. I flinched, which caused him to startle. "I'm opening the door," he said quietly. Which I saw was true, but also, our mutual embarrassment made clear it wasn't entirely true. Also, the door was already half-open. I ducked out and reported to the circulation desk for my shift.

I should have spent my time in the library drafting a Jane Austen paper, but I opened the file containing my project proposal instead. I couldn't help seeing what Seamus was talking about: It was obvious that I was reaching. *What kind of a church is focused on relentless expansion?* I'd asked. *What kind of a leader calls a committee to establish a building color palette?* The answers: Every church. Every leader.

Seamus wanted to know why I was angry. I had so many answers to that question I didn't know where to start. Because Mom left? Because of Pastor Mark's smug theology? Because of how everyone idolized Gary? Because Dad was so helplessly gullible?

Still insufficiently motivated to start my paper, I checked my email, found a message from Georgie.

> hey, wondering if it would be a good week to visit peabody. i could come thurs eve and stay thru saturday, if that sounds good. bus gets in at 6:30. should be fun!

I had to read the message again to confirm that Georgie's supposed question about a good time to visit was actually a statement about her planned visit. My first year here, I'd really wanted her to come see me. I was overwhelmed by how smart and accomplished the other girls were, and I longed for Georgie's unthinking approval. I wasn't lonely in an outcast way. Everyone was nice to me. I even had "friends." But still, I felt in almost every social situation like a wall hanging that looks less right every time you move it. Eventually, I gave up on Georgie, and on most social situations, too.

But now Georgie was asking to come, or had told me she was coming, and even if I kind of didn't want her, a part of me still did.

I HEARD THE HISS OF brakes before I saw the bus, which pivoted neatly into the lot, missing a lamp pole by three inches. Leaning against the brick wall of the bus station, I tried for a relaxed air. I didn't like that Georgie might be seeing all of this through the tinted windows. I also didn't like that I wasn't even sure she was on the bus. She hadn't responded to my most recent email, about what she wanted to do while she was here, and she hadn't answered my call when I tried to confirm she was actually on her way.

She was the fourth person off. Halfway down the grooved stairs, she turned to speak with the driver. She had on the same backpack she wore all through high school. It still had a wad of key chains hanging from one zipper. Under one arm she carried a sleeping bag. She was also wearing her big canvas jacket, the one I took that night I walked into the cold, and a T-shirt from her fifth-grade softball team. The T-shirt was snug on her now, threadbare in all the right places, like the fake-old shirts some girls at Peabody bought for fifty dollars. Her hair was wadded in a messy bun that perched on one shoulder like a scruffy pet.

Georgie had the singular gift of looking great even when, or especially when, she also looked like a mess. Maybe I was more accomplished, but she was at ease in the world. I sensed it more clearly than I ever had before: She was whole, where I was halved.

On the sidewalk now, my sister looked around brightly. She saw me, grinned, hugged me from the side on account of the sleeping bag. We dropped her things in my room and headed out again, supposedly to go to dinner, but she kept getting sidetracked, wanting to see the library, the student center. Now we were too late to swipe in for regular dinner, so I took her to the only open dining hall. They had an à la carte menu available until midnight. Georgie ordered a baked pretzel and a boat of waffle fries. I got grilled cheese, the cheapest thing on the menu.

Georgie couldn't know that this food wasn't covered by my meal plan and was being debited from the money in my student account, but I still felt like she should. I watched her wander until she found the condiments, pumped ketchup into pleated cups.

"Cool spot," she said, when she found me at a table by a wall of glass. Outside, the duck pond fountain made its final spurts of the night and shut off. "Do you come here for all your meals?"

Did she really think I subsisted on grilled cheese and waffle fries? "I usually have dinner earlier, at a different hall. There's a whole buffet. This is just what's open now."

"What about breakfast and lunch?" she asked, sucking ketchup from her fingers.

I was weighing how to answer when my eye caught Lily, who was approaching us and waving. "Is this your sister?" she asked. I'd run into her earlier and told her Georgie was coming. Now I saw that Morgan was behind her, unwrapping a Drumstick.

"Georgie," I told them, while my sister offered each of them the hand whose fingers she'd just pulled from her mouth.

"You two do not look alike at all," said Morgan, pointing her ice cream at Georgie, then at me. Lily had a raspberry sorbet in a narrow paper cone.

"I'm sure Jo is relieved to hear you say that," Georgie said, grinning as she screwed her ketchupy fingers into a balled-up napkin. Morgan tipped forward as she laughed, and a few drops of melted ice cream landed on the table. "Oh God, I'm sorry," she said. But Georgie deftly wiped the drops with the napkin, then asked, "Want to sit?"

Morgan dropped into the chair next to Georgie. "Sweet jacket."

Lily, sitting next to me, said, "I see a resemblance. It's here." She drew a circle around her eyes.

"You said your name was . . . ?" Morgan prompted.

"Georgie," said Georgie.

"Georgie and Jo," said Morgan. "Did people ever think you were little boys before they met you?"

"Sometimes people thought I was a little boy *after* they'd met me," said Georgie, which made Morgan laugh again, a little too loudly.

"Is Georgie short for something?" Lily asked.

Georgie intoned her legal name, as if, when she was done, some other version of her might stroll into the room.

"Whoa," said Morgan.

"I know." Georgie shrugged. "It was our mom's doing. Her parting gift."

"Did she die?" Morgan glanced at me, alarmed.

"Jo didn't tell you? She left." Georgie swept her hand as if knocking a figurine of our mother off the table. "Took off for California to write for tele—"

"Can we not?" I asked. I didn't mind telling the story myself, in certain circumstances. I liked the way it surprised people: *Your mom really wrote for a TV show?* But I already knew I wouldn't like Georgie's telling. She'd emphasize all the wrong things.

After an awkward silence, Morgan said, "I didn't know."

"Jo is good at keeping things to herself," Georgie said. I could feel her realize she was saying too much, because then she asked, "What's going on tonight? I'm up for whatever."

That, I thought, was Georgie for you. She couldn't bother with an associates' degree at a community college, but here she was prepared to do *whatever* at 8:51 p.m.

Lily said, "The field hockey team is having a low-key thing. We were about to head over. You should *both* come," she added, as if she knew I was already working on an excuse.

Georgie's version of getting ready involved adding a flannel under her jacket, then retying her hair in the exact same messy bun. She stretched out on my bed, hands under her head like she was watching clouds, while I stressed over what to wear. I picked a blouse with a cherry print. It was what I thought other girls here would wear if they were also limited to the choices available in my closet.

Naturally, as soon as we were outside, I hated what I had on.

Morgan and Georgie got ahead as the four of us crossed campus. Their easy chatter made the quiet between me and Lily seem stiffer.

"Whose party is this again?" I asked.

"Field hockey," Lily said, bundling the entire team into one party-making entity. She added, gently, "It's not a *party* party."

"I know," I said, too defensively. Another unfortunate silence fell. This was the first social event of any significance I'd attended in at least a year. As a first-year I did go to real parties, but I developed a horrifying pattern of getting very drunk and then bawling very hard in front of everyone. I knew this because I heard some girls from my hall talking about it. "Do you think something is wrong?" one of them asked. "Or is she just one of those drunk criers?"

"I'm sorry about your mom," Lily said. And then, "I get that you don't want to talk about it. I only wanted to say I'm sorry that happened to you."

"Thanks."

"Did she really write for TV?"

"Yeah. The show was called *Good Guys*."

"No kidding! I remember seeing ads for that show."

"Almost no one saw more than ads. It aired right around 9/11. People weren't in the mood for a new sitcom after that. Just bad luck, I guess."

"You sound pretty balanced about her being gone."

Did I? I liked the idea that I could be balanced about it. I said, "She got pregnant young and never got to do what she wanted to do. And my dad wasn't right for her. So it sucks, but she had a hard choice. I didn't want her to leave, but what am I going to do? Stay mad at her forever?" Once I'd said it, I felt like it could be a little bit true.

"You arrived at this perspective on your own?" Lily asked.

"More or less."

"Jo," she said, laughing, "some people spend thousands of dollars on therapy to be able to say something like that and mean it."

"Well," I said, pleased, "I never had that kind of money."

She laughed again. "Very resourceful," she said, and for a moment it seemed the night would go okay.

WE WALKED INTO A YELLOW mansion that had been converted into dorms. The large entrance room downstairs, where everyone was gathered, had high ceilings and dark paneling on the walls. A huge stone hearth had been blocked up with cement. A resident, definitely not an art student, had painted logs and flames on poster board and tacked it where the fire should be. I wanted to point out the sad humor in this to someone, but I was already on my own. Lily was hugging girls she knew and Morgan was pulling Georgie around by the elbow to meet people, then pointing back at me for reference. I watched my sister scoop a can of beer from a slushy bucket, wipe the top with her flannel shirt before cracking it open. She was so natural about it I had to assume she'd started drinking. I was surprised that she drank, then surprised by my own surprise. Of course she had grown up in my absence. She looked the same, she wore the same clothes, but she was different, too. I mindlessly accepted a cup of punch, found a seat next to a girl in my Jane Austen class. The only topic of conversation I could come up with was our next paper. She made an excuse and wandered off.

Now Georgie was with the volleyball twins, Sharon and Sheila, both of whom had gleaming black braids to their waists. Their height made them physically imposing, but their gigantic smiles made them less intimidating than the basketball players, who had a way of looking through me like I wasn't there. In sync, the twins threw their heads back at something Georgie said.

I had considered it pathetic, an example of Georgie's tiny, homogenous world, that she'd thought a single Somalian immigrant who was hired to work at the nursing home was worth mentioning to me. *I* went to school with people from all over the globe. *I* had been taught to say *American Indian* and not *Native American. I* had written a term paper on the legacy of Jim Crow. *I* had managed to be accepted, technically at least, into this elite, diverse student body.

But it was Georgie who already looked at home.

Lily brought another girl over, introduced us even though I already knew her name, and not only from Facebook. My first year here, I'd crossed paths with a delivery guy tethered to a cloud of balloons that were printed *happy birthday Helena!* The guy was so slight, and the balloons so oversized, that it seemed possible he'd be lost to the sky before he found his target.

Helena was tall and very blond, with a wide mouth and dimples. "Are you a first-year?" she asked as she and Lily joined me on the couch.

"I'm a junior."

"But I've never seen you before!"

But she had seen me before. For instance, when she looked around to see who was observing her receipt of nineteen gigantic balloons.

"I always say Jo should be a spy. She's seen only when she wants to be." To my knowledge Lily had never said this, but her comment softened the awkwardness. Helena and Lily fell into conversation about how busy they were with their extracurriculars. Lily was the president of the Korean Students Association, tutored at the elementary school, and helped found a campus group called PROTEST. "We advocate for survivors of sexual assault," Lily explained when she saw I didn't remember. I nodded abstractly. I wasn't in clubs anymore. When I first got to Peabody, I joined the newspaper, but I hated how heavily my work was edited, how wooden it sounded when it was printed. I quit after a year. I told myself I'd spend extra energy studying, and I did, but despite the extra efforts, my GPA wouldn't budge. A professor in one of my hardest lit classes actually called my final paper overwrought. *You're a skilled writer, but I think your work might benefit from* less *revision*, she wrote. *There is such a thing as an idea that has been clarified to death.*

I took the last swallow of my drink and stood. Lily looked at me with a question in her eyes. "Be right back," I told her. I walked toward the bathroom, then doubled back to the front door.

Outside I sat with my back against a gnarled tree. The punch had left a cough syrup taste in my mouth, and the alcohol was hitting me hard. I should have had more to eat than a flimsy grilled cheese. I could go eat in my room, but I also wanted Georgie to come find me out here. I stared up into the tree. Most of the leaves were gone, and what remained made a tattered black mess against the night sky. A wind started up from somewhere, rushed through the branches. We'd arrived at our house in Maine on an autumn night just like this one. As Dad drove us down the street, still unpaved at the time, he rolled down the windows. "Smell that air!" he called as gravel hit the undercarriage.

The move to Maine was because of Mark. Along the way to coaching Dad to a state title in the shot put, Mark led him to Jesus. When Dad got my mom pregnant the summer before his senior year, Mark was the one who helped him understand that God's plan was for Dad to marry Mom, not go to Ohio State on an athletic scholarship. Until I was seven we attended Maple Grove, a church in Canton where Mark was an associate pastor. But then Mark left to start a church of his own in Maine, and Mom left for the first time a few months later. She probably would've left anyway, but I couldn't help connecting her leaving with Mark's leaving. Mark had been the one to put our family together, so it made sense that without him, we fell apart.

As of our move, I still called myself a Christian. But in retrospect it became clear that my faith in God, my faith in faith, and my faith in my father had already started to come apart on that dark, tree-covered road, tiny rocks pinging our car. Our move felt too unscripted to be right. No one, it seemed, was really thinking about where all of this might go.

Our new house was a white, one-story ranch. The yard was a mess of overgrown grass and the garage door was hitched up on one side. We didn't have any furniture yet. Dad dampened a cloth to wipe thick dust from the middle of the living room floor, where we were going to spread our sleeping bags. The dark oval he made for us looked like the greasy thumbprint of a giant. "Georgie? Georgie?" I whispered, after she and Dad had fallen asleep. It was pitch-dark. Outside wind started and stopped, started and stopped. I knew I shouldn't wake my sister. But then she turned over and put her hand on my heart, which made it possible for me to breathe again.

Why, I sometimes wondered, did I still hold out hope that Georgie would be there for me in the way I most needed her to be? Then I would remember moments like that dark room. I once saw someone demonstrate how you could help a cat relax by grabbing the loose skin at their neck. It makes them feel like they're kittens being carried by their mother. Georgie could be like that with me, knowing exactly how to help me surrender my will, if only for a minute.

But only, that is, if doing so suited her. And it so often didn't suit her.

I WOKE TO FIND GEORGIE curled on the floor of my dorm room. She hadn't bothered to get into her sleeping bag, and was still wearing her clothes from the night before. The jacket blanketed her midsection. I wondered if she'd even brushed her teeth.

I quietly fixed myself breakfast, then studied at my desk until she woke, scrubbing at her eyes and stretching in ways she seemed to find painfully gratifying.

"Can I have some?" she asked, nodding at my bowl of cereal.

I gestured toward the drawers under my bed. "Help yourself."

"You could feed an army," Georgie said, rooting until she found two single-serve boxes of Special K with Red Berries. I was eating out of the only proper bowl I had, but Georgie dumped the cereal into an old yogurt container without comment, then drowned her breakfast in a dollar's worth of milk. She sat cross-legged on my bed, her back to the wall, facing me while she crunched cereal off a spork. I slammed my highlighter onto my desk.

"I can't think with you chewing and staring at me," I told her.

"I'm not staring at you." She sighed, dropped the back of her head against the wall. "Look. I know you're mad because—"

"I'm not mad." Obviously I was mad. I stared at the next sentence in the article on my desk. I knew what the words said, but I still couldn't get the meaning.

"You think I ditched you at the party last night."

"It wasn't a *party* party," I corrected her. "And you did ditch me."

"I figured you were going to bed. You should have told me if you wanted company."

"It's so convenient," I said, spitting each word like a bitter pebble, "for you to decide I'm all right. Then you don't have to know what's really going on. You don't have to be responsible. You can live your blissful life where everyone likes you and you don't have to care what happens to me."

She gave me a hurt look. "I do care about you, you know," she said.

"I have class in ten minutes," I said, though it was more like twenty. "I'm sure you can find something to do while I'm gone. Maybe Morgan's available."

Now Georgie frowned.

"She was all over you last night," I said, to remind her that she was in the real world now, not in a Word of Life bubble.

But Georgie said, too slowly for comfort, "I'm dating someone else."

"Did you tell Morgan that?" I retorted, wanting to make sure my gibe landed before we moved to the matter of Georgie dating.

"I told her when she invited me back to her room. She was cool about it. Can you back off for one minute? I'm trying to tell you something."

I was scared, but couldn't put my finger on why. Too much was happening in the same conversation. Morgan had invited Georgie to her room? Georgie had casually said no? Georgie had a reason for coming to Peabody, and it wasn't that she owed me a visit. Even Gary's death hadn't brought her out to see me, so what was it?

"Is Dad okay?" I asked. Fear tightened my voice. I didn't know something important. Without giving her a chance to answer, I asked, "Who are you dating?"

"That's not what I—" she started, and sighed. "I guess we can start there. Tara Clemmens."

"Tara *Clemmens*?" My mouth spread in a crazed grin. Was I hearing her right? I started to laugh. "How is that possible?"

Georgie looked hurt. "She's different now."

"I'd imagine so!" I laughed harder, but only out of relief. This I could deal with. It wasn't what I expected, but I could deal with it. I took the measure of my surprise, found myself more taken aback than shocked. Maybe, I thought, Georgie's sexuality had been quietly between us, all along, keeping us apart. Maybe she had wanted me to know, but I had never bothered to look hard enough. Maybe I'd even let her down by never seeing this part of her.

That sobering thought, along with Georgie's expression, brought me back. "Okay," I said. "How long have you been together?" And then, more seriously, "How is she taking Gary's death?"

"That's what I want to talk to you about."

"Wait—did you tell her about me and Gary?" No one, absolutely no one, was supposed to know anything about me and Gary except that we were briefly dating in a church-approved way. She knew this.

My sister said, "It does have to do with Gary."

Or what, I wondered, did Gary tell Tara, and Tara tell

Georgie? Did Georgie want me to know that word was going around? "Georgie—!"

"If you'll shut up, I'll tell you."

The air between us crystallized into something shatterable. I glared at her. What did I care about what anyone at home said about me? I was gone from that place. I would never return. As for whom Georgie was dating, well, I could find a way to not care about that, either. "You know what?" I said. "I have to go. I don't want to be late." I started gathering my things.

"Stuff happened before he died."

I shouldered my bag. "I really, really, really don't care."

"I'm trying to do the right thing," she said.

"Too late," I snapped. But I didn't leave. Still wearing my backpack, I sat. I waited for what my sister had come to say.

GEORGIE

CHAPTER SIX

In early November, Marlene—Good Old Marlene, as I thought of her, the one who got herself to dinner two inches at a time—fractured her hip coming out of the shower. I found out when I showed up for work the next morning.

"At least she doesn't need surgery," Rita told me. She'd found me in the staff room, hanging up my coat. I was eight minutes late for my shift because I'd driven straight from Tara's. Rita was studying me in a way that made me worry she knew this somehow, had seen me hit snooze twice, then do an ugly dance into my scrubs as Tara urged me to be careful, to not hit a deer. "Small miracle, really," Rita went on. "But she'll be in pain for a while, and being in bed is getting her down. I'm putting you on breakfast delivery because she likes you." I didn't know why she was frowning at me, but then she said, "Georgie. You've got to do something about your hair." I put a hand to the side of my head. Even without a mirror I could tell that sleep had mashed my hair flat on one side.

"Sorry," I said, yanking at the double elastics twisted around my bun. "I overslept."

"So it would seem." I thought that was the end of our conversation, but Rita added, "Don't give me too many reasons not to promote you to evening lead."

I stopped raking my fingers through the tangles. "What?"

"Daniel's moving in a few months. I'm going to need to replace him."

"Wow. Thanks." Evening lead was, as Rita herself put it, her right hand. It would probably come with a raise. "Don't I need to go to college for that?" I asked.

"Not if you have a plan for getting your associate's within a few years."

"Seriously?" This was the most satisfying job I'd ever had. The prospect of a promotion made me wonder if I could do this kind of work until I retired. Or at least for a long time.

"Cool it. I'm not offering you the position right now," Rita said, but she was pleased she'd made my day. "Other people have more seniority. I just like you better."

"Why?" I needed to hear her reasons. No one had ever gone out of their way to tell me I was good at anything. It was Jo who had made a point of excelling, Jo who got the praise. I had spent years thinking I could squeeze in anywhere, like a puff of air, take shape in whatever space I was given. Now I was glimpsing evidence that I already had a shape. I was made for something. Kind of like Mark had always said—*God has a plan and a purpose for you.*

At that moment, I believed it.

But Rita, true to form, said only, "Because you're the salt of the earth, Georgie. But that doesn't mean you get to skip brushing your hair."

AFTER MY SHIFT, I WENT straight home. Dad had an appointment he wanted me to come to. I'd always been happy to tag along with him, for PT, for the occasional X-ray. He mostly wanted someone to chat with in the car, in the waiting room. He said being a patient made him feel like a chart, not a person.

Today he was seeing someone new, in South Portland. On the drive down, I told him about my conversation with Rita.

"I'm happy for you," he said, but he didn't sound happy. Each time he changed his grip on the steering wheel, he seemed to squeeze it harder. The afternoon was clear and bright, but he leaned forward as if he were staring through blinding rain.

"Do you want me to drive?" I asked, but he didn't respond.

Tara had told me I shouldn't feel guilty about not being able to fix Dad's life. But I felt guilty about so many things—lying to him about where I was, spending so many nights away, not knowing how to help. And Dad had already lost Mom and Jo. If I left, too, he'd have no one but an arthritic old dog I wasn't always sure he was well enough to care for.

Tara was talking about moving in together. She said we could find a place closer to Pine Creek in the spring. The more we talked over the idea, the more I could see it. Maybe I still wasn't sure about being together forever, but maybe I'd never feel that way about anyone. I'd started to see that, day to day, I was more confident of our relationship than not.

Because of my confidence in my relationship with Tara, I was starting to regret telling Jo about the photos. But I wasn't worried about Tara discovering what I'd done for two reasons. First, all Jo said when I told her was that she wished I hadn't done that. When I awkwardly suggested that she use the photos as a story for her writing class, she looked at me with a mixture of pity and disgust. I could read her thoughts perfectly. What did I know anyway about writing assignments at a top-ranked college? What did

I know about the topics Jo might be most interested in? Second, Tara was not getting much of a response from the Army, and was starting to talk about what going to the press on her own would look like. Once the story came out because of Tara, it would be everyone's story to tell.

The Peabody trip, which started out well, took a nosedive starting when I looked around at the party and didn't see my sister. I knew I was supposed to go find her, but I let myself linger a little while before leaving. I was having fun. I was letting myself imagine, for the first time, what it would be like to go to college myself—not take classes here and there as time allowed, but live in a dorm with a bunch of friends, go to classes and events. I was surprised by how much I liked the girls I was meeting. And I could tell that Morgan liked me.

I had planned to apologize to Jo, something about how I'd looked around for her, and how someone said she'd probably left early—all true. I'd still left the party early, for the record, to make sure she was all right. As I approached her dorm, I saw a light in her room—I knew it was her room because I could see that wave-crash painting on the wall. I went to call her dorm so she could let me in, but my phone was dead, so I had to stand around until someone happened to come along, during which time her light blinked out.

At least she'd left her door unlocked for me.

Our pattern was exhaustingly well worn. Jo spent most of the time wanting little from me. Then, every once in a while, she would ask me to be there for her in a way so subtle and fleeting I would inevitably miss the cue. Then she would retreat, hurt, and I would fumble an apology that wasn't really an apology because I was mad she hadn't given me a real chance.

Anyway, by the time she marched off to class, I saw that the visit had been a bust. Which I took as a cue to make my exit.

IN THE EXAM ROOM IN South Portland, Dad and I sat on chairs so close together our elbows and shoulders touched. A doctor with curly gray hair came in. He was older than Dad, but had a spryness he seemed to flaunt a little as he scooted his wheeled stool around.

"Peter," he said, and smiled at Dad with practiced generosity. "What brings you here?"

Dad started in on an explanation of the accident, the first surgery, the second surgery. The doctor nodded energetically as his fingers skittered across the keyboard. Paper mill warehouse, thirty-foot shelf, box of luncheon napkins stacked wrong. This time Dad didn't make a joke about the napkin pack that broke his back. Come to think of it, I couldn't remember the last time he'd made that joke. All he said was "There were sixty packs of a hundred napkins each in there." And "It's heavier than you'd think."

The doctor grimaced. "I can imagine." The sympathy heartened Dad, who leaned into the details of each of his surgeries, his record of physical therapy, how he wanted to be of use so he volunteered at his church. What he meant was that he hated being on disability. Again the doctor nodded with sympathy.

"But," Dad said, "honestly, I'm finding that even everyday tasks are too much. Georgie"—I straightened a little, not having expected to be drawn into this—"has been a huge help, but she's got to move on. She can't stay with her old man forever." He sounded almost jovial, admitting this, but I knew how much it took for him to breathe even a word about needing help. I wished I could tell the doctor this. And now Dad said, "She's a caregiver at Pine Creek, where apparently there are higher doses being administered than the one I'm on."

His words made me want to drop through my chair. I didn't want the doctor to think I was giving my dad medical advice. I did remember him asking me what oxycodone prescribing was like at Pine Creek. I'd told him what I knew.

The doctor gave me a brief, forgiving glance. "Doses differ in a hospice setting," he said. "We hope you live for decades longer."

"Wasn't there a hundred-and-sixty-milligram pill?"

"It's been discontinued."

"Why would they do that? People like me—I'm in *real pain*—I'm a big man—"

The doctor sighed with regret. He said he was sorry. He could send Dad to another specialist if he wanted to.

"*You're* the specialist I was referred to!" Dad was shouting now. His hands were wrapped around the narrow armrests of the chair he'd squeezed into. The doctor was saying something about alternate treatments when there was a knock at the door. A man I first took for a police officer, but then realized was a security guard, stuck his head in. "Everything all right, folks?"

Dad staggered upright. "I am trying to do this *right*," he said, his voice trembling on a knife's edge between shouting and weeping. "In four years I've never taken more than I've been prescribed. I haven't taken a single dose even a minute early. I *know* all those stories about people getting hooked and they're *not me*!"

The doctor had stood, too, as if to absorb the force of Dad's fury.

"There really are some promising alternative therapies," the doctor said softly.

"I've tried *everything*!" Dad was shouting now. "I've done *everything* I was supposed to!"

"Easy, buddy," said the guard, taking a step toward Dad, who made such a sudden movement in return that we all started. But he was only lurching toward the door.

The doctor stopped me on my way out. "You might need this," he said, pressing a brochure into my hand.

"He's a good person," I said.

"Pain does things to people," the doctor said, sounding weary for the first time. "Even good people."

I glanced at the brochure as I followed Dad down the hall. *Are you worried about a family member's use of pain medication?* it asked. I dropped it in the nearest trash can.

On the drive home I kept looking over at him. This must be what it was like to raise teenagers, I thought—a struggle to decide whether it was a good moment to say something. Or whether you should say anything at all. The thought made me realize how much things had changed between me and Dad over the years. The tide was so far out I could barely see the waterline.

"I need help," Dad said.

"I know," I said.

"You don't." He was curt, even cutting. "I need *real* help."

I decided against agreeing again. Then I thought about what he'd said to the doctor—*I've tried everything*. Although he'd stopped short of anything he suspected of being non-Christian, a category that included acupuncture, crystals, and hypnosis, he *had* tried everything. Wherever you looked in the disorganized house—and it had gotten much messier since Jo left—there were signs of his commitment to healing. Books with titles like *Prayers for People in Chronic Pain* and *God Will Work a Miracle—in YOU!* Exercise DVDs—*Building a Pain-Free Back* and *Home Workouts to Transform Your Body (No Weights Required)*. There were resistance bands and foam rollers, sticky notes with inspiring Bible verses Dad left where he could see them. There were supplements in the fridge and odd-looking tools advertised to help with fascial release. It used to seem he would limp along like this forever, periodically energized by some diet plan or prayer practice, otherwise okay.

"And no one's going to help me," Dad concluded.

It felt like an accusation. Hadn't I tried to help him? Did trying to help even count for anything when someone needed *real* help, though? I had to admit, to myself at least, that things were worse than I'd cared to think about. In addition to his church attendance being down, I couldn't remember the last time he'd earnestly told me about something he'd prayed about, some sense of a promise God had given him. His expression had become grimmer, his movements more mincing, his words fewer.

And, possibly because I couldn't stand to watch this, I'd been putting distance between us.

"Have you talked to Pastor Mark?" I ventured.

"Pastor Mark has other things to think about."

"I thought he was back at church."

"He's leading services, but, Georgie. His son was just killed. It's not fair for me to burden him."

After a moment I started, softly, "I really think he'd want to know—"

"I'm not talking to Mark!"

Another awful silence. He almost never yelled at me. "Sorry," I murmured. I waited, then, for him to apologize, too. *Georgie, that was out of line. I'm sorry.* Of course I would forgive him. *No problem, Dad. I know you're going through a hard time.* But he still hadn't spoken by the time we got home, and after he parked, he wordlessly eased his frame out of the truck and went inside. His halting walk made me look away. My big strong dad. The summer before he got hurt he'd taken me to the high school practice fields a couple times to teach me shot put. He had hopes for me. I had his build and strength, and he was sure that, somewhere deep down, I had his dedication, too. I wanted to believe him, despite all the evidence to the contrary—my report cards, consistently Cs and Ds. My general lack of motivation.

But I liked practicing shot put with him. No matter how uncoordinated my efforts, he'd remind me that form took years to perfect. My favorite part was watching him throw. There was more to it than power or talent, though he had both of those. It was the surprising grace of it—the spin, spin, *launch*. The way the heavy ball rose like a soul heaving itself toward heaven. I always expected the weight to disappear into the blue.

I knew Jo thought Dad was naive, that he put too much trust in Mark. She probably had similar thoughts about me. I wasn't sure if she understood how much of my belief was because of Dad. Could she not see what a good guy he was, giving up his scholarship so he could be, well, Dad? So he could work blue-collar jobs his whole life and take care of us? It would've been so easy for him to spend the rest of his life telling a story about what should've been. To allow himself flashes of fantasy: The Olympics. A college coaching job. But he'd always been clear on what mattered—his daughters, his responsibilities, God.

Whenever I felt inspired toward something, it was usually

toward being like him. Trusting, patient, enduring. You could do a lot worse than that, I thought. And yet somehow, for all of his efforts, here he was suffering more than any person could handle. I knew he'd tried. I knew that even a well-meaning doctor couldn't appreciate what he was going through.

He did need real help. More than that, he deserved it.

I HAD THE NEXT DAY OFF, and was back at work again for the morning shift the day after. This time, I was five minutes early. Rita put me on breakfast rotation again. When I brought Marlene her meal—scrambled egg crumbles and a puddle of Cream of Wheat under a heavy plastic dome—I found her in bed, mouth open, breathing lightly.

"Breakfast?" she asked, faintly.

"Yes. Do you want some now?" My voice, full of false cheer, sounded as loud as a car horn. More quietly I asked, "Would you like to sit up?"

"Please," she said, nodding, and I held down the blue button on the side of her bed. She winced halfway up, but managed, "I'm all right. Keep going."

I swiveled the hospital table so it extended over her tiny lap, uncovered the plate, set out her napkin and utensils. "Would you like help?" I asked, and she shook her head. With a shaking fingertip she nudged dry egg bits onto her spoon. I sat. After she'd swallowed her second bite, she said, "You're quiet today."

"Just tired," I said. "Who sent the flowers?"

"Flowers?" She followed my gaze to the carnations at her bedside. "Those are from Pine Creek. They give flowers to anyone who gets hurt or sick."

"Oh." Now the flowers seemed cheerless and cheap.

"But I did get something from my granddaughter." She lifted a small white book that had been at her hip. "Kind of a silly thing," she said, handing it to me. Marlene opened it using one of the colored ribbons sewn into the spine. "This is the page she marked for me." The heading read *Prayers for Difficult Times*. The first prayer began, *God, I know that my present suffering is not worth comparing to the glory* . . . I couldn't help smiling at the old memory verse. I'd never been good at memorizing anything, either for school or for church, but the benefit of church was that I kept encountering the same verses, year after year, so many times that a few of them eventually stuck.

"What?" Marlene asked, watching my reaction.

"That's from Romans, I think." I handed it back to her.

"I didn't take you for a church girl."

"I used to be. I don't really know what I am anymore." I had figured, once Tara and I started dating, that I would become the kind of Christian she was—political, progressive. Someone who talked about the importance of interfaith groups and who casually used a four-letter word here and there, because God cared a lot more about feeding the hungry than whether you sometimes said *shit*.

But this version of faith didn't always feel like it was working for me. I didn't want to go back to assuming every Republican politician was doing God's work, and I was relieved to officially believe that Muslims and Buddhists and everybody else had the same access to the divine that Christians did. But I also wanted to know what it meant for me to say *God*. And I didn't anymore.

And that meant, somehow, that I wasn't sure what I meant when I said *I*, either.

"Huh." Marlene was looking at me closely. Her focus seemed to have dulled her pain. "I find that more interesting. Not knowing what you are."

"Yeah." I knew I sounded unconvinced, but Marlene didn't comment on that.

"What I want to know is why so many Christians feel like they need to convert everybody around them," she said.

"It's a Christian teaching. 'Go make disciples of all nations,' I think is how they put it."

"There are lots of Christian teachings. That one seems to get a bit overemphasized, don't you think?"

She was right. "Probably it feels good to get someone else to believe what you believe. Maybe if you convince them, what you believe seems truer."

Marlene nodded sadly. "That's it. My granddaughter means well, but she wants to feel sure of herself in this world. I've lived a long life, though, honey, and I can tell you that being sure is just a state of mind." We were quiet for a moment. "Which is why," she concluded, "I think you should be sure only that you don't know who, or what, you are."

"Thanks," I said. I knew she was trying to help, but the thought was depressing. I didn't need answers like Dad did. But I still wanted to be around people who had answers. Well, Tara had some answers. But were they the ones I needed?

"Will you put this back for me?" Marlene asked, tapping the book. "I can't reach that drawer."

I slid open the bedside drawer, pushed aside Kleenex, lozenges, a plastic comb with a few silver hairs in its teeth. I saw the orange prescription bottle with the E-Z Off cap. *OXYCODONE 40MG.* The label was from the hospital pharmacy.

"Whoa," I said. "They gave you the good stuff."

"I told them I didn't want to be dopey on pain pills, but they insisted. They don't understand that I'm content with my 'present suffering.'" She chuckled at her joke, then winced.

I heard myself say, "I'll take them to the nurses' station for you."

She nodded, closed her eyes. "That'd be fine."

THE HOUSE WAS SILENT WHEN I entered. Then I heard the click of Hulk's nails on the floor. Dad was lying on the couch with the footrest levered up. But when I rounded the edge of the couch I saw that his eyes were open. He moved his gaze toward me, then wordlessly back at the ceiling. He was wearing the same sweatshirt and sweatpants he had been when I left yesterday morning. His stare meant he was feeling what would make another person groan out loud. But you can't spend your whole life making sounds like that. He'd learned to swallow it. Still, I knew it echoed inside him, a cry that never ended.

When I put the pills on the folding table next to him, Dad looked from the bottle to me with a wonder that I thought might break my heart. He picked up the bottle, read the label. A question flared in his eyes.

"I've always been very careful about this," he told me.

"The doctor on staff thinks you should have access to more pain meds. He says to keep this quiet. It's not official. He just had some extra. Because like you say, you're a big person." I paused, flailing now. I hadn't expected anything but gratitude. I thought about apologizing, snatching the bottle back, never mentioning it again. But Dad had wrapped his large hand around it now. Only a fraction of the white plastic cap was visible.

Finally, he said, "Will you thank him for me?"

"Sure," I said. "Sure I will."

I DIDN'T THINK OF IT as stealing, let alone criminal. I wasn't holding up a pharmacy. I wasn't selling anything. Marlene simply didn't want her pills, and I knew someone who did.

If I'd really thought about it, I would have known how serious it was. But I didn't really think about it. Dad was suffering too much. The memories of his old self made my throat ache. When Jo and I were kids he once bought a sandwich and a Coke for a woman sitting alone at a truck stop. Even from a distance you could see she wasn't as good-looking as she was trying to be. Her makeup was too heavy, her shirt too worn. Up close, she smelled. When Dad asked if he could pray for her, she said why not, she'd tried everything else. He prayed with his hand on her shoulder, and she cried, then told him he was an angel. Next she turned toward me and Jo. Something fierce and defensive had gathered within her. "You two are lucky, you hear?" she said. "Lucky to have a guy like him for a dad. Don't give him trouble. Make him proud." We nodded dumbly. Dad, fumbling, said, "They sure do, ma'am. They already do."

There were other stories. It hurt too much to keep remembering how he used to be.

You have to understand I was living with the person I felt more loyalty to than anyone else. You have to understand how much I missed the person he'd been. I even would've taken the version of Dad in the months after the accident, when he was *hard pressed, but not crushed*, as the Bible says. He still insisted, back then, that God would use his injury to glorify Jesus. But Dad had long since stopped saying it. And I, for one, couldn't see glory anywhere, in any of this.

WITHIN A DAY, DAD WAS better. He raked part of the lawn. He took Hulk on a slow, long walk. He took a nap that left him refreshed instead of more beaten down. He asked me to play cribbage with him after dinner. We hadn't done this in a while. "Where are you off to so much these days?" he asked, after he'd dropped his cards in the crib, which was mine that turn. I was deciding whether to keep my seven, eight, and nine together in hopes of a double run or keep the fives and a face card. "You have a secret boyfriend or something?" he asked. Then he said, "You know I can't approve of you spending the night at a boyfriend's house." I gaped a little, felt tears sting my eyes. He said, "Georgie, hun, I'm not trying to read you the riot act. I just need to be clear with you about my priorities."

But I wasn't crying because of his reprimand—or, I was, but only because he'd regained that old voice he used when he was worried and fatherly and not sure what to do.

The only thing I could manage was a lame "It's not like that."

He nodded seriously, then gave me a long look that made me feel warm and safe. "I trust you," he said, at last.

I dropped the fives. Dad split the deck and I turned over an eight—double run for me.

CHAPTER SEVEN

JO

Usually I worked well ahead of my school deadlines, but I'd been avoiding the investigative project since Georgie's visit. I had hoped some new idea would present itself, or that I would regain my interest in the story I'd proposed. But as the due date for a two-thousand-word draft approached, I still had only two possible topics. One I knew how to approach, and one I didn't.

The night before the draft was due, I went to a quiet corner of the student center, where there was a long counter equipped with study lights and, importantly, outlets.

It was the eve of my birthday. Earlier in the week I'd gotten a card from Dad with a twenty-dollar bill in it. Georgie had called. Nothing from Mom. Based on experience I had a fifty percent chance of hearing from her. I'd seen her only three times in the last ten years. Once she came for a short visit, and twice I flew to LA for a week. The last time I'd seen her had been shortly after I'd been accepted into Peabody. She'd taken me out shopping for my college wardrobe, and I picked out that cherry-print shirt. For my birthday freshman year she sent full-length curtains I couldn't hang because even if she'd sent the rod I needed, which she hadn't, I'd also need access to an electric drill. Sophomore year I got nothing, not even a card. This year, I didn't know what I wanted. I mean, I wanted something from Mom, but I also knew that anything I got would leave me disappointed. And I was tired of being disappointed.

My student mailbox had remained empty all day.

I hadn't told anyone at Peabody about my birthday. Lily might try to do something celebratory, but it would be a favor I couldn't return. Also, because everyone around me was turning twenty-one, birthday celebrations defaulted to a bar. I didn't want to draw any attention to the fact that I was turning nineteen.

I took the spot farthest from the chaos of the student center's common area. The bar-height chair of highly curved plastic made me feel like an egg nestled into a carton. I'd written some of my best papers at these seats. I didn't come here often because I didn't want the setting to lose its potency.

Seamus had warned us that the draft would be difficult to write. The purpose, he said, was to identify gaps in our stories. "My whole project is one big gap," Morgan moaned to me, Lily, and Susan. She was writing about the firing of her high school's drama teacher. "At least you have *one* interview," said Susan, whose topic was the finances of her hometown's equestrian team's scholarship fund. Lily, who was looking into the college's maternity leave policy for non-tenure-track faculty, said nothing. We all knew her project was going well, and she didn't want to rub it in.

I had been trying to stick to my original story, but my "investigation" yielded nothing. I'd talked to my old Sunday school teacher and to Word of Life's former secretary, but they just seemed happy to hear from me and asked a lot of questions about how I was doing, which I felt forced into answering mostly dishonestly, which made me incapable of conducting a good interview.

I didn't want to write about what Georgie had told me, in no small part because Georgie assumed I would want to. I didn't have a history of accepting advice from Georgie and I didn't plan to start now.

"I'm not sure why you're telling me this," I told her, after she'd finished her disjointed story, which she clearly wanted me to see as a personal favor. But if she was trying to build a bridge between us, wasn't she also using a boy's gruesome death and disfigurement to bring us together? And wasn't that kind of messed up?

Her eyes roved the room, landing everywhere I wasn't. She said, "I thought you'd want to know. Maybe you could use it to help you process what happened? Or we could talk about it?"

"Honestly?" I said. "I wish I didn't know."

As if I hadn't spoken, she went on, "Or it could make a good topic for your class?"

So Georgie was repaying her old debt. Or trying to.

Merely by sitting on my bed she'd rumpled the covers to the point that I'd have to make it again. The gap between us was no more than four feet. It would take two steps to reach her. I could curl up next to her, maybe even put my head on her lap. She might put a hand on my shoulder, and I might melt a little, let my fists uncoil and my jaw unclench and something in my chest fall ajar. I might tell her that she didn't need to use that boy's death to bring us together. That there was enough between us already. I could describe the Frida Kahlo painting, say, *That's us. Fixed together by blood and by clasped hands, their connection one part biology and one part choice.*

But the idea was too dramatic. Wasn't it long past time I stopped entertaining these little fantasies about the affection between me and Georgie?

Georgie was waiting for me to respond. I said, "I really do have to go to class. I'll be back in an hour and a half." I sounded, I thought, as weary as I felt. If I didn't leave right away, I would do something I wasn't sure I was ready to do. Like, for example, forgive Georgie. Say something like *I know you were lost back then. I was too. It's okay. We can move on.* Wordlessly I left the room, pattered down the stairs. I couldn't help wondering if her eyes were on my back as I crossed the quad. I refused to look.

During class, though, I found myself increasingly anxious to return to Georgie. Halfway through her lecture, my professor gave me a puzzled look, and I realized I was tapping my pen on my desk hard enough to draw her attention. I stilled my hand. Minutes later my knee was going up and down. By the time I was striding back to my dorm, I thought I might be ready to talk.

When I got back to my room, though, there was a note on my desk.

> Figured I might as well head back.
>
> Thanks for having me, thanks for the cereal.
>
> Love Georgie

That was it. She couldn't give me ninety minutes to think things over. It wasn't forgiveness she wanted but acquittal. And I couldn't give her that.

Now I had something else to forgive her for, too.

Georgie might be right that the photos would be a good topic for the class, but in addition to my instinctive reluctance to use it, I had two concerns. First, the sheer gravity of the situation seemed to call for a professional. How would I go about writing about pictures I hadn't seen? Also, I suspected I knew only slightly more than the average American about the war. The national fever after 9/11 had long since worn off. The news coming out of Iraq and Afghanistan had become a narrow and repetitive stream, and I'd stopped paying much attention. If anyone asked, I was uncomfortable at best with the war in Afghanistan and firmly against the Iraq war. Beyond that, what was I supposed to do or think? I was eleven when the planes hit the towers. I didn't feel responsible for what happened next, and there was so much I didn't understand anyway. The one time I'd tried to read up on how it all unfolded, I got lost in a maze of older histories. I trusted I was capable of learning it all, but not of keeping up my GPA at the same time.

My second concern with using the photos for my class project contradicted the first. What if the photos represented only a general horror of war? It was all too easy to imagine sitting across from Seamus as he told me again, in so many words, that I didn't really understand how the world worked.

I HEARD MY NAME. Lily was striding toward me carrying a box the size of a large microwave. She leaned to look at my blank screen, asked, "Writing going well, huh?" I knew it was meant to be a gentle ribbing, but I was irked. Perhaps sensing my irritation, she hoisted the box onto the counter next to me, shook the ache out of her arms. "You're coming to the Right to the Night event?"

"The what?"

"Right to the Night. It's being put on by PROTEST."

I remembered now. It was a "community awareness and support" event for "survivors."

"We're trying to get a really good showing," she went on. "We don't want it to be, like, five of us marching around. I've got all these T-shirts to give out. Will you come?" She saw my hesitation. "I wouldn't ask you to do this if I didn't think it was really important for the whole campus to show up for rape and sexual assault survivors. I know you're super busy with everything you have going on," she went on, somehow managing to earnestly insist on what we both knew wasn't true.

I heard myself say, "Okay."

Lily hugged me. "Let me give you a T-shirt. We made them big so we can wear them over jackets." She drew out a huge white shirt that said, in block print on the front, I HAVE A RIGHT TO THE NIGHT.

I wasn't comfortable with the shirt, either its style or its noisy sentiment. But Lily was so enthusiastic about it that I took it from her, draped it over my lap like a blanket.

"Meet outside Carter Hall, nine o'clock. And *thank you*," she added, pressing the words hard into my consciousness, so that I could feel their imprint after she was gone.

Someone opened the door for her as she walked out with her box. I wiggled my finger on the trackpad to wake my laptop. There was a delay so long that I wondered dully, and then with growing fear, whether the computer had made its final gasp and I'd be banished back to Jarrett. But the screen blinked on, showing me the same blank Word document, cursor beating its slow rhythm.

I remained surprised that Gary had taken pictures. For all the ways in which Gary wanted to draw attention to himself, he had a secretive side. Not that he told me any real secrets. I just sensed they were there, somewhere under the bluster. In fact, I sometimes wondered if he liked drawing attention to himself because then he could direct where the attention went.

But the pictures were a fact. And I needed two thousand words on *something*. Why should it bother me what Seamus thought of my new topic? He already didn't want me writing about the one I'd chosen, so it wasn't like disappointing him with the new one would change the situation.

For a few minutes all I could think about was everything I didn't know. I had to wake my computer twice more when the screen blinked out. Unfocusing my eyes, I went over what I did know, letting images and snatches of conversation and church gossip swirl in my head. And then a little bit of magic happened: I got a first sentence. It landed whole in my consciousness. I typed,

> At the memorial service for his son, held in a high school gymnasium well past capacity, Pastor Mark Clemmens read from the Gospel of Matthew.

Then I got another sentence, and another one.

I was surprised by how much I could say without having done formal research. Or, better yet, without having realized that I was doing research. I could report on the funeral because I'd read news articles. I could report on what people said about Gary because I had access to Facebook. I could report on the photographs because Georgie had arrived ready to tell me as much as she knew. I was rearranging the last paragraphs of a rough draft when something hit my chair. "Whoops, sorry," said a voice. It was a guy about my age, pushing a yellow mop bucket on wheels. The bucket had careened into my chair.

"No problem," I said. I was almost done anyway, and surfacing from deep thought made me feel strangely chatty. I gestured at my laptop. "Got this draft due tomorrow."

"What class is it for?" he asked, pulling a thick black lever to wring out the mop. He had high cheeks and thick dark brows, and his skin was lightly pocked with acne scars.

"Investigative journalism."

"You're taking Seamus Matthews's course?"

"Oh," I said, surprised. "Yes."

He smirked. "I may be a janitor, but I know a few things about this college."

"I wasn't suggesting—" I said, but I was. I wanted to tell him I'd mopped floors, too, back at Betty's, but didn't know how to say it without making the entire exchange more awkward. I wondered if there was any place in the world where I would feel like I belonged.

BACK IN MY ROOM, I layered a fleece over a hooded sweatshirt, stuffed mittens in the pockets, pulled the T-shirt over the whole bulky top. Even with all those layers, I swam in the T-shirt's cottony expanse. I could only hope everyone else looked as silly as I felt.

Descending a shallow hill toward Carter, I could just make out a few dozen people gathered by the front door. Other figures drifted toward the group like metal shavings toward a magnet. Seconds after I attached myself to the ragged edge of the crowd, someone gave me a candle in a plastic holder. It was identical to what I'd get at church for Christmas Eve services. A deacon always started the service with a lecture about how to light our candles, by tipping the *unlit* candle toward the *lit* one, not the other way around. Because most people didn't listen, Georgie and

I always had to stay late after the service because Dad was one of the people who'd go around with a butter knife scraping up the wax droppings.

I spotted Lily in a group of girls, one of whom was using a flashlight to illuminate a clipboard. Lily was wearing her T-shirt over a puffer jacket, but she'd knotted the shirt at her hip so that she looked like a tidy marshmallow. I, on the other hand, looked like a kid wearing one of my dad's old T-shirts as pajamas. I put the unlit candle between my knees so I could style my shirt the same way, but too late: Someone had struck a lighter, and now the flames around me were multiplying too fast for me to fix my outfit.

An organizer stood on her tippy-toes, called out, "One little flame was the source of all the light we carry! Think about that for a second! Think about what one act of courage can do! Now—are we ready to march?"

The group responded with a half-hearted "Yeah!"

I dreaded the predictable pump-up—*I SAID, are we ready to MARCH?!*—but it didn't come. Instead, the same organizer called, "Our first stop is Romley Hall. We want to be heard at the highest levels of the Peabody community!"

Romley Hall was the administrative building. Half of us cheered loudly and the other half didn't make a sound. The mood still hadn't settled between solemn and raucous.

A cold breeze pushed through the crowd, raising gasps of alarm as some candles were snuffed. They were quickly relit, then cupped by protective hands as we shuffled along.

Romley had about a dozen low, semicircular stairs leading up to the main doors. Lily mounted the stairs. We waited with the anticipation of a Sunday congregation.

"Tonight we're going to hear from survivors," she said. "I don't need to say anything except that these stories matter." Then she stepped down. I couldn't help being impressed by the brevity of her remarks, how right they felt at this moment. Lily was so socially adept that I sometimes found myself thinking, ungenerously, that she was too self-satisfied. But then she'd go and do something like this, making it clear she was the last person she was thinking about.

I recognized the girl replacing Lily at the top of the steps. Her small but wide eyes gave the impression she'd been newly popped from a mold, as if she experienced every second as a fresh shock of exposure. I was blanking on her name.

"I'm Rochelle," she said. She held her candle higher than she needed to. "When I was five my parents split up. The next year my mom remarried and we moved to Colorado. We lived in a little yellow house, and I had a room with lace curtains." She blinked at us and then said, somewhat mechanically, "My stepdad raped me repeatedly over the next three years."

I could barely make out my own shoes in the dark, past the candle's weak light. What did I expect, coming here? Euphemism and insinuation? That we would all be in agreement that it's best not to name the horrible, bodily truth? I focused on the candle in my hand, pulled the flame toward me so I could feel its heat on my chin. The girl in front of me had her hair in two braids. I studied the curled lock she'd missed at the nape of her neck.

Lily had told me what the event was about, but I'd still managed to ignore the real purpose, which struck me as useless. Maybe it helped some people to *tell their stories*. I couldn't imagine it helping me.

Rochelle was telling us about how her high school guidance counselor said she had a chance at a scholarship at Peabody. How this scholarship, this opportunity, had changed her life.

So Rochelle was one of the Presidential Scholars. I knew my surge of jealousy was insane. Still. Being a Presidential Scholar was more than a full ride. It got you special access to internships, alumni. The website for past Presidential Scholars listed their achievements. They were impressive.

I'd once imagined my name on that page.

Rochelle said that even at Peabody it was still hard. "It follows you wherever you go," she said. "It's followed me, anyway." She waited a few seconds, trying, it seemed, to find the right way to end her short speech. Then she said, "I think that's all I have to say." Girls put their arms around her shoulders as she came back into the crowd. An organizer ordered us to Brentwood Hall. We begin walking again. My candle was two-thirds as long as it had been when we began, and I was getting cold. I wanted to slip away, but leaving would be too obvious. For one thing, I was wearing a white T-shirt as big as a sail.

I was surprised to see that Helena, Lily's friend, was the next to speak. Helena was, I'd decided, the Barbie version of Georgie. They were about the same size and had similar coloring, but where Helena was smooth, tan, satiny in her prettiness, Georgie looked, at best, like she'd been crumpled and hastily smoothed.

Helena spoke more easily than Rochelle, and I could tell she'd told this story before. It was her senior year of high school. She was dating an older guy. Her parents didn't know. She always had an explanation for them. A sleepover at a friend's, a weekend soccer camp. A few days after she graduated, her boyfriend took her to a club, got her in through the back door. She only wanted to have some fun. And it was fun, for the first hour, the dancing and colored drinks. Then someone brought her a third drink. That's about where her memory stopped. Next thing she knew she was on a bathroom floor, being prodded awake with the business end of a mop. Her purse was gone. The guy she was dating was gone. Someone took her to the hospital, she had a kit done. The guy she'd been dating said he thought she'd left the club. He agreed to be tested. It wasn't him. And that was all she knew about the night she was raped.

"My parents don't like me talking about it," she said. "They tell me they're not ashamed, but that I might not want this to be public information down the line. I think they mean well, but their interest in secrecy isn't helping. It's driving the problem deeper into the shadows. The thing is," she continued, "I don't care about the judgment of people who don't care about me. And anyone who *does* care about me will understand the unjust stigma of the crime committed against me. Yes, the same girl who was on high honor roll all through high school, the same girl who captained the soccer team two years in a row, the same girl who threw my parents a huge surprise anniversary party and never got so much as a speeding ticket—that girl woke up on the broken tile floor of a club whose name she didn't know, her jeans around her ankles and her favorite thong torn on the floor." She looked at us fiercely, and then her features softened into weariness. "And still, every time I tell this story I realize someone is probably judging me for going to a club with an older guy and taking drinks out of the hands of God knows who."

"We love you so much!" someone yelled.

Someone else called, "You fucking rock!"

Helena's eyes shone, but she was smiling at her friends in the crowd.

I thought about how Helena had so much more going for her than I'd ever had going for me. But how she still wanted an older boyfriend who was probably even richer than she was. She wanted to sneak into a club, she wanted to drink with adults.

Not that she deserved what happened to her. Still, I was aware of a kernel of judgment lodged at the base of my thinking. My judgment made me feel ashamed, then defensive, then ashamed again.

Now she said, "What I want to say to anyone dealing with this is, it's not your fault. It doesn't matter what you wore. It doesn't matter if you were drunk or high. It doesn't matter if you flirted. If you thought at first you wanted it. If it was someone you knew. If you were on the wrong street, or at the wrong party, or in the wrong car, or if you'd lied to your parents and everyone else about where you were. If you'd slept with a hundred people before. You can always find a way to blame the victim. So I want to do something right now." She moved her candle from one hand to the other and smoothed her hair. "This is spontaneous, but I want to try it. Sorry if it sucks." A ripple of laughter. "I want to share a thought. I want us all to be really clear, mentally, about something. If you are a survivor, I want you to tell yourself, 'It's not my fault.' And if you are not a survivor, but you support survivors—and why else would you be here?—then I want you to think about the survivors in this gathering, the ones you know and the ones you don't. I want you to tell them, in your mind, 'It's not your fault.' All right? Go."

It was like a race I hadn't signed up for was underway, and I was scrambling for a starting line I didn't even want to take. *Not my fault?* Immediately I was dive-bombed by qualifications. This was why I didn't think about it. I could drive myself crazy trying to pick apart exactly what I was and was not responsible for. I'd liked it the first and second times Gary kissed me, and stopped liking it after that. That was weeks before we'd had sex, though in retrospect it never felt like *we'd* had sex at all. The most grammatically correct way to put it, I realized, was always that *he* had sex with *me*. But did that make me a *victim*? If I'd never done anything to try to stop it?

I thought of calling Georgie from the motel. Hadn't I tried to stop it then?

And now another memory surfaced from that night. I hadn't been able to stomach as many drinks as the times before, which made Gary experience me as, I guess, less pliant than usual.

"You can't tell me you don't want this," he said. He was already on top of me, his forearms around my head like a frame. From outside my body, I saw myself as a work of art: *Head of a Girl*. Better yet, *Girl Without a Body*.

"I don't," I said.

"Sure," he said. Then he said, "Scream if you want me to stop. Or even try to fight me." His tone was light. His eyes were doing that self-satisfied dance.

And I lay silent and frozen.

Standing in the well-meaning crowd, all I wanted was to edit my history the way I might edit a draft of a paper, peeling that crucial paragraph open, adding the sentences that would convince him, convince me, convince anyone who read it that *I did not want this*. Why hadn't I done more to stop him? Why didn't I scream?

But I knew why: Because I'd decided that I might as well bear these few minutes so it could end as soon as possible. Because these minutes seemed more bearable than any drastic steps I might take to stop it. Because I did not understand what a few minutes would cost me.

Then again, what if I had screamed, had struggled? Would he have let me go? Or would he have muffled my cries? My strength was no match for his. A sudden heat inside my jacket and a chill at the back of my neck told me I'd broken into a sweat.

I wondered what the "survivors" around me would make of me asking, *What if resisting only makes it worse? Isn't it rational at some point to make a kind of bargain, to step into a stretch of time as you would into an awful hallway, trusting that you will come out the other side, capable of closing the door behind you and never going back?*

I thought of the looks I'd get. The unasked, horrified question I'd see in their eyes: *You* let *it happen?*

Fine, I thought. *Yes. I let it happen.* I had to think of it that way. I had to believe that I'd had a choice. Because the alternative, that in that moment I'd had no power and no choice, was worse.

Because then it could happen again.

Now, though, my cold, wet neck was prickling with the knowledge that the people around me were silently telling me *Not your fault.* Mentally I shoved it back their way.

It's not your fault.

It is my fault!

Not your fault.

Yes it is!

I'd missed a cue. Everyone was walking again, sliding past me like a river around a rock. I blew out my candle and walked away.

• • •

AN HOUR LATER, LILY AND Helena knocked at my door. Still wearing their big white shirts, they came in like detectives entering a crime scene, mincing but attentive. My makeshift bed skirt was hitched up on one side, revealing a neon CLEARANCE sticker on the butt end of a bag of bagels. I positioned myself, casually, I hoped, over the gap while Helena helped herself to my desk chair. Lily handed me a small red package that depicted a cross section of a little cake.

Lily leaned against my dresser. "My grandma was just here. Don't worry," she added when she saw me hesitate. "I have plenty. My dorm room currently looks like an Asian market." I tried to find her well-stocked room as funny as they did.

She was too kind to turn down, and anyway, dinner already seemed like it had been days before. I peeled open the wrapper, hefted the palm-sized dessert before lifting it to my mouth. Its chocolate shell broke delicately between my teeth. The cake and marshmallow layers inside were light and not too sweet. Lily and Helena watched as I ate the whole thing, then wiped my lips. Already I felt a little better.

"Thank you," I said.

Lily said what we'd all been waiting for her to say. "We heard you looked upset when you left. We wanted to make sure you're okay."

"I was getting chilly," I explained. I gestured at some books. "And I remembered I have to . . ." But I was too tired to finish inventing the lie. I said, "I did want to support survivors. I mean, I do support them."

Lily and Helena looked at each other. Helena said, gently, "Can I close the door?" My fearful shrug was taken as a yes.

Once the three of us were sealed off in the small space, Lily said, "It wouldn't be fair for us to ask you to share anything you're not ready to. And we don't make assumptions. But just to let you know—we're here to talk about anything you need to."

The two beautiful girls waited patiently. A powerful feeling of déjà vu resolved when I realized that this was what an altar call at church felt like. *Tell us what we want to hear,* they'd say, *and in return we'll take care of you. We'll give you the right things to believe and say and do, so that everything works out the way it's supposed to.*

I knew how it would go. I would tell them what happened. They would make soft sounds in their throats. They would sop up my every word. We all would forget about the time. They'd stay here as late as I wanted them to, growing in our resolve and trust. At some point we'd start laughing, even.

And that's almost how it happened. I almost told them the whole thing, the plain ugly truth in plain ugly words. But then I thought of what would come next, in the days and weeks after. For a while, I might feel unburdened, like I'd given the memory away. Like it was off my shoulders for good. But then, at some point, Lily and Helena would introduce a plan for me. Counseling. Maybe a police report. They'd remind me I was brave. Then, in a few months or next year, they'd approach me about how, when I was ready of course, I might consider *telling my story.* Could they pencil me in for standing on the steps of Romley next year, holding a candle high to light my face and speaking through lips numbed by cold?

But I didn't know how to be a Survivor. I didn't have the right ratio of strength to weakness. I would seem too fine, and then too damaged. I seemed that way to myself.

I said, "I think you have the wrong impression." I sounded as nervous as I felt. "I was really touched by the stories tonight, but not because I'm a—" I couldn't meet their eyes. I found myself trembling, which I knew preceded either throat-closing panic or the kind of ugly self-pity I really didn't want them to see.

"It happened to my sister," I blurted. And I burst into tears.

"To Georgie?" Lily asked, gravely.

"It was this guy she was dating in high school," I said. "He was older. I know stuff happened. I think it was okay at first. They were just dating. But then things changed. It wasn't good."

I looked at them to see how my story hand landed. Their expressions were pinched in concern. They nodded slowly, assimilating each detail. Troubled, but not surprised. There was a skill to this kind of listening, which conveyed that they were upset without acting upset.

"I don't know much more than that," I went on. "It was a really hard time in our family. Our dad was in the hospital. I wasn't really paying attention. I don't even have clear evidence that anything happened. I mean, I don't know if there was a crime. But I think there was." I felt a little breathless. But awake, too, and strangely alive to possibility. I knew I sounded brave as I forged on. "I didn't help her. I didn't do anything," I concluded. Tears again, but they were in a slow drip now. Lily pulled me in for a hug, rubbed gentle circles on my back. "I'm so sorry," she said. "So, so sorry. For you both."

"Does she know that you know?" Helena asked.

I nodded into Lily's shoulder. "It took me a while to bring it up. When I finally did, she said she didn't care."

"It would be normal for you to experience some denial when it happened," Helena said. And then, "It's also normal if you feel some guilt. Not that you should. It's just normal."

"Thanks." I hadn't had a good cry like that in a long time. A new space had opened in my chest. Lily slipped out of my room, returned with neatly folded toilet paper. I blew my nose. All three of us laughed at how much snot came out.

They asked me how I was doing now, and whether I'd be okay tonight.

"I'm fine," I said, and I meant it. More hugs.

"We can talk more tonight, share ideas about how to help her, but only if you want," said Helena. "It'll be totally up to you."

I said thank you. Then they left. I couldn't sleep, so I put on my jacket and walked loops around the pitch-dark campus. I didn't know if I'd go so far as to say *the truth set me free*, but it sure did take a weight off. Of course, it wasn't the full truth. I was still warming up to that. I'd say it eventually. Maybe in a few years, to the next person who needed to hear it.

Back in my room, I booted up my laptop. Without even skimming the proposal again, I opened a new email.

> Hey, Seamus. Got a new topic for the project. See the attachment. Still a little rough, but what do you think?

I still didn't feel sleepy, so I got out my reading for PoliSci. I got less than three pages in when my laptop dinged. Seamus had already written back. He wanted to see me at nine.

• • •

FIVE HOURS LATER I WAS at his office door. It was 8:58. I'd slept maybe two hours, but I still didn't feel tired. Maybe I would never feel tired again. Maybe my half-truth had cured me of all fatigue. I knocked and he called, "Come in."

The overhead light in the office was off. Behind Seamus was a large window, leaving him backlit in a way that made it hard to see his face. Hard to gauge the mood in the room. I sat across from him. He was staring at his lap, where he held a printed document. I saw that it was my proposal. He dropped it gently. It caught on a pillow of air, then fell two inches to the desk.

"Hi," I said.

He said, "You're sure about this."

"My sister knows what she saw."

"And she saw the photos how?"

"She . . . knows Gary's sister." Instinctively I left out the part where they were dating.

He put his hand to his cheek, stared at me. Down the hall, someone greeted someone loudly. Finally he said, "Gary was the son of the pastor who went around wanting money from everyone."

"Right."

"It does make the money thing more interesting," he mused. "That could be a sidebar."

"Oh?"

"If there's one thing I've learned being a journalist," he started, and I wondered if he knew how many things he claimed were the one thing he'd learned as a journalist, "it's that crimes of significance are at the center of any number of other moral failings.

Which makes the father's habit of coaxing money out of other people more interesting."

"You think I should write about Pastor Mark?"

"I'm saying that now the dad is good background for a story about Gary." He folded his arms on the desk and leaned toward me, his shoulders up at his ears. "This Gary guy—tell me more about him."

"Well," I said, trying to remember what I'd already said in the proposal. "Gary was one of those guys who could seem perfect even when he got in trouble. What I mean is, the right kind of trouble is a good look for some people."

"You need to put that line in there—'the right kind of trouble.' That's going to be key."

"Okay."

"You know you have quite a story on your hands?"

"I guess?" I said. But then I said, "Not really," because I wanted him to keep convincing me.

"I *knew* there was something going on back there, that day we talked," he said, drawing little circles with his fingertip in the direction of my brain. I didn't contradict him. Didn't say, *No, what you saw was something else.*

"I wasn't sure it would work for class," I said.

"Screw the class! This is salable. Do you see that?"

"Salable as in—?" I knew what he meant but still needed him to spell it out.

"To a national magazine. This is your break." His enthusiasm seemed tinged with dismay. Was he jealous that I found this story? Or was he dismayed because this was what real journalism was like? Because you could never be happy about an ugly truth?

I said, honestly, "I wasn't sure this was a big deal. It's horrible, but it's war."

"War *is* horrible, but it's not supposed to be deliberately grotesque. It's not supposed to be saving body parts. That's what the Geneva Conventions were for. That's why we have court-martials."

"I guess," I said.

"You're unconvinced."

"Men get away with a lot. Especially the ones everyone likes." Did he know I'd put him in that category? Not that I thought he'd commit atrocities. Still. I suspected, given his teaching practices at least, that he'd gotten more passes than he deserved.

"Of course they do!" he exclaimed, so loud I started. "That's the point of journalism. You hold to account the powerful, the popular. The well liked." He was looking at me earnestly. "If American soldiers are doing that, the public needs to know."

"Gary is dead," I pointed out. "So it's not like he can be brought to justice."

"That makes things simpler for you as a writer. He can't come up to you with puppy-dog eyes, begging, 'Don't do this to me!'"

I gave a little snort. I couldn't imagine Gary doing that in real life, either.

"Jo." Impatience put new force in his voice. "What's giving you pause?"

"I'm still surprised you think the story could go somewhere. I thought . . ." But I'd already said what I thought.

He seemed to finally register how far forward he was leaning, because all at once he dropped back into his chair and crossed his arms. He was giving me that curious, tipped-head stare I was familiar with by now. "You have a pretty cynical outlook," he declared. Without waiting for a response, he said, "No, I get it. The world is shitty. But then the question becomes—do you *do* something about that? Or do you sit around and say, 'Too bad the world's so shitty'? Maybe your one article won't change national policy. Maybe no one will be brought to justice as a direct result. But what if there are other articles? What if what you write contributes to a shift in public opinion? What if you prevent even one act of violence? Wouldn't that be worth it?"

Both of us knew there was no point in answering the question.

"Here's what I'm thinking," he went on. "First, take some time with it. It has to be your decision in the end. If you decide to go for it, I'll start bugging my contacts. Annie at *The Atlantic*, Jim at the *New York Times Magazine*. See if I can't find an interested editor. Someone who wants to work with a very talented budding journalist." He grinned at me. I couldn't maintain eye contact. "I'll be here to help you, but the byline should be all yours. You should be prepared for how time-consuming this will be. I know some people here might want me to remind you of the importance of your studies, but I think you know your college transcript doesn't matter unless you're trying to get into med school or law school. So, pass your classes, but otherwise screw your transcript. All right?"

"All right," I said, but I was thinking about how my scholarship required a minimum GPA of 3.25. I tried to do some math. I probably couldn't afford anything lower than Cs for one term. At Peabody, a C still took work.

"First steps: Read up on military policy, war crimes. Make a list of things you remember about Gary. Put that list away and make another list. Scrape the corners of your memory for every detail. Think about who you can interview. Not just war buddies but his old coaches, his old teammates. And, of course, get those pictures."

"The pictures?" I said faintly.

"You have no story without the pictures."

Of course I didn't. What did I think, that I could write a story saying they existed? That I could present them to the world when I hadn't even seen them?

"How do I get them?" I asked.

"You ask his sister to give them to you. Everyone likes being the person who tipped off the news." He paused. "Do you want me to contact her instead? My name recognition might help."

"No," I said quickly. "I'll get them."

"Your reading list should include examples of structures and approaches you might want to borrow from. Do you start with scenes from his youth? A key moment in a basketball game? Do you start with the pictures? Did you say he comes from money?"

He'd gone so quickly from rhetorical questions to an actual question that it took me a moment to catch up. "Not really," I said.

"Just as well. Rich kids fucking up is too obvious—they fuck up because they know they can. A lot of them spend their whole lives exploring the strength of the net that will catch them." He paused, as if to make a note of his own thought, then mused, "It almost never breaks." I thought of Helena. Was this what Seamus would say about her? Her kindness had dissolved my judgment, helped me see more clearly. She hadn't been testing the strength of her safety net. Besides, how could what happened to her resemble *safety*?

I thought about saying something, but Seamus had moved on: "If he didn't grow up with much, what's the corrupting factor? Is it the military? His family? The church?"

None of this felt real. *The Atlantic*? The *New York Times*

Magazine? My big break? Meanwhile, Seamus was getting carried away like he did in class sometimes, delivering a monologue thinly disguised as conversation. I hauled my bag onto my lap to show I was ready to leave.

"All right," he said. "I need to let you go." He circled the desk as I zipped my coat, then stood about two feet from me, watching me thread my arms through the backpack's straps.

"I'm excited for you," he said. He was leaning against the wall, arms crossed. I noticed, then, that his door rested against, but not inside, its frame. Usually he made a show of propping it open. He was distracted, I told myself, but I let myself wonder if it was more than that. I made myself look at him. I liked the weathered skin around his eyes. I liked that one of his front teeth was chipped.

"It's my birthday," I said. I wasn't sure why I said it, except that I was deliriously tired and spinning with confused excitement.

Also, I didn't actually want to leave his office yet.

The news seemed to delight him. "Are you doing anything special? Is it going to be a late night tonight?"

"No," I said. And then, "I've got too much work to do. Especially now."

He gave me an exasperated look. "You have time for *one* fun thing."

"I don't think I do." I realized that, for the first time, I had the upper hand in conversation with Seamus. Had I figured out how to take it? Or had he given it to me?

"New assignment: Get your friends to buy you drinks. Wake up with a hangover tomorrow."

I scoffed. "I'm sure the college administration would be interested in this pedagogical method."

His expression hadn't changed, but I could tell he liked that I was teasing him. He unfolded his arms, worked his hands into his pants pockets. Had he always been nervous around me or was I only noticing it now? "I genuinely think," he said, his voice in a soft and sincere register I felt, somehow, in my knees, "you should do something fun. Or at least something interesting. Something to mark the occasion." He was looking at me.

I knew he was not going to do anything beyond allow this pause. I knew that whatever did or didn't happen next was in my clammy hands. I felt the last few years cresting now, at this exact moment, and I was afraid. But one of the things I was afraid of was missing a chance. Not being bold when I needed to be bold. Not going for what I wanted when I had the opportunity. Throat thick, thinking a dozen things and none at all, I gave the door a little push. It latched with mechanical finality. I took a step toward Seamus. His fingertips crawled into my hair.

CHAPTER EIGHT

GEORGIE

The first Sunday in November found me in a Word of Life pew, picking dog hair off my dress pants while Mark gave a sermon about the feeding of the five thousand in Matthew. Dad had invited me. Better yet, he'd said, "It's been a while since you came to church, huh?" He spoke in an easy, inviting tone I remembered from when I was a kid. The tone said, *Hey, I'm not mad. I'm on your side, asking something reasonable.* I'd always found it authoritative without being threatening.

Though I knew I could resist, I didn't want to. I was happy to let him be in charge again, happy to make him happy.

After I dressed I found Dad in the living room, contemplating everything he'd bought at Home Depot at least a week before. There was shelving for the garage and basement, vinyl plank flooring for the bathroom, and a garbage disposal.

"I'm getting started on this stuff today," he told me.

"Great," I said.

Feeling better had made him anxious about the state of the house, which had gone from disorganized to chaotic. I'd tried to keep on top of it for a while, but dating Tara had hampered my efforts. The truth was that Dad and I were both ashamed, a problem we dealt with by not talking about it.

He also had a new habit of nodding off at weird times, which was why I knew he wasn't going to finish those projects. He probably wasn't going to start them.

"Let's put yourselves in the moment for a second," Mark was saying. "You've walked with your family half a day to see this man who does miracles. Yet it's also true that you're getting hungry, your children are getting hungry. You see the disciples beginning to pass out food to some gathered. There are five hundred people between you and the food. And you're starting to feel pretty stupid—why did you come all this way just to hear some rabbi talk?"

Dad's breathing had changed; his exhales were now little puffs of released air. I didn't have to look to know he'd fallen asleep. Slowly, inconspicuously, I pushed my elbow into his side. He straightened, then looked around in mild wonder, as if drifting from one dream to the next.

I knew it was the pills. Another bottle of oxycodone had showed up in Marlene's drawer, and I took that one, too, this time while she slept. I knew it wasn't a long-term solution, yet both times I'd handed him a bottle, I'd half believed that *these* pills wouldn't run out. Mark was saying that the loaves and the fish showed how God provides even when it seems like there won't be enough. But when I put myself in the moment, as Mark suggested, all I could think about was those people, how desperate they were for that little bit to last.

Everyone, I thought, knows what it's like to have a little bit of something that's running out fast. That's what I would talk about if I were preaching on this Bible story.

The people I'd grown up with had studied the Bible like it was an object. But I was starting to see it more like a memory. People kept retelling it and saying it differently every time.

Talking with Tara had been giving me room for thoughts like this. For the first months we were dating, I didn't know how to think for myself about Christianity. I just wanted her to tell me what she thought. Over time, I found that I had ideas of my own. At first I felt silly—they sounded dumb in my head and worse when I said them—but then Tara would give me this *look*.

"Are you sure you don't want to go to seminary?" Tara had asked me recently.

I wanted to laugh at this. Tara claimed that lots of churches hired women. Even if they did, she seemed to be forgetting the fact that I'd almost failed out of tenth grade. And anyway, it was one thing to practice having ideas and another thing to stand in front of a bunch of people and say them like they were true, when I would know they were, at best, optimistic possibilities.

What, at the end of the day, or even the end of my life, could I know, beyond a doubt, was lasting and real? And if the answer was, as I feared, "nothing," then why bother with the attempt at all?

This was the other reason I'd agreed to come to church with Dad. I wanted to try on the old teachings, like shirts pulled from the back of a closet, to see if they fit.

Of course they didn't.

Tara didn't know I was here. I didn't mean for it to be a secret but I knew it might end up being one anyway. Things between Tara and her parents had been bad for a while, but after she talked to them about the photos they got a lot worse. Mark started inventing other explanations, and Miriam was sure Tara hadn't understood what she'd seen. Tara said her dad had shouted her out of the house when she told him she'd contacted the Army.

Watching Mark now, it was hard to imagine him shouting anybody out of his house. When I was a kid, Dad had said to me, "If you ever hear anyone call Mark intolerant or discriminatory, you can be sure they haven't actually met him." Mark had unwavering opinions, but he had a way of saying them while sounding concerned, not angry.

I knew now that a person could be discriminatory without raising their voice. But even so, I still had a hard time picturing him yelling.

Mark had finished warming up to the topic and was in fine form now, gesturing one moment and leaning toward us conspiratorially the next. He was captivating even with Gary's death still pulling on his features.

The sanctuary windows were high and small. All I could see of the outside world was a few brown leaves being blown by. I stepped on Dad's foot until he lifted his chin from his chest again. I was surprised to find Mark finishing the sermon already. Maybe his sermons had become shorter since Gary died. As the worship band played the last song, though, I saw other glances of confusion.

After the benediction, Mark stood motionless at the top of the center aisle until the after-service murmuring died down. We all sat, some of us actually on the edges of our seats. He smiled at us as if to say he understood our confusion.

"I need to make an announcement." He waited for complete stillness before continuing. "Since Gary died, I've been seeking God's will from, you might say, a more urgent place." He turned to Miriam, who was sitting in her usual spot, second pew on the right. "Actually, Miriam, will you come up here?" he asked, extending a hand toward her. We waited while she joined him. She took his hand and gave us all a strained smile.

Mark scanned the room and, amused, said, "Come on, dummies. I'm not quitting my job."

This drew relieved laughter, which made Mark smirk at us. People loved to talk about how "real" Mark was. They meant that, on one hand, he could say things that would sound mean if they came from anyone but him, and on the other hand, he could say things that would sound sappy if they came from anyone but him.

"No," he said, when we were quiet again. "I'm not leaving. We built this place together—me and many of you. Ron, Bob, Dale, Larry, Peter . . . There are others, but those guys have been a backbone of this church since ninety-five." Dad dropped his head, embarrassed but pleased at having been named.

"Fifteen years ago," Mark said, "I heard a calling. God wanted me to plant and grow a church. And by God's grace I did that. We did that. This is a beautiful, God-centered place of Christian worship. But Gary's death—" He fixed his eyes on an upper corner of the room, dropped his voice. "Gary's death showed me that I have been complacent. Satan's forces are still here. They come, as the Bible tells us, wrapped in sheep's clothing. These forces are social relativism, sin masquerading as acceptance. These forces would destroy the institution of marriage, murder unborn children, and take away our religious rights in the name of pluralism."

He spoke calmly, but even so, I knew I was hearing stronger language than I was used to from him. As if to confirm my suspicion, I saw Miriam adjust her grip on his arm. The movement was so slight it would be easy to say it meant nothing. I knew better. Tara had told me that her mom was more accepting of her than her dad was, but that Miriam defaulted to Mark's opinions because he was the head of the household. "Sometimes I wonder who she'd be without him," Tara had said.

"So I am here to announce a new capital campaign," Mark said. "It's a big one. I don't have any materials printed up, so you're just going to have to listen to me tell you what it is." He let us wonder for three, then five seconds. "The Garrett Joshua Clemmens Memorial Gymnasium." Another long pause. "You're wondering why. I know. We're a church, not an athletic club. But that is exactly the point. If we are going to reach people today, we need to think about how to meet their needs. And what do people need in a world numbed by television and video games? We need a space for community recreation. We need to host men looking for a pickup league, travel basketball teams—we need kids on roller skates, we need a rec space for our growing youth group. Now, I know that this project is larger than any we've undertaken as a church. But I'm past the point of cowering under a plant, like Jonah. And let me tell you something: God is already at work here. I have a combined forty thousand dollars from some individual donors already. We're just going to need about two hundred fifty thousand more dollars."

Someone drew an audible breath.

Mark smiled. He was equally fatigued and resolute. He said, "Remember the loaves and the fish. Arithmetic isn't a problem for God." Then he nodded at all of us, as if he trusted us to do the right thing with this insight, and made his way to his usual spot by the sanctuary's double doors.

Dad, who always had his checkbook in church for the offering, didn't stand until he'd finished writing a check, which he carefully shielded from view. As we stood in line to greet Mark on our way out, I imagined ways to pull Dad out of line, get him straight out to the car. I imagined slipping the check out of his pocket, tearing it into confetti I'd dribble out the window as we drove home to safety.

Jo hated how much money Dad had given to the church. She used to sneak into his room to look at financial records, emerge white-faced and furious at the thousands he tithed, especially each time Mark had some building project—new windows, a renovated foyer, fresh pavement on the parking lot. When I asked her if he had the money to give, she'd snap, "That's not the point. What about his future? What about yours?" But here, for all her smarts, Jo had missed the obvious point—that my future had never really concerned me. *Tomorrow will worry about itself*, Jesus had said. It was one of my favorite verses.

I was always of the mind that Dad could do whatever he wanted with his money. I didn't even worry about him saving it for later. If he needed help when he was older, he could come live with me. Simple.

But I did not want Dad to give Mark that check. When the church bought the building in the early nineties, it had been a garden center on a hill with a sprawling gravel lot. The brick store in front became offices, and the huge display room in back was the sanctuary. When we followed Mark to Maine, the congregation was sitting on metal folding chairs. The floor was poured concrete. You could still faintly smell dirt.

Now nearly every aspect about the church was different. The brick storefront had been rebuilt three times as big, for the fellowship hall, offices, and extra Sunday school rooms. The sanctuary was carpeted, padded pews installed. A giant sound system hung from ceiling cables. A slit in the ceiling opened to lower a projector screen, which rolled down like a scroll from on high.

And now a gym? It hit me wrong.

The line moved. When Mark put his hand out for a handshake, Dad pressed the check into it. Mark made a weak attempt not to take it. "You've given so much," he told Dad. "No one's asking for more from you."

"God is," Dad said, and tucked the check into Mark's jacket pocket. They embraced. Now the two of them were gripping each other by the upper arms. "We've been through so much together," Mark said.

"I know," said Dad.

"We're not done," Mark said, and gave Dad a pat that sent him in the direction of the fellowship room, where there were butter cookies and coffee.

When I shook Mark's hand, he said, "Good to see you here."

"You too." I tugged a little on my hand, but he wouldn't let go.

"What's been keeping you?" he asked.

"Work. I got a job at Pine Creek."

"We miss you here, though."

"I'm trying to change my work schedule," I said lamely. I hated lying, but it was my only option if I couldn't stand up for myself. Which I definitely could not do with Mark Clemmens.

He gave me a sympathetic look, which made me think I might be free of the conversation, but then he said, "One more thing. Tara's back in town—did you know that?"

"I think I heard." I spoke haltingly, knowing I should proceed with caution, but also knowing that I didn't yet know what the catch to this might be.

"Do you think you'd want to hang out with her again?"

"I could do that."

"Do you have her number?"

"I think so."

His forehead bunched. "Are you sure? She didn't get a phone until she moved back to the States."

"Oh. Maybe not." The knowledge I was flushing only made me flush more.

"Let me write it down for you." He patted his pockets but, not finding any paper besides the check Dad had just written for him, said, "Come with me." Not seeing any other choice, I followed him to his office, which was separated on one side from the fellowship hall by a wall of thick glass cubes, textured so you only saw watery, warped shapes though them.

Inside, Mark picked up a book of Post-it notes. Instead of writing anything, though, he fanned the stack repeatedly against his other palm. It sounded like he was shuffling a deck.

"You know," he said, "Tara did recently imply that you two were seeing each other. Regularly, even. Which makes me wonder why you wouldn't want me to know that."

Mark's voice sounded measured, pained. But there was something hard in his eyes that I could neither meet nor avoid.

Too late I remembered Tara telling me that she'd told her parents we'd hung out, in case they ever asked me. But she'd told me this in that stiff and slightly angry way she had whenever the subject of my preference for secrecy came up. So I'd been focused on defending myself, not on what she said.

"Georgie, look at me." My eyes had dropped to somewhere around his mid-chest, to the sleek red tie draped there. I raised them like a child in trouble.

"Does your father know—" he started, but Miriam opened the office door. "Georgie, your dad needs you. He took a spill."

I found Dad sitting against a wall of the fellowship room. He was between Dale Feeney and my old high school teacher Mr. Gromberg, each of whom had a hand on one of his big shoulders. At least five other people were standing around him. At first I thought, in horror, that Dad had wet his pants, but it was coffee. There was more coffee on the floor, which another of the church ladies was already coming to clean up.

"I think he fainted," Dale told me. "Celinda's going to check if there's a blood pressure cuff in the car." Celinda, his wife, was a nurse.

"I didn't pass out," Dad said.

"You sat down with your coffee and cookies," said Rose Scarry, who'd been my Sunday school teacher for three years and who, with her long face and dyed-black hair, did seem kind of scary. "I looked away for a minute," she said, "and then you were on the floor."

"I just need to get home," Dad said. "I just need some rest." He started to stand up, but Dale and Mr. Gromberg held him back.

"He's on a new medication," I said. "The doctor said this might happen. I'll keep an eye on him." I put out my arm, and Dad accepted the help.

"Can we help with the stairs?" Dale asked.

"I've got it," I said. "My job is to help people with stairs." It was my third lie in five minutes—there were no stairs at Pine Creek—but everyone believed me. I knew what they were thinking, too—look at Georgie. Sturdy, capable Georgie who's here to do the right thing.

I needed them to think this about me. It was the next best thing to thinking it myself.

WITHIN A WEEK, SOMEONE HAD printed up one of those weatherproof canvas signs and stretched it out between stakes on the front lawn of the church. FUTURE SITE OF THE GARY J CLEMMENS MEMORIAL GYMNASIUM, it read. Below that, in smaller font, FOR WE ARE GOD'S HANDIWORK, CREATED IN CHRIST JESUS TO DO GOOD WORKS, WHICH GOD PREPARED IN ADVANCE FOR US TO DO. EPHESIANS 2:10. And below that, DONATE TODAY!

Following Jo's lead, I'd snuck a look at Dad's checkbook. He'd given two thousand dollars. Two thousand dollars was more than the disability check he got every month. It left him with one hundred sixteen dollars in his checking account.

The shelves and the garbage disposal were still on the floor.

Right after his injury, when a doctor took me and Jo into a room with padded chairs and tissues to tell us that Dad might never use his legs again, my thoughts had gone to a story I'd once heard, of a woman who broke her neck but then learned to paint with her teeth. In an instant, I'd decided that Dad could do something like that. I imagined him carving intricate wooden toys, becoming famous for his craft. The idea stuck with me for months. I often felt impatient with Jo for being panicky about the future of our family. I told myself she would see. Things would turn around. And they did—for example, Dad regained the ability to walk.

After his injury and the first surgery, he got his commercial driver's license and spent a year driving a bus for the Westbrook school system. Bus driving worked for his back until it didn't, and he finished the school year by force of will alone. He lost something like twenty-five pounds between January and June because, when he wasn't driving a bus, holding still was even more important than eating. Sometimes I heard him sobbing in his room. The sound throbbed slowly through the house like a bass drum. And I was often the only one home to hear it, because Jo had gotten a special permit to work part-time at Betty's, and then additionally because she started dating Gary Clemmens, of all people. It seemed she came into the house only to get what she needed—food, sleep, maybe a few hours in her room for homework—and then drifted out again. When I came home that fall and heard her and Gary having sex in her room, I stood stock-still, feeling my heartbeat echo in my limbs. Feeling, for the first time, truly furious with her, and only partially because of the sex. I mean, it was very uncomfortable to hear my sister having sex. But I'd already decided that Mark and the other church leaders were a little obsessed with the topic of purity. I was still a virgin, but I'd let a few guys put their hands in my underwear and found afterward that I felt none of the guilt that I did after, say, lying.

Still, something about Jo and Gary was off. I, at least, was mediocre at everything—no one expected me to do anything more than half-heartedly, including, I assumed, being pure. Jo, though—I expected more of her. Which didn't mean she wasn't allowed to have sex, exactly, but did mean that it shouldn't be with Gary, who was not as great as everyone liked to think and definitely too old for her.

He emerged from her room in boxers, all muscle and self-satisfaction. I gave him the straightest, flattest stare I could summon and turned on my heel.

I wasn't proud that I didn't wonder how Jo felt about what was going on. It was also true, though, that this happened in the lead-up to Dad's second back surgery. He was desperate for this one to work and was leaning on me a lot.

The surgery and recovery were just as arduous as the first time, and I spent hours taking care of him. He insisted for a while that this had done the trick, but when his recovery period was up he found he couldn't go back to bus driving. Also, he now owed the hospital ninety-six thousand dollars. At first he thought the bill was a mistake, because his insurance company assured him the procedure was covered. Then he learned the hospital he'd used, same as the one for his first surgery, was now out of network.

That spring, newly unemployed, he saw a TV ad for a work-from-home medical billing course. He said it was an answer to prayer. Here was a job that paid well, that he could do from home, and that built on his recent experience with the hospital and insurance company.

Three weeks after his CDs and study guide came in the mail, he started looking for work again. It was Jo who told me it was a scam—"Obviously." She brought me Dad's study guide, yanked it open to the table of contents. "'Overview of Job *Summery*'?" she asked, pointing at the chapter title. "I mean, the spelling, but also the redundancy." She flipped to another page, jabbed a sentence with her pointer finger. "They don't even know how to spell *deductibles*." Now she threw the book aside. "Total scam."

"Why didn't you say something?" I asked.

"You think he consulted me in the twenty minutes that passed between his seeing the ad and ordering this junk? You think they have a refund policy?"

"Wait," I said. "How much did Dad pay for this?"

"Fifteen hundred dollars." She closed her eyes as if summoning patience, but I knew it hadn't arrived by the time she opened them again. "It's pathetic," she said.

I didn't think fifteen hundred dollars was a lot to owe on top of ninety-six thousand. "That's not too bad."

"It's fifteen hundred dollars he doesn't have!"

"He doesn't *want* to be in debt," I snapped. "He's trying as hard as he can. If he makes a mistake here and there that's—"

"You defend him," she interrupted, "so you can defend yourself."

"What are you talking about?" I demanded. I was angry, but it was also a real question.

She gave me a pitying look. "You feel good when you think about how much worse everything could be. But it could be a lot better, too."

THE TUESDAY AFTER MARK'S GYM announcement was cold and windy. As I drove, small clouds migrated overhead. The trees kept getting light and dark like someone was playing with a switch.

I'd left Dad sleeping on the couch. I didn't even want to wake him to say goodbye. He'd spent the first part of the week leaping into action to help Mark raise money. He'd joined the fundraising committee, started making phone calls. Dad had this idea for a hoop-a-thon, where people would shoot baskets or play three-on-three to raise money. I wasn't clear on the details. The committee's first meeting was that night, and I suspected he was going to miss it.

He'd taken the last of his pills that morning. He should have had more from his regular prescription left over, but he didn't. I already knew he was going to wake in pain while I was at Tara's. I knew I'd have to tell him about her soon. It was a terrible irony that he was in the worst possible shape to receive the news.

your dad confronted me in church, I'd texted her.

he has suspicions, she wrote, *but no real evidence.* Then, *you went to church?*

long story, I responded.

My low mood, which followed me into the Pine Creek lobby, was immediately worsened by Martha, who stood behind the desk with glasses on the end of her nose. Without looking up from her computer she said, "Marlene is close."

"Oh." I knew it wasn't unusual for someone to die quickly after something that shouldn't technically have killed them. It happened to Walter soon after I'd started at Pine Creek. He'd been walking ten laps around the garden every day, even in winter. Then he got a sinus infection and died a week later.

But I'd barely known him. Marlene I knew, and liked.

"You never know when it's time," Martha was telling me. "Everything's just humming along and—" She snapped her fingers. Martha liked to present herself as an expert on death, but the only insight I'd ever heard from her was that death could be unpredictable.

When I brought Marlene a new diaper, she tried to smile at me, but the expression didn't land the way a smile should. "Glad it's you," she said. "That other girl . . ." She had to pause for a breath. "Has no idea what she's doing."

I didn't bother smiling back, because her eyes were already

closed again. I put a hand on her bony wrist. Her skin was cool. The whole thing—slowly getting her into position, removing the old diaper, putting on the new one—took a while. Sick old people aren't like babies. You can't just yank them up by the ankles. I didn't mind taking my time. Being next to a dying person had slowed my thoughts almost to the point of stopping them entirely, and I needed some quiet in my head. Marlene stared at the cracks of light coming through the horizontal blinds as if she'd never noticed them before. I carried the used diaper into the bathroom. It was barely wet. I thought about how the shower when she fell would be her last. And I wondered if everybody makes such a big deal about first things—first steps, first paycheck, first time having sex—because we know they're the first. Maybe we're trying to make up for the fact that we almost never know if we're doing something for the last time.

I returned to Marlene to make sure she was properly tucked in. The prayer book was back on her side table. Her carnations were turning brown. I wanted to say more to her, but she didn't open her eyes as I adjusted the blankets. Distracted as I walked out of her room, I almost collided with a guy in a white knee-length coat. Each of us exclaimed our sorrys. Then he said, "Georgie! What's up?"

It was Lee Volk, a pharmacy tech at the company that filled the orders for Pine Creek. I'd known him in high school. He'd been skinny and pale-haired back then, and was still skinny and pale-haired now, though he was taller and the worst of his acne had faded. He'd been popular with a certain crowd because his family could afford a swimming pool and a trampoline. Even now, he grinned at me like a salesman about to tell me he was offering a once-in-a-lifetime deal.

"Making the rounds." I didn't mention the diaper duty. Complaining about body functions was boring. People expected me to be disgusted by them. They weren't pleasant, but I wasn't disgusted, either. They were just a fact of life in a place like Pine Creek.

"You take care of Marlene regularly, don't you?" he asked.

"Yeah," I said, then lowered my voice. "It's a bummer to watch her like this."

"I thought I might ask you something." He looked over my shoulder, then took my elbow and steered me to a little alcove at the end of the hall. Brenda was going by with a huge wheeled tub of sheets. He nodded at her and she nodded back. I pulled my elbow away from his grip. I've never liked it when guys move me with a hand on my back or arm. They don't do it to each other. "What?" I said.

"It's about the opiates Marlene was prescribed at the hospital. I heard she was refusing them, and I went to collect them. But they were gone."

I steadied my expression. I was finding it hard to read his smile. He had to know something, or else why would he want to talk to me? But then, why would he be smiling at me like we shared a good secret?

Marlene must have told him where the pills went. Obviously. I could hear her saying it now: "Georgie took them back to the nurses' station for me."

I was an idiot.

I said, "I don't—maybe she—"

The more uncomfortable I got, the more easily he spoke. "We're contracted to keep tabs on all the prescriptions that come in and out, even the ones we ourselves don't prescribe or fill. Just wanted you to know how we work and what we do."

"Okay," I said.

"Have a good one," he said, nodding at me and walking off.

In the next two hours I went over the conversation repeatedly, but all I could find was a friendly warning. He knew, or guessed, what happened. If he wanted to get me in trouble he'd have done so already, or asked different questions. Still, I was shaken. Rita had to snap at me, because I didn't hear her ask whether Paul had gotten his dinner yet.

On my fifteen-minute break I took a coffee in a Styrofoam cup out to the car so I could sit somewhere private. It seemed if I held still for long enough my nervous energy would stop crashing around inside me and I could go back to the calm face I liked to present to the world. And to myself.

I opened my phone, saw I had missed a call from Jo. No voicemail, though. I called her back.

"Hey!" She sounded upbeat, especially given how our last interaction ended. "Sorry I keep missing you. I'm slammed with schoolwork."

"No problem."

"I was thinking about coming home for Thanksgiving," she said. Then, "I shouldn't have been so mad about what you came here to tell me."

"I get it," I said. "It was weird of me to bring up."

"I needed time to process." A delicate pause. "I'm making the photos the subject of my journalism project after all."

"Your professor liked the topic?"

"He definitely thinks it could work."

"Nice." I tried to sound enthusiastic. I tried to remember why it had mattered to me so much that she would use the photos for the project. I tried to remember why I was in this parking lot while Jo was at one of the best colleges in the country. A gust of wind lifted the corrugated lid of the dumpster next to my car. It fell with a bang.

"My professor says I need the photos, though."

"That might be a problem."

"Tara still has them, right?"

Bang. "Yes. But it would be pretty tricky to go to her now."

"Are you saying you're not going to ask her?" Jo's voice was businesslike.

"She made me promise not to tell anyone." The lid dropped again. I felt like I was sitting next to a giant, slow typewriter.

"You said she contacted the Army. She's not trying to keep it a secret."

"That's true. But she also wants to manage who knows it."

"Didn't you tell me because you wanted me to know about it?" Jo asked.

I squeezed my eyes shut, grabbed the bridge of my nose, like I was trying to hold in a sneeze, or something more guttural.

"I really need those pictures for the project," she stated. Whenever she talked like this she reminded me of Mom, unable to see any logic except her own.

"Are you asking me to steal them from her?"

"I thought she might give you copies if you asked."

"Asking means she would know that I told you, and that wouldn't be good."

"Well," Jo said, an odd lightness to her tone, "let's forget I asked, then. I don't want to put you in a tough position."

"Thanks," I said, uncomfortable. Jo didn't tend to give up so easily.

"Maybe when I'm home for Thanksgiving we can go visit her. I want to meet your girlfriend, you know? I mean, meet her again."

What choice did I have now?

WALKING BACK IN TO FINISH my shift, I thought about how happy Dad would be that Jo was coming home for the holiday. Of course I wanted him to be happy. But some forms of his happiness could be hard to be around. Imagine one of those inflatable yard decorations people put out around Christmas, but in your living room.

Thinking this made me feel small and mean. Dad had so little to look forward to. Then I thought of how dismayed Jo would be by the state of the house. I had a little time. I could clean it up.

I was ten paces from the automatic doors when Lee exited wearing a long, dark jacket over his white pharmacy coat. The combination made him look like a priest.

"You're going back in?" he asked.

"I was on break."

"Ah." He was doing that looming and smiling thing again. He said, "Following up on what we were talking about earlier, I want to make sure you know who to ask if you need anything. What I mean is—" He stepped toward me and cast his eyes to either side to be sure we were alone. He looked conspicuously like someone who thinks they're inconspicuous. "I can help," he concluded. "If there's a need."

"No need," I said quickly.

"I'm telling you," he went on, "I have access. I wouldn't say this to anyone, but I trust you."

"Are you seriously saying this out loud?" He'd forced me into a familiar, hushed tone I'd never used with him before.

"What?" he asked, baffled by my anger.

"What if I walk in and report you right now?"

"I'll tell them you're lying and give them evidence that you stole that Oxy from Marlene. Come on, Georgie. I didn't know you were such a square."

"I'm not," I said, but I sounded like one.

"All I'm doing is making a little extra money. Having some fun on the weekends. You should come over for one of my parties. They're chill."

"They're not for me," I said. "The pills."

"For your dad, then?"

I shouldn't have been surprised that he guessed. Curtisville wasn't a tiny town, but it was small. When I was out shopping for groceries or getting the car serviced, people still periodically asked me how my dad was doing. I gave the tiniest nod humanly possible. "It was a one-time thing. Bridging the gap before his script got refilled. Look, sorry," I went on. "My break ended two minutes ago, and you know how Rita—"

"Go, go," he said, waving me away. "But think about my offer. I'd give you a good deal because we're friends."

Those two words, *we're friends*, echoed uncomfortably as I walked away. I glanced back and saw him waving cheerily at me, coat billowing in the wind.

JO

CHAPTER NINE

Georgie was waiting in the short-term lot when my bus arrived at the Portland station. From my high perch I could see her leaning against the hood of the car. Despite the drizzle, she looked neither cold nor wet.

When she released me from her hug, though, I found I was damp.

The ten months I'd been gone, my longest stretch away, still didn't seem long enough to make coming back feel so significant. As I lowered myself into Dad's old Taurus, though, with the passenger seat spilling its stuffing and that same old beaded anklet hanging from the rearview mirror, I felt as though I were falling back in time. The car was a familiar mess. Empty iced tea jars and takeout wrappers littered the floor. The tray between the front seats was full of dirty coins and pens that didn't work.

As Georgie turned onto the main road, I reached over to click on her wipers. She gave me a look. "It's raining," I said.

"I know. I could see fine."

I said, honestly, "I didn't come here to give you a hard time."

A slow moment turned over. "I know," she repeated, and something cleared, slightly, between us. As we exited the highway onto Seaside Way, I cracked the window and pressed my nose to the opening, smelled the soft putrescence of low tide. I rolled the window back up.

"I tried to neaten up around the house," Georgie told me.

"Thanks," I said.

"Don't thank me yet."

"I was never under the impression that our house was very clean."

"Well," she said, and took a breath. "It's a bit of a disaster." It was out of character for her to admit this. Then she said, more quietly, "Everything is kind of a disaster."

"How so?"

"Dad hasn't been doing so great."

"He hasn't been doing great for a while now." I didn't like admitting this, because it meant I should be helping more.

"He's worse. I wanted to prepare you."

"You could have told me," I said.

"I'm telling you now."

The porch was chilly, but I found myself taking my time with my shoes anyway, bracing for however I might find Dad. The wall hooks were smothered in coats. When I tried to hang mine, four others fell in a whoosh.

Then the smell hit me, something more musty than foul, but not pleasant, either. Was the smell stronger, or was I more sensitive to it now? Had I really lived all those years in a house that smelled like this?

Maybe Georgie had done some cleaning up, but her efforts couldn't hide the fact that the mess I'd always known had accelerated, picked up more mess, more neglect, the way dust picks up dust. She'd vacuumed, but dog hair lay thick where she hadn't touched. Everything around me was piles of papers and bags stuffed inside bags, boxes that were probably supposed to help but that in the end had only contributed to the problem.

"Is that Jo?!" Dad called from the living room.

Georgie was coming in behind me with my duffel and

backpack, moving through the tight space without, somehow, knocking cereal boxes from the counter or toppling the precarious tower of recyclables that rose from the bin by the closet. "I'll put these in your room," she told me.

Hulk limped toward me, stopped a few feet short to wag his tail and duck his head. He remembered I didn't want the full-on greeting, and I appreciated this. I told him hello, actually bent to scratch his ears so I could avoid thinking about everything else for a few more seconds.

"How was your trip?" Dad continued to exclaim from the couch. "Here, have a seat." He was patting the cushion next to him.

Eyeing the dog hair on the couch, which it seemed Georgie had tried to vacuum but was now topped with hair rolled into snakes of fur and lint, I said, "No thanks. I've been sitting long enough."

"Well, how are you?" He lifted the remote toward the TV, and a female voice blared, "BUT THE COST OF THE IPHONE STILL—"

"Whoops," Dad said. "I meant to mute it."

How could Dad sit here not knowing whether the TV sound was on or off?

"Classes are good?" he asked.

"Yeah."

"I bet you're acing every one of them."

I wished I could find a volume button for his exuberance. I said, "I'm doing fine."

"Great. That is excellent. Really excellent." He smiled while he waited for the next subject of conversation to occur to him. He said, "I'd help you with your things, but my back is acting up again."

"No problem. Georgie's got it."

"We're both so glad you could join us for the holiday." He made it sound like I was the overbooked vice president of a midsize company instead of an undercommitted college student who definitely could've come home at least twice in the last ten months.

"I'm planning on grilling the turkey tomorrow," he said, relieved to remember we had holiday plans to discuss. "Georgie's on stuffing and sauce and mashed potatoes. Actually—Georgie?"

My sister appeared in the doorway on the far side of the room. She was quiet and unreadable, like a servant. This bothered me, though I didn't know which of them to blame—Georgie for taking on the role or Dad for allowing it.

"Before you go out to the grocery store," he asked, "will you see if there's anything special Jo would like you to pick up?"

"I'll shop with Georgie," I offered.

"That'll be so nice," Dad said. "Thinking of you two out there together."

"Let me make a list," said Georgie.

I waited for her by the side door, aware that I was standing as close to an exit as possible. It was embarrassing to come home and have Dad treat me like the prodigal son. Most tellings of the story I knew emphasized a young man who foolishly squandered his wealth in sinful living, but I now wondered if the shame he felt as he returned home wasn't about what he did in the world. Maybe his shame came from knowing he shouldn't have left his family in the first place.

As Georgie approached me, stuffing her arms into the sleeves of her jacket, a snore erupted from the couch.

"His pain meds make him sleepy," Georgie explained. She had her hand behind my headrest as leverage to help her look behind us as she backed out of the driveway. The gesture had been Dad's, and the memory of him confidently maneuvering a car unlocked others. He used to delicately carry pieces of furniture a single man shouldn't have been able to lift on his own. The year before his accident, I got a flu bad enough that I was briefly admitted to the hospital for an IV and observation. I didn't remember much about my stay, but I did have a vague memory of waking to realize Dad was holding me to his chest. I remembered the heavy thump of his heart and hallucinating that it was pumping blood into my body. I remembered believing that this would heal me.

"That's new, right?" I asked, about Dad's fatigue.

"Different dose."

"Is he still on OxyContin?" I asked.

"Yeah," Georgie said.

At first my awareness of the drug had been vague, informed by headlines I skimmed, snippets of news I might catch on TV. My perspective had changed the spring before, though, when I was crossing campus and came up behind a girl who was sobbing into her cell phone. "He'd never even *tried* Oxy before," she'd wailed. "And now he's *dead*."

Now I asked, "Do you think it's causing too many problems?"

"He has a prescription," Georgie said, a little curtly. "I'm keeping an eye on him."

This was more than I was willing to do. I decided not to wonder out loud whether he needed more than Georgie keeping an eye out. To account for my concern, I told her about the conversation I'd overheard.

"Recreational use can be dangerous," she said, sounding less defensive now. "You know Dad's not like that."

"You're right," I said. Of course he wasn't.

• • •

IN THE GROCERY STORE WE each took a basket, parted ways to make the errand brief. I collected powdered gravy and a stuffing mix, browsed the frozen pie selections. I remembered I was low on tampons. As I stood skimming my options, my eyes landed on the dreadfully titled Family Planning section of the aisle, to the row of the also dreadfully described Personal Lubricants. I fled the aisle clutching my Tampax.

The day after we first kissed, Seamus emailed me to ask if I wanted to come over for dinner that Friday. Was it that simple? I wondered. Did I walk to his apartment and knock on the door? Would I be seen? Did I want to be seen?

When he opened his door, he was too carefully scrubbed. He offered me wine: pinot or Malbec? Or, he added hastily, a glass of Perrier? "Wine, I guess," I said, and then, "I honestly don't know which to pick." I wished I didn't notice him checking his reflection in the glass of a cupboard door. He poured me samples so I could decide which one I liked. I said I liked the pinot and was glad he didn't ask me why. I wasn't even sure I liked it better. I chose it because it tasted different from the Malbec, which I sampled first.

Next, Seamus pointed at two Chinese takeout boxes on the counter. He'd picked vegetarian for me, and pork for himself, but we could switch if I wanted.

"I thought you might be a vegetarian," he explained.

"Not at the moment." I'd never been a vegetarian, but here I was trying to ease that truth onto Seamus, making myself sound like if he'd asked me a week ago, I would've said I was.

"It's because you're a principled person. Principled people tend to be vegetarians." I could tell that he'd wanted to say this once he'd gotten confirmation that I was a vegetarian, and now that he knew I wasn't, or wasn't really, he still wanted to get credit for his line of thinking.

I laughed. "You're making me sound like a fusty prude."

"That," he said, as he rotated the bottle of wine to cut off the flow, "you most certainly are not." I couldn't look at him as he slid the glass toward me.

GEORGIE HAD HER BACK TO me as I approached her at our designated meeting spot near the checkout lanes. I wanted to tap her on the shoulder, whisper, "I had sex with my journalism professor." But I wouldn't do that here. Maybe later. I wanted to say how Seamus didn't offer me a fork, and I struggled to control my chopsticks without looking like I was struggling to control my chopsticks. I wanted to tell Georgie how, at some point in the middle of the meal, I realized the whole thing was going well. That I was having fun. That I saw Seamus more clearly than I had before, as exceptionally if oddly handsome and slightly eccentric, as permissive and tireless, as eager and afraid. That we kissed for so long I became impatient with kissing, but then, when his hand finally crept under my shirt, I instinctively flinched in a way that made him jerk back. "I'm sorry. I'm so sorry. I should have asked." Nothing I could say would let him do anything but continue kissing me. I left his apartment with chapped lips and cheeks and a grin I couldn't keep down. I slept poorly because of the wine. I went back the next night, and we drank all the Malbec and had sex. After undressing, he'd produced a bottle of lubricant.

"Do you want me to use this?" he'd asked. I didn't want to ask what it was, so I said, "I haven't tried it before." He said, "You might like it." He was right. Now, in class, he carefully avoided eye contact with me unless he was calling on me with such measured neutrality I wanted to laugh. Somehow, we held it together.

All of this I wanted to tell Georgie. I wanted to explain how standing in the grocery aisle, I was stirred all over again. I felt desire, yes, but I also enjoyed my desire, how it was clean and direct. I hadn't known I could feel this way about anyone. How did it match up with Georgie's feelings for Tara? I considered asking her once we were headed home, but she was the one to break the silence in the car: "I made plans for us to go to Tara's. This Friday." It was dark, and the road home had almost no lights, but my sister was anticipating every turn with professional ease.

"Great. Th—that will be nice." I'd almost said *thank you*. More quietly I said, "Do you want to talk about what I—"

"That's exactly what I don't want to talk about," Georgie said, and I hurried to say, "Sure, of course." I was watching the faint line of black trees whiz by when Georgie braked so suddenly I cried and threw out my hands, catching myself on the dash. Then I saw the little figure ambling in front of Georgie's headlights. A skunk. I had no idea how she'd seen it in the dark.

"As a reminder," Georgie said, once we were on our way again, "Dad still doesn't know about me and Tara."

"You told me," I said. Actually she'd told me at least twice. "You can't keep it a secret forever."

"Tara keeps telling me that."

"Then she and I will obviously get along."

"That," Georgie told me, "is the problem."

I laughed. "You don't want us to get along? You came to visit me and all my friends fell in love with you. Actually, I think one of them fell in love with you for real." Morgan had asked me twice when Georgie might visit again.

Georgie said nothing. I thought of the four different cables I'd bought at a RadioShack in Springfield. "You should have brought the camera with you," the clerk said. He was upset that I was buying three more cables than I needed. He fretted over all of the options before announcing that he was ninety-six percent sure one of these cables would fit the camera I'd left at home. "Are you sure you don't know the make or model?" he asked one last time as I made for the register.

I'd borrowed Seamus's car to go to Springfield, but hadn't invited him or even told him where I was going. A few days before, I'd said, "What do I do if Tara refuses to share the photos with me?"

He shrugged, then said, "You use every resource at your disposal."

That was my initial reason for coming home: to use every resource at my disposal. My primary resource being, of course, me. Now that I was here, though, I saw other reasons for my visit. Like getting caught up with Georgie. We could go to Pizza Loft, above Betty's, and gossip about the people we used to know. I could help her try to do something about the house, about Dad.

I remembered a phone call I'd had with Mom after the first time she went to LA. When I asked her how long she would be gone, she said, "I don't know."

"Why don't you know?"

She sighed. "You're not old enough to understand."

"I'll understand. I promise."

She laughed, but not unkindly. "You really promise you're going to understand?"

"I'm mature," I reminded her. Everyone said that about me. Then again, I realized as I said it that a truly mature person probably wouldn't describe themselves with that word.

I was afraid Mom would laugh again, but she didn't. "You are mature," she said, half musing, half agreeing. "Let me put it this way. People will praise your talents and tell you to make the most of them. But you will find, eventually, that people do not actually want you to make the most of your talents. What people want is for you to be normal. Have a family. Raise children. Stay put. Pipe down."

I wanted to say, *I never wanted you to be normal.* But I'd agreed to understand.

"Promise me," she said. "Promise me you won't settle. Promise me you won't waste your talent."

I was vaguely aware that what this promise entailed was beyond me. But I was aware, too, that this was the point of the promise. It was meant to be an anchor for all the times I would be tempted to do things differently.

Like right now.

THANKSGIVING DINNER WAS LATE and haphazard. Dad kept announcing he was about to start the grill before falling asleep. Georgie eventually put the whole turkey in the oven without realizing how long it would take. Two hours in, we burned our fingertips dismembering the bird so it would cook faster. By the time we sat to eat it was after eight and Dad was looking tired again anyway. Georgie and I passed rolls we'd bought frozen, instant mashed potatoes, and messy plates of turkey meat back and forth while we tried to make conversation with him. He got through dinner and two bites of pie before he returned to the couch.

I knew there was something wrong, but the more time I spent at home, the more I saw how deep and intractable the whole thing was. I told myself that not all problems were fixable. It sounded like a borrowed thought, but I didn't know from whom. Probably Mom, but I couldn't remember her saying it.

When Georgie and I left late the next afternoon to go to Tara's, she told Dad we were having dinner with friends, that we'd be back late.

"Sounds fun," Dad said. To me, he added, "You haven't seen some of those people in a while." I was only glad he didn't ask for more details.

On the drive to Bear Pond, Georgie told me little stories about Tara: how she'd stood up to a sprinkler company that lied about work they'd done, how she'd made friends with Crazy Ted, the guy who sat outside the Hannaford's supermarket in nearby Lakewood. Crazy Ted wore Oakley sunglasses and a knit hat year-round and talked to himself on the bench. Georgie said Tara got his life story and corrected anyone who called him Crazy Ted. "His name is Teddie," she would say.

None of these stories seemed to accomplish what Georgie wanted them to, though, because she concluded each one by saying, "You'll see." Then she'd pause, and start another. I stopped listening after a while. Currently the only thing I was seeing was a tangle of dirt roads so complicated I was sure Georgie had lost her way. Abruptly she turned, and we were in a clearing. I craned my head to make out the first stars as Georgie parked next to an old Subaru. Before the headlights winked out I saw the white-and-brown trailer. Given my knowledge of Tara, I'd expected a quaint cabin with chintzy decor.

But of course Tara wasn't who she used to be. That's what Georgie had spent the drive trying to tell me.

We crunched across a few feet of gravel, mounted wooden stairs. "Hello?" Georgie called as she shouldered the door open.

I heard Tara striding toward us before I saw her. She was wiping her hands on her thighs. We shook. Her hand was small, but its strength briefly overwhelmed mine. She looked as narrow as she had in high school, when she ran cross-country. For a long moment I tried to sort out what percentage of what I was seeing was Tara as I used to know her, what percentage was Tara as the person who'd grown and changed, and what percentage was Gary looking out of her eyes.

She did look more like Gary than she used to. I wished Georgie had warned me about that.

"You two didn't eat yet, did you?"

"No," Georgie said, leaning in. I busied myself with my coat, but couldn't help listening for the quick kiss. Were they acting differently because I was here? Or were they being normal, which would make me the one incapable of normalcy?

Georgie told me, "Tara has a thing about making me eat here."

"That's because you don't eat real meals on your own," Tara said lightly.

I knew why this was. Dad tried to take over making dinner every night after Mom left, but it was a struggle after he'd put in a full day of work. For a while Georgie and I tried our hands at Hamburger Helper and Velveeta, but the results were mixed at best, and side dishes were beyond us. So as a family we kind of gave up. Our fridge turned into a hodgepodge of three different sets of food preferences. We were never hungry, but we were never really sated, either.

Georgie plopped onto a plaid couch. I followed Tara into the kitchen and offered to help. She handed me potatoes to cube, then stood next to me peeling the plastic from a Styrofoam tray of chicken breasts.

"I'm really sorry about Gary," I said. The blade was so dull I had to press down with both hands to get the knife through the potato. I added, truthfully, "I don't know what that must be like."

"I hardly do either," she said. "But thank you. I'm sorry that blade is so dull."

"It's about as sharp as the ones we have at home," I said.

"You're doing great." She gestured toward the potato I'd already cut. "Very even pieces." Then, as she poured oil into a frying pan, she said, "It's the weirdest thing, but I feel like I still have a relationship with him. Like some give-and-take is still happening. Is that even possible? Can you have a relationship with someone who died?" She was using the only other knife to cut the chicken into strips. "Probably not, right? But it doesn't stop me from trying. Or wanting one. I don't know." Her shrug sent a ripple of quiet through the kitchen. "Thanks for asking," she said.

"Thanks for telling me." I found myself hungry for more of this honesty, which didn't come with requests or guilt. Was this how she talked to Georgie? And Georgie listened? What did she say in return?

"So how's school?" Tara asked. Then, "I don't mean that in a parental way. I mean how you find it. I've heard good things about

Peabody, but I don't know anyone who's gone there."

I didn't want to launch into my usual spiel, which went something like, *It's great, the professors are great, last year I was in a seminar with only five other students and a leading Renaissance scholar.* The class had five students because the leading scholar had standards that were impossible to discern, never gave feedback on papers, and frequently started class five minutes early and marked you late for arriving on time. I should've dropped, but I wanted to prove to myself that I could do it. I worked way harder than I should've to wind up with a C-plus, my lowest grade so far.

"Honestly?" I said. "Not as great as I thought it would be. Most of the girls there went to private high schools. They have parents in the State Department, CEOs for dads. I thought it was a coincidence that this one girl's last name was the same as the science center, and then I learned it was because her family paid for it."

"Are they nice? The girls?" she asked, scooping the potato cubes onto a baking sheet.

"You know when everyone's nice to you, but you know it's because they're trained to be nice? And you're pretty sure they think they're better than you?"

"You mean like how most Christians treat gay people?"

I had to laugh at this. "You get it." When I thought of how Lily might feel if she overheard me say all of this, I added, "I actually do have some good friends there."

"Individuals have a way of complicating any story you tell about a group."

"Exactly," I said.

When I heard the snap of a magazine page, I knew Georgie was listening. I knew she was hearing me say things she hadn't heard me say before, and that she didn't want to reveal how interested she was. *You should have asked*, I thought, though I knew it wasn't fair.

"So do you regret going to Peabody?" Tara asked as she pushed the strips of chicken into the shimmering oil. We took a synchronized half step back, out of range of the splatter.

"I think I'm going to get a lot out of it," I said.

"I felt that way about the missions program I worked with," Tara said. "Though I'm not sure it's helped me in the long run yet. And like you, I did make some friends."

I was considering how to angle a question about this when Georgie called, "Smells great. Can I help?"

After dinner Tara announced that she would do dishes herself and Georgie and I should look at the stars. I zipped my jacket up to my chin, followed Georgie out to the water. Georgie was carrying her second beer, which she handed to me so she could rummage for something under the trailer. I had declined a drink, but even so, the fullness in my stomach gave me a happy warmth that made me feel tipsy. Georgie emerged with a log. "For you to sit on," she explained.

A few feet in front of the water's edge were two much wider stumps. They looked five times as comfortable as what I was being given, a narrow log for splitting, but I didn't complain, and Georgie didn't make any offers. I could tell she was uneasy. I sat on the cold, hard log, watched a breeze riffle the pond's inky surface. I stuffed my hands in my pockets. I wished I had a hat.

Georgie was staring up, her chin in the air. I followed her gaze. The Milky Way looked like glittery dust swept in a loose line by a wide broom. Feeling the cold on my neck, I retracted my chin turtle-like into the warmth of my collar.

"It's nice," I said.

Georgie grumpily said nothing, and then, "This feels wrong."

"You wanted to get the word out about this." It came out too snappy. "I think it's the right thing."

Georgie glanced over her shoulder. Satisfied that Tara wasn't coming out yet, she said, "Honestly, I don't know if Tara and I are going to last. So maybe it's not the worst if she finds out about the photos."

"Do you think we can just ask her?"

"No. Definitely not." Georgie exhaled at the sky, watched her breath plume and dissipate.

"She seems great." I knew this point was counterproductive to my aims, but I couldn't help making it. I really liked her. Tara was another person that I liked. I didn't think I disliked almost everyone before Lily, Morgan, and Susan joined me at dinner, but then again, hindsight was making me feel like maybe I had.

"I can tell you think so," Georgie said.

"Are you not ready for a relationship or not ready to leave Dad?" I asked. "Or are those the same thing?"

"I'm not sure I'm ready to be with her. In general."

This was not the answer I expected. "You don't think it's wrong, do you?"

"No," she said, and then, "I think it might be wrong to lead her on."

I could imagine the dynamic: The more Tara tried to establish things her way, the more Georgie might quietly, stubbornly resist, if for no other reason than that she didn't want Tara's conclusions to be her own. If I wanted to try to save their relationship, I might tell Tara not to try.

But I wasn't trying to save their relationship.

"I think you have good taste," I said. And then, with a confidence that surprised me, "I think you both will be okay."

The screen door banged shut behind us. Footsteps brushed the gravel. "Thanks," Georgie said. "I appreciate that."

Tara settled between us quietly, seeming to take the temperature between us. I felt her waiting for a good moment to speak. I liked knowing she wasn't going to ask us what we were talking about. Georgie had told me that Tara was considering becoming a counselor. I could see it working for her. She had this goodness. It was a private goodness, I thought, all the more real because it wasn't for show.

Georgie could use someone like that. Thinking this made me hate even more what I was going to do.

It wasn't too late to change my mind. I could tell Seamus I'd decided not to pursue the story. He would be incredulous, then disappointed. It might end whatever had started between us, but the thought didn't frighten me. I suspected I liked being *with* him more than I liked *him*. I mean, I liked him fine. I didn't love him, though.

But I was too frightened to turn back. I was frightened by a future that reverted back to homework and library time cards, obedience and predictability. I was frightened that I'd be forced to get a lifeless job whose purpose was to help me spend ten or fifteen years paying off my college loans, then twenty or thirty years paying off a house, which meant that my conservative estimate for being debt-free and reasonably able to do what I wanted was sixty-five, in time to retire and do what, and for how long?

I had always wanted more. Here, finally, was that opportunity. *Be bold*, I told myself. I stood a little too quickly.

"You okay?" Tara asked.

"I need the bathroom. I'll be right back."

Halfway to the door I turned, saw Tara lean into Georgie. I went inside. I'd left my backpack in an inconspicuous corner. I took out my laptop and turned it on to give it time to warm up. Tara owned so little that my search was short. I found the camera in a cardboard box marked *Gary* just as Windows was sounding its ethereal chimes. I took it to the ugly couch, which gave me an unobstructed view of the figures on the beach.

The second cord I tried worked, and I went through a set of on-screen prompts leading up to the download. For once, my laptop cooperated perfectly, and the whole thing was over faster than I could've hoped for. I put the camera back in the box and stowed the cord in my backpack.

Then I made the mistake of looking at the photos.

I'd told myself I only wanted to make sure I had them, but some part of me knew that I also wanted to see how bad they were. To encounter confirmation that this was the story Seamus thought it would be. To be sure there was something to say here.

I inhaled hard when the dead boy filled the screen. I registered the blood beneath him and the messy rose on the side of his head where his ear should be.

This was real. This boy was someone's kid. This boy was someone's friend. The awful truth wasn't new to me, but it felt new, and with this new feeling my motivations seemed mixed at best, if not shallow. Someone's whole life had ended right there, and I had let myself think about how I could use this ending to my advantage. That was wrong, wasn't it? But wouldn't it also be wrong to let this remain a secret?

I was startled out of my reverie by the sound of steps on the porch. Tara came in. "Is everything okay?" she asked. She sounded puzzled more than upset. I found my heart was hammering. Georgie, who had come in right behind Tara, was giving me a look of wild apology, and I knew she'd tried to stop her.

I gestured at the screen. "I had an idea for my Jane Austen paper," I said. "I wanted to write it down before I forgot." I thought my voice was surprisingly level, but I couldn't be sure. "I'll be back out in a minute."

"That's Jo for you," Georgie said, a little too brightly. "Doing homework on vacation." The comment, plus her bad acting, were agonizingly suspicious to me, but Tara said only, "Do whatever you need to do," took a wool blanket from the couch, and went back outside. Georgie waited while I closed my laptop, stowed it in my bag. I was afraid she'd say something to me, but we walked silently to where Tara was sitting. Tara fussed about the blanket until it was spread over all three of us evenly. We looked in silence at the stars.

Tara gasped. "Did you see that?"

"See what?" Georgie asked.

"A shooting star. Right there." She pointed.

"I missed it," said Georgie.

"Me too," I said.

Tara asked, "Are you serious? It was so bright."

"Maybe there will be another," I offered. And we all waited.

CHAPTER TEN

GEORGIE

"Where are you going?" Dad asked. He'd come into the kitchen to watch me stuff my feet into the boots I bought after I dropped Jo off at the bus station. I'd needed to do something to clear my mind, so I stopped at a vintage store in Portland. These boots, with their thick felt lining and wide red laces, had been seventy dollars, which was seventy more dollars than I should have spent on them. Also, they smelled awful if I wore them for more than an hour. But I still liked everything else about them, especially how they hung loose when I left them untied, so that my footsteps were messy and big.

"Out with friends," I said.

"Why don't I ever see these friends?"

I didn't respond. Dad ran his hand across a patch of counter as if noticing its height and texture for the first time. He'd been trying to cut back on pills again. When I told him that the doctor at work wasn't able to provide any additional pills, he'd taken the news in stride. He'd even said that it was all right, he wanted to wean himself off of them anyway. He'd talked before about getting down to zero pills. Every time he came back to it, the idea was as compelling as it had been the time before. More compelling, even, because this time he was more sure that he could do it. But each attempt only drove him wild, left him at the counter with a knife as he tried to approximate seven-eighths, then five-sixths of a pill.

Eventually, he'd get so miserable he'd take extra, feel great for a little while, then doze for half a day.

At work, I was doing my best to avoid Lee. In a moment of idiocy I'd let myself buy a bottle of forty-milligram Oxys from him, but the anxiety that followed the transaction left me sick. Lee had—according to him—made good on his promise to give me a deal, but I didn't appreciate this nearly as much as he expected me to. The exchange only left me all too aware I owed him something, a fact I was reminded of every time I saw him at Pine Creek, every time he grinned at me and called "What's up?" too loudly.

"Georgie," said Dad. "I learned something about what's going on in your life. But I want to give you a chance to tell me before I find out even more on my own." When I didn't respond right away, he said, "The first thing I want to know is, is it really happening?"

"Yes," I said, and then, "I'm sorry." Even though I'd spent months wanting Dad to know without actually having to tell him, I now realized how important it was that he hear it from me instead of Pastor Mark. "I'm sorry," I repeated.

"For wanting to live your own life? That's nothing to be sorry for."

Now I stared at him. "You're not upset?"

"I'm a little sad. I won't lie—it's kind of tough for me. But if it's right for you, it's what you should do."

"I don't know what to say."

"You should give me more credit," he said. Then he said, "Do you have a date yet?"

"A date for—?" Did he think that being with Tara meant we were getting married? Was that what Pastor Mark had told him, or—maybe worse—what Tara had told Pastor Mark? We couldn't even *be* married in Maine. What did Tara think, that we were all going to drive down to Massachusetts together? Why would she suggest this to her dad before she and I even talked about it?

But Dad said, "For moving into your own apartment. You left your search up on the computer last night."

"Oh," I said. "Yeah. No official plans yet, though."

"You were going to tell me, right, before you moved out?" He was trying to joke with me, but we both knew that what he said was too true to be funny. To whatever degree I could be said to have a plan, it was basically to spend more and more nights away from home, to fade pixel by pixel so that it would be impossible to say for sure when it was, exactly, that I was gone.

"Georgie," Dad said. "I want what's good for you."

"I know you do," I said, and meant it.

ABOUT AN HOUR LATER, WHEN I walked into Tara's, she asked, "Do you have rags?" I'd agreed to bring some when I came over. Tara had bought unfinished furniture and we were going to stain it together.

I groaned.

"We'll use old T-shirts," she said. "It's fine." She'd picked out a six-drawer dresser and night-stands. Two of them. They stood in the living room, which now smelled like a lumberyard. We lifted the dresser onto the newspaper and took out its drawers. Tara cracked the windows, then took a pair of scissors to a purple cotton shirt.

"I found an apartment," I said. "In Gorham." Tara had talked about finishing her bachelor's degree at the University of Southern

Maine there. I'd have a longer drive to Pine Creek, but not by much.

Tara was easing the brush out of the stain, waiting until all excess liquid dribbled from the bristles before she applied it to the side of the dresser. Though she kept moving, I could see that my words had stilled her, and that excitement had made her cautious. All she said was "Oh?"

"It's on the second floor of a big house. There are windows all along the side and front, and a big covered porch." I wished I could hand her the pictures I'd seen online. More than that, I wished I could hand her the sense of hope I'd had, looking at them. The vision of the two of us living there. I had been seized by happiness. "I think these would look nice there," I said, gesturing at the furniture. Then I said, "I guess I was wondering if we should apply."

"Is that what you want?" she asked.

"I think so."

"Could you give me a little more than 'I think so'?"

"Yeah. I mean, I want to."

Tara put her brush down and looked at me.

I looked back, helpless.

She picked up her brush again. "For Pete's sake, Georgie. I know you've needed time, but this is getting to be too much."

"I'm going to talk to my dad." I hadn't planned to tell Tara this—let alone actually talk to Dad about us—but it was clear that this was what I needed to do. Maybe, I thought, it was not so much my own doubt as it was Dad's not knowing that kept me frozen.

"When?" she asked.

"Tomorrow," I said.

I thought she was going to make me promise, but she was back to drawing the brush in neat strokes, then wiping the area she'd stained with a rag. She'd already covered more than half the dresser's long side. I, on the other hand, had done only one of the cross pieces along the front. Tara rarely looked like she hurried, but she left in her wake a trail of efficiency and accomplishment.

Eventually she said, "Okay." Then she said, "Rob doesn't actually need this place back in the spring. So I was starting to think I would stay anyway." This had been our reason for moving in together—Rob was going to move back in here and Tara would have to go.

I had trouble reading her tone. "Oh," I said, deflated.

"I want us to work out, but not so badly that I'm willing to wait forever."

"I said I'm going to tell my dad tomorrow."

"It's not only about that," she said. "I've been reducing everything to whether or not we'd move in together. And I realized that I could wait on that for a long time if I knew you wanted us to work out. But I'm not actually sure you do want us to work out." She said all of this without looking at me.

I didn't know what to say. I felt like I'd finally come over to her side only to have her step into the uncertain place I'd just left.

"Are we breaking up?" I asked weakly.

"I hope we're not at the moment," she said. Then she sighed. "I know it never works to put pressure on you. I know you'll clam up if I try to force you to say you're committed. So it's not fair for me to insist on that right now. But I have to think about what's fair for me, too."

"I know," I said.

"I don't want to make an ultimatum out of it, give you a date for a final yes or no. But it should be soon."

"Soon," I repeated. This felt doable. "I'm going to say I'm in, you know."

"Are you?" I couldn't tell if she was teasing me.

"I just need to find a way to say it."

"It's not that complicated. 'I love you and I want to be with you for the foreseeable future' would do just fine."

"I do love you and want that. But it's like you said."

"You don't want me to put you on the spot."

"Right."

We were quiet. I tried to peer through the murk of the coming days and weeks. I tried to see the day where we moved into the sunlit apartment together, where this furniture looked just right, like it had in my vision.

Then Tara said, "I have other news. You know how the Army investigation wasn't going anywhere." She'd told me about this—how she'd called at least twice more to see what they were turning up, how each time she'd been asked if she had new information, been told in so many words that she shouldn't be following up with them unless she had something new to report. As far as I knew, they still hadn't even asked her for the photos. "I got impatient," she said, "and sent messages to Gary's Facebook friends, especially the ones I'd heard him mention before. I didn't want to make anyone feel freaked out or investigated, so I started with general questions." Now she was carefully working her brush around the dresser's curved foot, the same way I knew she'd use to talk to the people who knew Gary—neat and controlled and slow.

"The guys from his squad mostly didn't offer anything beyond general condolences. But one guy, Dillon, seemed pretty open. He wrote that when he first met Gary he thought he was an asshole, but then over time he decided he was maybe less of an asshole." She gave a dry little laugh. "I guess this made me trust him, because it was my own experience of my brother. He's kind of an asshole, until you figure out that he's not actually totally an asshole. Dillon told me that Gary was the nicest of all of them to the Iraqi kids. He'd remember to bring little bottles of bubbles out with him, and he'd be mobbed by children. He was also, apparently, reading his Bible sometimes. People started calling him Reverend, which got shortened to Rev." Done with the first side of the dresser, she carried the can, brush, and rag to the other, knelt again. She studied the wood as if deciding where to begin, though I could tell she was actually deciding what to say next.

"After a few exchanges with Dillon, I was ready to allude to the photos. Dillon said he'd heard of some messed-up stuff. He said he would be willing to tell me what he knew, but that for now he needed to finish his tour. He'll be back in March. He said I could go straight to the Army with it, but he didn't think I'd get very far. He also said, 'I wouldn't jump to conclusions if I were you.' So."

I looked at my own work so far. I hadn't used the rag often enough, and the stain was blotchy in places. Also, I hadn't been consistent in my application. Watching Tara, I saw that the best way to work was by drawing the stain slowly across and down, like a curtain. But I had never settled on a single direction.

"This is all over email, by the way," Tara said. "I haven't actually talked to him."

I didn't know what to do—keep adding to the edges of the blob I'd already stained, or leave that and start over in a different corner?

Tara was waiting for a response from me.

"Huh," I said, two seconds too late.

Tara's only sign of impatience was a brief tightening of her lips. "So I'll talk to Dillon when he gets back, try to get the whole story. Maybe I can support him when he talks to the Army or even goes to the press. Reading between the lines, what he plans to do will not be popular. I think he's concerned for his own safety."

"Wait," I said. "So you think Gary's innocent?" I thought I'd been following, but I must have missed something, because Tara's relief was out of proportion with what she'd told me, which was that another guy said she shouldn't jump to conclusions.

"I'm not saying that," she said, exasperated. "I'm saying—" But even she seemed to have a hard time deciding what she was saying. "This may not be a big deal to you, but it is to me. It's the difference between 'my brother was a monster' and something like 'my brother got mixed up in something horrible but regretted it.' It's the difference between wondering whether I can even mourn him, or . . ." She trailed off. I could feel her gathering the effort to speak. "Or if I'm supposed to be glad he's dead." Then, quietly, "You've always seemed kind of neutral on this whole thing. Do you want him to be innocent?"

"Of course I do."

We went back to staining. For a while the only sounds were our brushstrokes, our rag wipes. Because of the cracked windows, the living room was now about as cold as it was outside, and my hands were red and smarting. I wished I could do better, for Tara. I should share in her relief that her brother wasn't a sicko collecting body parts, or that even if he'd participated, it might be somehow not as bad as it looked from the pictures. But I couldn't offer Tara much because I was thinking about Jo, wondering whether I owed it to her to give her this update from Tara.

I said, "It sounds like you're not planning on going to the press soon." Tara's growing impatience with the Army remained my primary hope for solving the issues of having brought Jo into all of this and having helped her get the photos. If Tara went to the press, the story was certain to come out before Jo finished her project, which I guessed would be due at the end of the semester.

Then again, because Jo was a college student writing a college paper, her work would never appear outside the classroom. Maybe her journalism professor would like it, but how would a story written by Jo get into the world? She was barely old enough to vote.

"Why would I go to the press when all I've learned is that the story is less certain than it seems?"

"I don't know. Maybe a reporter could uncover the truth faster."

She surprised me by nodding. "Fair point." Then she said, "Dillon really wants me to wait. I trust him. I'm going to give it a little longer."

I wondered only briefly whether I should tell Jo what Tara had said. It would seem like I was trying to defend Gary. And even if he wasn't the worst person involved in all of this, that shouldn't earn him a special prize.

I wouldn't interfere. Let her impress her journalism professor. He'd help her get a good job somewhere. Any rumors that came out of her project would allow a real journalist to investigate.

Everything would be fine, because it had to be.

THE NEXT AFTERNOON I DROVE home slowly, rehearsing what I'd say to Dad. I knew if you explained an apology too much, it stopped being an apology. But there *were* things I needed to explain. Like how much I really did care about Tara. How those moments, talking to her in the Yarmouth Dunkin' Donuts, had felt both electric and familiar.

Had Dad felt this way about Mom when he first talked to her? I pictured her stepping off the track, her small chest heaving, her usually neat dark hair in a matted mess around her face. Had he felt captivated like I had? Did all relationships start with something that felt like magic, even the ones that ended badly? Then how were you supposed to know whether it was a good relationship? Whether it was worth sticking around for?

Through the dusty windshield, I watched night chase the sunset in a slow cascade. I still hadn't chosen the words I would use with Dad. So be it. Sometimes the words you needed were the ones you didn't practice. I told myself that even if Dad didn't like what I told him, he wouldn't yell or threaten. He was a good person. I could trust him.

And that was also why this would be hard.

I entered the house to a shout, then the sound of a loud clattering. I ran down the basement stairs with my heart in my throat, found my dad with a drill in one hand and a set of shelves at his feet.

"Dumb mistake. I didn't tighten the screws all the way. Help me, would you?"

For the next half hour, we talked only about the job in front of us, which was installing the shelves he'd bought a month ago. We were both tired when it was over, and agreed to wait until the next day to actually put things on them.

"I'll put a pizza in," he said. We watched a show while the pizza baked. A confrontation in a kitchen involved someone brandishing a spatula as they made their allegations. The issue was resolved two scenes later.

As I set the table, my hip knocked against the coat he'd left draped against the back of the couch. I heard it—the unmistakable, almost cheerful sound of pills shifting in a bottle. Dad was rooting in the refrigerator for something, so I reached into the pocket and pulled out the orange prescription bottle. The doctor was in New Hampshire, and the prescription had been filled at a Rite Aid in Concord. It was in Dad's name, but this didn't make me feel better. If Dad was going to have more pills than he was supposed to, I wanted to be the one getting them. If anything, I was disappointed he'd gone out and gotten more for himself.

Dad and I dumped powdered Parmesan cheese and hot sauce on our pizza slices, ate in silence for a few minutes.

"I've got to sit down," Dad said. "I'm wiped." He went to the couch. Two minutes later he was snoring. I put down the pizza I couldn't taste anyway.

I'd always thought that Dad and I were a good pair because we mostly left each other alone. We each hated to bother the other. Now I wondered if maybe people who stuck together because they didn't want to be bothered should actually be bothered for that exact reason.

The phone rang. Dad twitched but didn't wake.

It was Pastor Mark. "Your dad there?" he asked.

"He's . . . resting," I said.

"I'm calling to see if he wants to be part of an outreach team for fundraising for the gym."

"I'll let him know you called."

"All right." A pause. "You take care, Georgie," he said, and hung up.

• • •

FOR A LONG TIME I sat on the couch next to Dad. He wasn't waking, though, so I draped a blanket on him, fed Hulk, and, though it was early, went to bed.

Sleep was usually my trick for coping with things that I didn't know how to cope with, or for ignoring what I knew I would never understand. I slept on the way into Maine, while Dad drove and Jo held her fingertip to a map to trace our progress. I slept the night after I learned that Jo was sleeping with Gary. I slept after I gave Marlene's pills to Dad. Sleep had always washed over me like water. I'd wake feeling clean and optimistic.

That night, though, I couldn't sleep. The rhythm of time was off, the sensation of being alive too strong. I had things that needed fixing—Dad, Jo, Tara, honesty. Me.

Jo had never slept as well as I had, and now I knew why. When there is a problem but you know you can't fix it, it's easy to sleep. But when you know there is something you need to do—and when you are ready to do it—you can't relax.

Finally I knew what it was like to need the future to give me time to repair the past. Finally I'd learned the difference between waiting for a new day to start and needing it to.

PART TWO

CHAPTER ELEVEN

JO

A cold, gray morning in January found me at my desk, one hand wrapped around a mug of instant coffee and the other resting on my laptop's trackpad so I could compulsively refresh my email. Though by this point, compulsive clicking had turned to desperate clicking. Such was the state of my research and writing process. The oak outside my window hadn't lost its leaves in the fall, and its dead and crumpled foliage permitted only shards of early-morning light.

It was the sixth day since I'd sent questions to Squad Sergeant Thomas Gadson. It was afternoon in Iraq. If he'd gone on any sort of night mission or patrol, he'd be back and would have made his report and slept and, I thought, should have had time to sit down at a computer. The time difference had a weird way of making him feel both close and far away. Far away because my morning was his afternoon, my afternoon his night. Close because I was constantly counting the hours between us, imagining his wristwatch marking the same steady march of time as mine.

For four days now my waking thought had been *Today Thomas Gadson will write me back*. Each day he didn't was another wasted day, because the silence left me too distracted to do any other reading and writing, though I tried. Seamus told me that putting the article together would take as long as it took, but I knew that, practically speaking, this was the last month I had to finish it. I had virtually no other obligations. Spring term would bring four new classes I needed to do well in if I was going to keep my scholarship. None of the editors Seamus knew were willing to contract with a new writer, so I was working on spec. No matter how much Seamus insisted I could sell it, I couldn't get out of my head the fear that I'd labor over this for months and then it would flop. By that point, Seamus, who had extended his one-semester visit to include the January term, would be gone, back to his apartment in New York, which for some reason I envisioned as looking not like his apartment here but like the office he was borrowing from a professor on leave, except with a narrow bed in the corner.

When Seamus suggested taking me on for the January term, I'd pictured the two of us leaning over my laptop together, arguing about paragraph placement and sorting through my notes, trying to piece together what happened like brainy detectives in a crime drama. That had not been the reality. Every morning I stopped by his office to update him on my progress, which at this point amounted to telling him what I was worried about. He told me not to worry, that patience and guts always win out in the end. He seemed to think that once you decided to write about something, all you needed was to keep believing the story would materialize while you threw everything you had at it. I could already see him using this approach on the story he'd recently started, something about Christian adoption agencies. The intensity he brought to his work was palpable. Each time I stepped into his office after breakfast, I'd find him hunched over his laptop screen like he was staring into a deep and exhilarating pool.

I knew he cared about my article. Actually, he seemed invigorated by the idea of the two of us working side by side on our separate projects, as if we could together ride our confidence to greatness. I was relatively confident in myself as a writer. I had a good record of wrestling words onto the page. It was the story on my hands that seemed weak. No matter what Seamus said about how I had more information than I knew, how I might have to go to press before I was sure of the entire story, how my job was to report on what *I* knew, not what *God* knew, I suspected I didn't have nearly enough. I needed more interviews. I needed more information. And so the words circled and circled like birds who wouldn't, couldn't, land.

By now I had two distinct relationships with Seamus. In the morning we met in his office, door wide open, while he said in a loud, teacherly voice, "*Insist* they talk to you!" Ten hours later he'd be letting me into his apartment, pouring me wine, poking fun at professors in the department and talking about how glad he was that he didn't go into academia. We'd established a tacit rule that I didn't sleep over. I preferred it this way, waking up alone in my own room and with my own thoughts, and I suspected that he liked how each morning I showed up in his office and we started all over again.

When my latest click actually brought a new email to my inbox, I thought I might be hallucinating. But there it was, an unread white bar sitting on top of all the grayed-out ones. Subject line: *Re: Follow-up Questions*. From: *Thomas Gadson*.

I hovered the cursor over the email. My pause was deliberate, full of effort, as if I could will the contents of the email to be what I needed.

Behind me came a smart rapping, not on my door but from inside my room. I almost knocked my coffee over as I spun to see who was there.

"Whoa, hey. It's just me." In a gesture of respect for my space, Lily had tipped only her top half into my room. I thought I'd closed my door, but I must not have pushed it hard enough to latch. "I haven't seen you in forever," Lily said, admitting the bottom half of her body.

I folded my laptop, tried to glance surreptitiously around my room to see what Lily was seeing: a jar of instant coffee, bananas badly bruised on one side. At least I hadn't dug into my oat clusters yet, because then she would see the battered box. I got it for fifty cents because it looked like someone had driven a forklift over it.

Lily put an elbow on my dresser. She was wearing black leggings, Asics, and a baggy sweatshirt. Her hair was pulled back, with glossy stands of it stuck to her temples. Probably she was coming from an early gym session on the elliptical. I imagined her dragging a highlighter in wavy lines across her reading while her legs climbed and climbed.

"I saw you last week," I reminded her. Her Jan Term class was on public health, and she'd come into the library to check out a stack of books on malaria.

"I mean we haven't hung out. I have no idea how you're doing. How was break? How are things with your sister? Did anything . . . come up?"

"Nothing new," I said feebly. Christmas had gone okay, if *okay* could mean worrying about Dad every time he got in a car, hiding in my room with a stack of books, and trying to wordlessly make Georgie feel better about the photos I'd stolen. There had been some nice moments, too. Georgie and I snuck boxes of Chinese takeout into a late movie, then listened to a burned CD of popular songs from high school on our drive home.

"At least nothing's getting worse," she said brightly, but I wondered whether she was disappointed there wasn't a bigger crisis looming. "Can I take you to breakfast? My treat," she added, too casually. "Let's go to Franny's. Don't say no. I've missed you."

I dressed while she went to get her car. It was weirdly easy to leave Gadson's email unopened, mostly because I didn't want to face the disappointment of another dead end. I could practically write it myself: *sorry i can't be of more help, i'd rather not answer any other questions, you could report this to the army offices, good luck*. The sorts of answers I'd already gotten from the other guys on Gary's squad. It was clear they were evading the topic, but reticence alone would not support a story.

In front of my closet I wondered what the right thing to wear to breakfast would be. I wanted to match Lily's style, leggings and a warm, sporty top, but I hadn't been to the gym and it wouldn't make sense to go right after breakfast. I knew it was stupid to worry about this. I knew Lily would tell me it didn't matter, that I could wear anything I wanted. I picked out a sweatshirt and jeans, pulled on a pair of wool socks Lily once complimented, slipped my feet into knockoff Birkenstocks I regretted halfway down the stairs, when I remembered yesterday's snowfall.

As I opened the door to Lily's car, she pulled CD cases, scarves, and a pair of sunglasses off the passenger seat. "Sorry, sorry," she said about the clutter. The air in the car was thick with powdery freshener. I'd never been in her car before. It was a pale gold Toyota. I sat on an old coffee stain the size of my palm. The car's heater was slow to get going, and we scrubbed our thighs to ward off the cold. The diner was in a trailer that had been retrofitted to look vaguely like a train car. Christmas lights still blinked on the roof.

"They have good pancakes," Lily said, to counterbalance the shabby appearance.

The woman at the register was counting crumpled bills. "Sit wherever, dearies," she said, without looking up or pausing her counting. I followed Lily to a corner booth. A teenage boy brought menus, mugs, and coffee.

"I'll have a blueberry pancake," Lily told him, without looking at the menu. To me she said, "Order whatever." A single blueberry pancake didn't sound like enough food for me, so I got a cheese omelet with home fries. The boy disappeared with the menus. Now there was nothing between Lily and me but our thick-walled mugs, which both of us gripped with two hands.

It was nice being off campus. Not only to Bean There, which could barely be considered "off campus," but somewhere we had to drive to. Our booth was upholstered in faux leather and the table was covered in glittery laminate. Above us, a fluorescent light shuddered. Steam rose from my oily black coffee, which I realized, when I sipped it, was very strong. I glanced around and then said, softly and quickly, "So I'm sleeping with Seamus."

Lily's eyebrows jerked upward as if yanked by strings. "Wow," she said. "*Wowww*." She seemed to start toward three different sentences before asking, "I take it that's what you want to be doing?"

"I'm—yes and no. I mean, I chose to. It's—" I sucked my lips to keep from smiling, or breaking into nervous laughter. "It's a good thing. But it's also—he's kind of in the professor category, you know?"

Lily nodded. "There's the age difference, and the power differential, too. That can be complicated." Then she hurried to add, "I'm trying to get to the bottom of 'yes and no.'" She flashed me a wicked smile. "Fucking a *professor*, Jo," she said, and we laughed violently, which helped clear away the awkwardness of my confession.

"You can't tell anyone," I said.

"I won't if you're okay," she said. "But don't blame me if anyone guesses."

"Are people guessing?" I asked.

"Susan has her ideas, but she has lots of ideas, too many to be serious about any one of them." She paused to drink from her mug. "So is it good?"

I laughed again and covered my face. I thought of how anxious and tentative Seamus had been at first. Even I knew he was being a buzzkill. So I got to be the assertive one, moving us along, until he was sure that I was sure that I wanted this. I liked his sudden boyishness, how at odds his bedroom behavior was with his classroom bravado. I liked how he looked me up and down slowly, like my body kept revealing its shape to him anew.

Lily concluded, "Seems like it's good." Then she asked, "What's the plan when he leaves?"

"We don't really talk about it."

"So it's just a super casual thing? And you're okay with that?"

"Yeah. I think so. I mean, yeah." When Seamus brought up my visiting New York, I was the one who'd been noncommittal. It seemed too complicated. Plus I couldn't imagine him remaining interested in me once he got back to his regular life. Putting more force in my words, I said, "It's casual, and that's what I want."

"Great. I just can't help asking. Like, what if you break up? Does that affect your grade? Then again, given the grading of Jan Term, that doesn't matter, right? It's pass/fail, and you'll pass.

Besides, if you two do get found out, he's the one who'll be in trouble, not you." She shrugged. "I'm thinking out loud. I don't mean to be a downer."

"No, it's fine," I said. Then I said, "He'd be in trouble?"

"Colleges have rules against relationships between faculty and students. It's to protect students. He's leaving anyway, though, so I'm not sure there's much they could do. Even if they found out. Which they won't." She lifted a hand to brush away the specter of concern she'd raised. "Once you've done enough training and volunteering and stuff, you can't shut it off." She mimicked herself with a high voice: "*Are you sure it's consensual? What if anything goes wrong?*" She laughed. "I am actually capable of being happy for someone who's in a relationship they want. If you're happy with it, then I'm happy for you."

"I'm happy with it," I said, though *happy* caught a little in my throat. *Happy* was sitting in a too-bright diner with Lily, high on caffeine and waiting for a hot breakfast. *Happy* were the increasingly rare moments I thought my draft might come together perfectly. Being with Seamus made me feel good, but I didn't know about happy.

I wondered, then, whether happiness meant understanding, or thinking you understood, what was happening and what might come next. And I wasn't clear on either of those things with Seamus. Which didn't mean I didn't like what was happening. Just that it didn't make me happy.

If Lily sensed my hesitation, she decided to move on anyway. "I don't even know what your independent study project is about," she said. "All I know is you're still working with Seamus. Are you extending your piece about the church?"

I hadn't told Lily, or anyone else at Peabody, about the photos and the change in my project topic. Only Seamus knew. It felt safer this way. I needed a sense of privacy to write. If my friends were asking me about it all the time, I would have trouble finding the mental quiet I needed. Now, though, I was starting to feel too isolated with my project. I wanted a voice other than Seamus's in my head.

Before I could answer, Lily looked past me and leaned back, signaling the arrival of our food. Her single pancake was the size of a dinner plate, studded with blueberries as big as marbles. In the center, a sphere of butter melted slowly, like a setting sun. My omelet, on the other hand, was covered with so many dark brown spots it looked like leopard print. There was a greasy smear on one side of my plate where the home fries had been shoveled into place.

Lily crinkled her nose at my breakfast. "That looks burned," she said. "Do you want to send it back?"

"It's fine," I said, picking up my fork.

"Are you sure?"

"Totally." The fact that she was paying somehow made her responsible for this dish, and I didn't want to appear ungrateful. I cut a corner bite. The omelet's overcooked skin was like cloth in my mouth.

"It's kind of a new project," I said.

"Can you tell me what it's about?" She sensed my hesitation, then said, "I'm not trying to pressure you."

"It's gotten kind of involved. Seamus thinks we can publish it somewhere." I paused. "I mean, that I can publish it somewhere. He wants me to have the byline."

"Publish it somewhere like—?" she prompted.

"He has some contacts at big magazines. *The Atlantic*, the *New Yorker*." I heard myself applying that half-casual, half apologetic tone I'd always hated hearing from the other girls at Peabody. Like the time a classmate had come late to a group project meeting because she'd been watching her uncle be interviewed on *60 Minutes*. "I thought he was going to say like two things," she'd explained. "But he went on for*ever*." I'd sworn to myself I'd never talk like that no matter what happened. Now that I wanted to explain something without seeming like I was bragging, though, I wondered how else I was supposed to do it.

"Are you serious?" Lily seemed more surprised by this than by the fact that I was sleeping with Seamus. "You're going to launch a journalism career while you're in college?"

"I mean," I said, "I'm guess I'm going to try."

"Holy shit, Jo," she said. She cocked her head. "You sure you can't tell me what it's about?"

The waiter came to check on us. I knew I didn't want more coffee, but I let him pour it to give me time to think.

"You need anything else?" he asked.

"I'm good," I said, and he retreated behind the counter.

"Jo the man magnet," Lily said.

"What?" I asked.

"He's been looking at you this whole time. Don't act surprised. You're very pretty."

I turned to glance at the counter. Indeed he was looking at me. "No. It's just because—" I started. But I didn't know what to say. No doubt Lily was prettier than I was. I'd never hoped to look more than fine. But was she right? Was I pretty, even *very* pretty?

For some reason, I didn't want to know. To change the subject, I said, "War crimes."

Her eyes widened, stayed wide. "Are you serious?" she asked, for the second time in as many minutes. "We don't hang out for a couple weeks and all of this happens?" She seemed to have forgotten the fork in her hand, the perfect bite of butter- and syrup-sodden pancake she'd cut. "You're not putting yourself in danger, are you? Not creeping down dark alleys to meet with sources?"

I had to laugh, especially when I thought about how much of my recent research had involved obsessing over the wording of Facebook messages I hoped were inviting but offhanded, specific but not too long. "Nothing like that. I haven't even met any of my interviewees in person."

Lily chewed thoughtfully, then said, "I guess I'm kind of jealous."

"I thought you didn't like Seamus."

"Not of that," she said, then noticed I was kidding. She rolled her eyes, but I sensed a mutual pleasure in my joke, which had taken even me by surprise.

She said, "You and I are at a top-ranked college to make connections and do cool things. To graduate with something besides a transcript that says we took Biology and American Studies and did all our homework. And that's what you're doing. You're . . . *beginning.*" She seemed to have forgotten that, until very recently, a transcript was going to be all I graduated with. I thought of Lily's clubs and activities, the way she wanted to befriend everyone, even me, because she was afraid of missing out.

I could discern the shift in Lily's mood as she cut another soggy piece of pancake and I forced down another leathery bite of omelet. Lily signaled for the check, then turned to me. "I keep being a downer about all your news," she said. "I really am happy for you." I knew she was, or was trying to be, which was more or less the same thing.

I thought of what was waiting for me back in my dorm room: A small pile of evidence that hadn't resolved into a story. A pit of anger so deep I wondered if even writing and publishing this article could fill it. A series of ghastly photographs that felt connected and yet also unrelated to what Gary did to me. An email from Thomas Gadson that was sure to say nothing at all.

"At this point I'm not sure the story is going to work out," I told her as we walked to her car.

"Will you let me know if I can help?" she asked.

"Sure," I said. "Thanks."

"In ten years I want to be able to tell people that Jo Prescott, the Pulitzer Prize–winning journalist, was my college friend."

"I hope we're still friends in ten years," I said, then worried I'd said too much.

"We will be if I have any say in the matter," she said. It had started to snow, dry occasional flakes that slid up the windshield as we drove. Lily gave me updates on the various committees she was on. I knew she was trying to remind herself that she was *beginning*, too. I couldn't offer her a story about her future as tidy as the one she'd predicted for me, but I wanted to show her how much I believed in her. Then again, because our respective futures were the undercurrent of the conversation and not its actual topic, I could only offer things like "You're doing an amazing job" and "They're lucky to have you," which, despite sounding superficial, I really meant.

When she dropped me off at my dorm, she said, "Don't disappear on me for another month, okay?"

"I won't."

"Promise?"

"I promise," I said.

IN MY ROOM I FOUND my cold instant coffee, my laptop screen folded down to shield Thomas's email from Lily. The sun, having cleared the oak tree, was beaming straight into my room. I adjusted the blinds, sat at my desk, tapped the space bar to wake my computer, and waited.

Facebook had given me a lot of context. I knew, for example, that Gary's squad was led by Sergeant Gadson. Devin Cozens posted a picture of them all hanging off each other like a middle school basketball team. The description on the photo said, simply, *SQUAD*. He'd tagged Russell Duquette, Thomas Gadson, himself, Luke Sauceman, Jeremy Lard, Nick Lanzi, Gary, and Dillon Washington. Gadson was the one as tall as Gary, and Dillon Washington was the only one who was smiling. I'd sent Facebook messages to all of them. Only half of them replied in the first place, and Russell Duquette was the only one who'd continued to respond to me. But he'd been less helpful as time went on. He claimed his sporadic responses were because he couldn't get online regularly, but I kept seeing that he'd liked or commented on another post since I last wrote to him, so I knew he was avoiding me. "It's not necessarily a problem," Seamus told me. "Probably he wants to talk but knows he can't yet. Maybe he'll talk to you once he's home."

"That will be months from now," I'd groaned, but Seamus said, "It will take as long as it takes." Easy for him to say. Besides,

Seamus wasn't consistent on the topic of patience. One day it was "A well-reported book that takes ten years is worth fifty books that got dashed off in six months." The next, it was "Journalism is all about timeliness. Old news is old news."

Russell had told me he wasn't there the day the boy died, but that the boy had been holding a grenade. When I asked why Gary took pictures, he wrote *your going to have to ask someone who was there cuz like i said i wasnt.*

When I asked about the photos of the ear, the fingers, he wrote *i dont know anything abut that.*

I'd copied every exchange I'd had with the guys into a Word document I'd read over and over. I even found myself wondering if the haphazard spelling would reveal something to me.

My computer screen was still blank. I tried the space bar again. Nothing. I checked the power cord. It was plugged in, and the little light was on to show that it was connected. I held down the on/off button, waited. Still nothing. My panic felt like a buoy whose line was too short to let it break the water's surface. It kept wanting to rise, and it kept finding no release. The fact that I was loaded up on very strong coffee didn't help. My hands shook as I tried the power button again and again in a kind of hopeless, technological CPR.

THE COMPUTER SERVICE STORE WAS on the far side of town. It took me forty minutes to walk there. The store itself didn't inspire confidence. It had torn gray carpeting and shelves lined with yellowing computers that made me think of sixth-grade typing class.

I entered on a wave of my own urgency but was brought up short by the fact that there was only one person working, and he was already helping the guy ahead of me. The customer was going on about a Windows service pack. The man behind the counter listened with the air of someone quietly entertained by the fact that they are humoring someone else. Even though the guy in front of me was skinny as a rail, I shifted back and forth as if making sure I could be seen past him.

Finally the man at the counter, who had a goatee so long it brushed his chest, flicked his eyes toward me. "Can I help you?" he asked.

"My laptop broke," I said.

"Put it here," he said, tapping the counter. The customer moved aside without backing away, as if we were all going to examine it together. I slid my computer onto the counter. The customer whistled. "Your first mistake was buying one of those things," he told me. He was about my age, with dark hair and light, darting eyes. He was familiar somehow, but I couldn't place him.

The goateed man, whose plastic name pin said WES, and OWNER under that, asked me a series of diagnostic questions. When did this happen? What was I experiencing before it happened? While we talked, he kept three fingers on the closed laptop, like he was taking its pulse.

"Sounds like a system crash," Wes said. "Probably you've got a bad sector on your hard drive."

"Or a missing system file," said the skinny guy.

"You could try to fix it yourself," said Wes.

"Get an external housing for your hard drive," said the skinny guy. "You can take the hard drive out yourself. Get your data back that way if the file system is still working." He added, "It's really not difficult."

Wes looked at me as if he was the one who'd last spoken. Why did he think I understood anything the young guy said? Why did he want me to take care of the problem myself? Didn't he start this business to take care of other people's computer problems?

"I could work on it for you," Wes said. "Problem is I'm backed up about three weeks."

"I don't have three weeks," I said.

He opened his palms toward the stained ceiling tiles. "Can't help you there," he said.

A thought occurred to me. "You *can* get what's on here, can't you?"

He made the same gesture. I thought I might cry. I didn't back the photos up anywhere. Why didn't I back up the photos?

"I need what's on this computer," I told him, hating how desperate I sounded.

"I could work on it for you," said the skinny guy. "Have it back to you in a couple days, probably. Maybe even sooner. How did that journalism project turn out?"

"What?" I asked, jolted by surprise. Then I recognized him from the student center. I should have done so earlier, but I had been too upset to put it together. "This is actually for—" I started, then went back to keeping things secret. "I just need what's on there."

"I'd be happy to help you with it," he said. "And I'd be cheaper than this guy." He tipped his head at Wes, who said, "You haven't even told her your name."

"I'm Brett," said Brett. "Two *T*s."

"Brett knows what he's doing," Wes said. "I'd hire him to work here, but . . ."

"You don't like my opinions on Windows," Brett said, grinning. "What's your number?" He plucked a ballpoint pen from a dirty cup, poised its point over the back of his hand. "Go for it," he said, when I hesitated. After I told him, he said, "If I can't get the whole thing up and running again, I'll put anything I can retrieve on a thumb drive. Assuming you don't have hours of video on here?"

"No video."

"Great." He tucked my laptop under his arm. "You brought your power cord?"

As I plundered my backpack for the cord, I realized I had broken into a cold sweat. I hated the expectation to go along and not slow things down with questions or concerns. I wasn't ready to part with my laptop, especially not to a guy who didn't even work at the computer shop, but I didn't think I had a choice.

"The stuff on there is private," I said.

"Course it is," Brett said cheerfully. "I don't go poking around in anyone's stuff." He waggled his eyebrows. "Unless it's juicy."

I felt my cheeks flame. "It's not," I said.

"All right. I'll get to work." Looking at Wes, Brett touched a fingertip to his forehead. "Think about what I said. Think about what you want from WPA security." He left without saying goodbye to either of us.

I looked at Wes. "He doesn't even know my name."

"I can take your name if you want. He's in here a lot, as you might guess."

I gave him my name, dorm room phone, and email address. I found myself lingering, as if some final exchange could make myself confident I was doing the right thing. Wes, who was finally softening to my anxiety, said, "Look, it's a good thing Brett was here. He'll probably have it done by tomorrow. It'll be okay."

With only those words for comfort, I headed back to campus. The cloud cover was so thick I couldn't tell where the sun was. Cold stung my cheeks and the tips of my ears. What I would've given for the weight of the laptop and power cord, with its heavy black brick, pulling at my shoulders. How could I have been so stupid as to not save the photos? I didn't have a good answer. And now my laptop was in the hands of a teenager who didn't think I should've bought it in the first place.

Even though I was hungry, I went straight to Jarrett, took my old spot in the lab with the whooshing vents, tapped out my login on keys that felt as big as ice cube tray wells compared to my laptop's delicate ones. At least I could still read my email on the school computer. Not that I thought Gadson's message would be of any help. The ranks had closed around Gary. The only complete story I had about him was the one I couldn't tell.

Gadson's email was a rectangle of text. It took me a read and a half to compute what he was saying.

> Hey jo, sorry I've taken so long to get back to you. Truth be told it's been hard for me to decide what to do about Clemmons. I had my concerns but I didn't have proof, and then of course he died. And that is horrible no matter who he was, and I needed to be taking care of my guys. With me being in a leadership position, there's a way in which what he did reflects on me. That's not fun to admit, but at the end of the day I have to do the right thing. So

> yes I will talk to you. I'll have a week of leave starting in ten days and you can call me then. I have to be anonymous. The higher ups don't like us talking to reporters, especially stuff like this. —TG

I closed his email, then opened it again, as if I could prolong the echo of excitement rattling through me. When the door to the lab opened behind me I closed the message again. I knew I was being silly, but I couldn't help it.

I waited for the girl who'd joined me to print off three articles, at least twenty pages each. As the acrid smell of ink filled the room, a clear feeling grew inside me. This would work out. Gadson would tell me what I needed to know and Brett would find a way to save the files on my computer. I didn't need to even trust them much as individuals to know that they would do these things, because most guys would go to any lengths to be a hero.

GEORGIE

CHAPTER TWELVE

It took me until a few days after Christmas to actually tell Dad about me and Tara. But I found myself hesitating anyway, not so much because of what Dad would think but because of how he was doing overall. Then Jo was home for the holiday and I didn't want to ruin her visit, so I waited until she left. I knew my waiting would look bad to Tara, so I kept up a steady stream of texts about it. *he's not feeling well today. jo will leave this afternoon.*

She responded, *just do it when you're ready.*

The day was warm for late December, somewhere near forty by the afternoon, and Dad was out back tossing worn tennis balls to Hulk. I joined him there. He was wearing his new flannel shirt from me and the Peabody knit hat that Jo had given him. She'd given him a similar one her first year at Peabody, which both of them seemed to have forgotten.

For a while we watched Hulk obligingly trot after the balls. Then he quit in the form of lying down in front of the door. Afraid that if I didn't speak now I would never say what I wanted to say, I said, "Dad, I have to tell you something. I'm dating Tara Clemmens. We've been dating for a while. I'm sorry I didn't tell you sooner. I know things are hard right now and I didn't want to make anything more difficult. But I'm sorry. Because I should've told you." I could hear my words starting to loop back on themselves already, so I made myself stop.

We stood for a long time, not looking at each other. I knew better than to try to take the measure of his emotional state. Dad needed time. I could give that to him. I had usually known what he needed. I had been here for him. He had to see that I was still trying to be here for him, in my broken way. Finally I stole a glance at him. He seemed pensive, looking at the jagged line separating trees from sky.

"Does Mark know?" he asked.

"Not yet. But he asked me about us."

"What did you tell him?" Dad meant, *Did you lie?* Dad hated lying. He called it cowardly.

"Our conversation was interrupted. But Tara's going to tell him now that I told you."

He nodded faintly. "I guess I should have seen, with you not getting your start in life and all, that maybe there was something keeping you back."

"What do you mean?"

Hulk heaved a sigh, but neither of us moved to let him in.

"I think I understand now. You found yourself wanting . . . that kind of relationship, and you weren't sure what to do about it. So you stuck close to home. You ended up hanging out too much with me." He tried to chuckle but the sound came out sad. "I'm sorry. I don't know what else to say."

A crow flew overhead, folding its wings and screaming. I let the weight of Dad's reaction sink in. He thought my being in a relationship with a woman explained the fact that I hadn't moved out yet or made more of myself in life—none of which I'd thought was a problem in his eyes. I'd even thought he liked having me here. That I made things more pleasant, or at least not as lonely as they could be.

Apparently, all this time he'd been wondering what was wrong with me. And now he had an answer.

"Well," I said. "If you don't know what else to say, then there's nothing else to say."

"Georgie," he said, sounding pained.

"What?" I asked, equally pained.

Neither of us wanted to move either forward or backward. And so we moved, as was typical, sideways. Dad said, "Better let the dog in," and I mumbled about whatever it was I had to do, and the moment we reentered the house, it was as if we agreed not to speak of it, at least not inside. In fact, we carried ourselves into the evening with more kindness than usual, as if to store up whatever goodwill we could before the days ahead.

TWO WEEKS PASSED. TARA AND I were working on getting an apartment—not the one with all the windows I'd first located, which Tara had deemed too expensive, especially if she was going back to school, but a small bright space in Westbrook. The white paint on the walls was literally still drying when we toured it, and I thought the carpet was rough and ugly. I still liked the vision of that second-floor apartment with all the windows. "We'll get there," she said, because she had seen the pictures and liked it, too. "But we don't *start* there."

I still didn't like this apartment. Yes, it was clean and got good sun, and it was obviously better kept than where I was currently living. But it also felt industrial, even cold.

"We'll put up decorations. We'll make it our own," Tara promised.

Then the landlord was out of town, and then he needed more

financial proof from us, and then he was worried about my lack of a credit score. After a few days he agreed that Tara alone could be on the lease, and then for some reason he had a change of heart and emailed the lease over to be signed by both of us with a twenty-four-hour deadline for returning it, which Tara suspected meant that he'd gotten interest from someone else he preferred to rent to, because Tara had told him she didn't check her email often and that the best way to contact her was by text.

Which is how Tara and I ended up needing to sign the lease the morning of Martin Luther King Jr. Day, which happened to be the morning of the Polar Plunge fundraiser for the Garrett Joshua Clemmens Memorial Gymnasium. Fundraising had started out strong—within weeks of announcing the project, Mark had seventy-five thousand dollars promised—and then petered fast, after he'd gotten what he could from all the contacts he already had. Tara, who had been helping with the planning, said that for all the effort that had gone into the Plunge, the event would net at most about ten thousand dollars. "It could be more, but Dad's already spent a bunch on a DJ, special prizes, and radio and newspaper advertising," she said, and shrugged. "He'll probably spend the rest of his life trying to raise all the money it will take to build the gym." Then she said, "I guess there are worse things he could devote himself to."

The day was clear and very cold, with a predicted high of about twenty, though as of when everyone was gathering at the parking lot by the beach, the temperature hovered around ten. Dad was checking people in and making sure they'd signed all the appropriate waivers. I was helping at the warming tent. Tara was on safety checks, counting people as they went into and came out of the water.

I was one of five people in the tent, where tall narrow heaters made the air shimmer. Participants plunged in waves of five, then ran shouting for the warming tent as if running for their lives. We would hand them towels fresh off a heating rack, have their change of clothes ready.

I'd volunteered for this mostly because it seemed like an opportunity to appease Dad, Tara, *and* Mark. I hadn't expected to have fun. It wasn't surprising that the people coming out of the water hooted and shrieked, but it *was* surprising how naked they seemed, and not only because they came in dripping in their bathing suits. The water seemed to have temporarily washed some sense of themselves away, and they stayed like that, bare and open to me, for the whole time I helped them towel off, dance into their clothes, and get a cup of hot chocolate into their bright red hands.

I was so busy with each wave of people—toweling, laughing at their shock and exuberance—that I didn't see Dad coming until he was right behind me.

"I didn't know you were doing this!" I said. I hadn't seen his name on any of the bags of clothing and towels people had dropped off at check-in.

He grinned at me. "I thought you might try to stop me."

He was right about that. "I'm not sure I have clothes for you," I said.

"I left them in the car. I'm just here to warm up for a bit." I could tell the water had brightened him, too, and while he seemed in one sense like all the other stripped-down humans I'd been tending to all morning, the exposure seemed to have calmed him, quieting the noise in his body rather than causing him to spill outward like everyone around him. It was so like him, I thought, to robustly take a shock of cold. Even in his state, so compromised compared to what it had once been, he could bear quietly what almost no one else could.

I draped a spare towel around his shoulders. The scarring from his surgeries looked like the faint fossil of some long and many-legged insect. At first his scars had been hard to look at—I had been in charge of changing bandages because Jo was always busy—but over time they'd faded. The weird thing was that, now that they seemed like a relic, they also mattered more than ever.

"I'll tell you something," he said, as if he could read my thoughts. "Right now, I feel no pain at all."

"That's great," I said. "But I don't want you to catch a cold."

"The truck's right there," he said, pointing to remind me. He had maybe ten yards to go.

"Okay," I said. "Go dress quick or I'll be in trouble."

After one more wave of people, the event was over. Participants had already started leaving by the time the DJ stopped playing. People were breaking down tents and tables; Mark was circling the area officiously. He looked like a football coach with his long puffy coat and clipboard. I could see his breath when he gave orders and shouted thanks. I suspected this was the best he'd felt since Gary died, and I couldn't help being glad for him.

"Hey." Tara was approaching with a folder. "Time to do this. I'm going to drive straight over to drop this off before the deadline." We were bent over the last standing table, pushing our names onto the paper in blue ink, when we heard a voice from right behind us: "Seriously?"

We turned. Mark folded his arms and tilted his head. "You two are seriously going to do that right here? Right now?"

You would have thought we'd been making out or something. His anger was sudden and intense, an odd but somchow logical match for the good mood he'd been in only minutes earlier.

Though Tara didn't discernibly move, I sensed that she had dropped into a mental crouch, tensed and ready for a fight. Maybe because she hadn't said anything yet, Mark took a step toward us and, dropping his voice, said, "I can't believe you'd do this at this event. For Gary," he added, as if we didn't know.

"Gary didn't give me half the grief you have," Tara said. "So I don't think he'd mind." She handed me the pen. "You have to date it," she said.

My hand shook a little as I wrote. There were a few people nearby, but I didn't think they could hear us. Even so, I hated that this had to feel public. I wasn't ashamed by what we were doing. My shame was the result of this scene. I wanted my life to be scene-free.

Mark was standing there like what he was, an angry parent trying to decide what to do with his problematic child. Tara was standing there like what she was, an adult who was going to make her own decisions.

"Just as a reminder," she said, her voice soft, yet also trembling faintly, "you already lost one of your children. It's up to you whether you lose another."

"Don't threaten me," Mark said.

"Like you yourself used to say, it's not a threat. It's a fact."

Miriam had appeared at her husband's side. "Is everything okay?" she asked. She was talking to Mark and not to us.

"These two are signing a lease together," Mark hissed.

"Tara, do you have to do this right now?" Miriam whispered.

"Yes, Mom, I do." Raising her voice now, Tara said, "Would you like us to go sit in the car while we sign? Would that appease your sense of righteousness?"

"Honey, it's fine." Miriam's whisper was more strained. She started tugging at Mark's arm. "Come on." Mark looked like he might be going with her, but then his eye caught on the figure of my father, now in his long jacket with the big hood, wandering toward us.

"Do you approve of this?" he called. "Peter, what do you think of this?"

"What's that?" Dad pulled down his hood as he came closer. "Didn't catch that."

"Our daughters. Moving in together." He hesitated, and then, as if to rebuke his own hesitation, he said, "*Living in sin.*"

Dad gave a little grimace, as if empathizing with the difficulty of Mark's situation. He tucked his hands into the coat's big pockets. The coat wasn't zipped, and I could see his old Ohio State T-shirt underneath, the one they'd sent him when they offered him the scholarship. He said, "Dawn has always made the choices she wanted to. No matter what I said to her. So I can't say the situation will be helped. I always knew she wasn't coming back, but I had to believe differently." He paused and looked around at all of us. He seemed to register the collective confusion and concern, because he added, "We have to have faith that in the end it will be okay."

"Dad?" I said. "I'm Georgie."

He squinted at me, then grunted. "Course you are."

"Are you okay?" I asked.

"'Okay' is a matter of prayer," he said. "Prayer is what I've devoted my life to, only not always, because sometimes I fail. So often I fail." He'd started to cry. "Jesus, save me!" He wandered toward the parking lot. Miriam said, "I'm not sure he's okay," and went after him. I thought about telling her of course he wasn't okay and I knew why, but I kept this to myself.

Mark turned to me. The strangeness of the interaction seemed to have brought him back to himself. "Aside from the rest of this, I have to tell you, I've been worried about your dad. He tells me he's fine and then these odd things keep happening. You see that, don't you?"

I nodded.

"You have to think about what you owe him," Mark was saying. "What he gave up for you."

Miriam was shouting, "Georgie! Mark! Get over here!" She had a hand on my dad's neck, another inside his coat. "He's hypothermic. Where's the heater?"

"It's gone," Tara said. "They packed it up."

"For God's sake, then, get your car started."

I fished Dad's keys from his pocket and revved the truck's engine. The dashboard thermometer said seventeen degrees. How long had Dad been wandering around in the cold with an unzipped jacket? Plungers were required to have wool socks, boots, thick pants, and a coat and hat to put on. Dad was wearing his usual cotton socks and New Balance sneakers. Plus he hadn't spent the required fifteen minutes in the warming tent. Miriam and Mark were helping Dad into the car. "Take him to the hospital," Miriam told me.

"Are you sure?" I asked. I imagined them doing some sort of blood draw, figuring out that he had way more oxycodone in his system than any single doctor would prescribe. "Don't we need to just warm him up?"

"Take him *to the hospital*," she said. So I went.

• • •

"IT LOOKS MORE SERIOUS THAN it is," an ER doctor told me. She meant the fact that Dad had an IV drip and a mask over his face. "We're just taking extra measures. He's been responding well." Dad was sleeping now, his breath long and even. I knew when he woke up he would need another Oxy, and I was trying to think about how to get my hands on some.

"My pastor's wife said to bring him in," I said, apologetically.

"It's good you did," she said briskly. "I'm not suggesting otherwise. We had a teenager die of exposure just a few weeks ago. He might have lived if his friends had brought him in ten minutes sooner." When she saw the shock on my face, she said, "Bodies don't argue well with cold. I'll check back in in another hour or two, and if all is still good we'll get you two on your way." With that she swept out of the room, and I was left with Dad's breathing, with his still form, and with all the strange things he'd said to me on the way here—"I always did want to live in Florida," and then, "Do you plan to stay this time? Don't say yes if you're not going to." And then, "The girls miss you, you know. They should have a mother. I'm not enough for them."

"Dad," I kept saying. "Stop. Please."

"Why did you leave them without a mother? It was wrong. I forgave you, but can they?"

I turned on the radio to try to drown him out.

I'd always thought it was inconsistent of Jo to, on one hand, be so mad about Mom leaving us and on the other hand seem to idolize her. I'd always thought that, by not thinking about it much and not having strong feelings any way, I had the more reasonable view on Mom. But now I saw how not thinking about it was not the same as not having strong feelings. Why *was* I doing this alone? Why *hadn't* Jo and I had her in our lives? If Mom had died, that would've been one thing. Awful, but clear. Likewise if she'd moved across town and remarried, but still shared custody. But what did it mean if your mother moved across the country and only sometimes returned? Did it mean she didn't like you, or that she didn't care? And why did it matter that I still couldn't say?

For a few minutes I sat there seething, tracing it all back to Mom and her inability—her unwillingness—to do the one thing a mom was supposed to do, which was be there for her kids. Then my senses slowly returned to me and I was sitting in a hard, square hospital room again, breathing sterile air and feeling an ache in my tailbone. I thought of Mom as a teenager, first meeting Dad. Had she been impressed by Dad's seriousness and commitment? Had he made her laugh? I'd always thought Jo was like Mom and that was the end of it. But what if Jo and I just had different pieces of Mom in us? Jo got the piece that made her need to leave. I got the piece that first made her want to be with Dad. Because, see, if you suspected that you weren't all that good yourself, your next best option was to be with someone who was.

CHAPTER THIRTEEN

JO

I waited for Seamus to finish reading my draft. The Jan Term ended in two days and he would leave for New York two days after that. I'd written and revised for eight hours that day. Through his office window, snow reflected an evening palette of blues and violets.

"It's very good," he said, tapping my draft against his desk so the pages lined neatly, then laying them down.

"But?"

"No buts. It's very good."

But there was a *but*, and we both knew it. I watched him avoiding my gaze. I could feel him decide, finally, to level with me. "I do wonder if you have enough material here," he said.

"You said I was supposed to trust what I had!" The irony was incredible.

"And that attitude works for most cases. I'm not sure if it works for this one. I think you need access you're not getting yet—probably another two or three months of research. This is good. It's just not ready to send out."

"I finally have my phone interview with Gadson today," I reminded him. He was, at last, on leave, and I'd set the earliest date I could. "Once he fills in the missing parts . . ."

"And maybe he'll give you something good," Seamus said, without sounding hopeful. "You're right. The jury's still out. I'm really trying to be . . . collegial here. As your college professor, I can say 'A-plus' and end it at that. We both know that for student work it's already exceptional, and will be even sharper once you get Gadson on the phone."

"It's been a while since you were *just* my college professor."

Seamus's eyes bugged out a little as he glanced at the open door behind me. After he shut it, he said, quietly, "I could be overthinking this. I've never been in this position before. I mean with a . . . mentee." I wondered what other words he had weighed.

"Would you send it to Jim or Annie? If my interview with Gadson is helpful?" It was strange how fluidly I could now use their names. Being mad had given me the right.

"Yeah. I bet I would," he said.

Only a week before, I'd wanted nothing more than to convince him how doomed the whole thing was. Now I wondered if I'd wanted him to be worried because then I would have something to resist other than the stiff headwind of my own doubts. I stood and collected my draft, slid it into the empty laptop pocket in my backpack.

"Talk to me," he said.

"There's nothing to say. I'm going back to work."

"So you're not quitting."

"No." I couldn't help smiling at him, though it felt more like I was smiling at myself. Of course I wasn't quitting. I never quit, no matter how much I wanted to or how much I threatened to.

He gave me a smile that was a little tired and surprisingly tender. "Do you want to go to the Dirt Bar later?" he asked. "I think it's late enough that we can be seen together. Anyway, I'm leaving town if we cause a stir."

The Dirt Bar was the trendiest bar in town. Its walls were bloodred and covered with abstract sculptures made from scrap metal. They had something like a hundred craft beers on tap. But they carded everyone.

"I can't," I said. And then, because we seemed to be saying things we'd been previously withholding, and because I knew everything between us was winding down anyway, I said, "I'm not twenty-one."

Seamus's face fell in surprise, then became uncertain, and then afraid. "I thought you were a senior? How old *are*—?" And then, shakily, "Do I even want to know?"

"I'm a junior. I'll be twenty next fall."

"You're nineteen." Then, remembering: "You turned nineteen the day we—" He took a deep breath. "I can't believe you didn't tell me."

"You didn't ask. I'm a legal adult."

"Don't you think I would've liked to know?"

"You're acting like I'm *fourteen*," I said.

"You were fourteen five years ago." This upset him at least as much as anything.

"Yeah, and in just two years I'll be twenty-one. The arithmetic works both ways."

"I don't think it does." I could tell there was more he wanted to say, despite the fact that we were in his office, but I wanted to leave. Was this the end of us? I didn't want it to be, but I knew I would survive if it was.

"I have to get to my interview," I said.

"Okay. Can I see you again before I leave?"

"Maybe," I said.

"I'll be packing tonight. You can stop by. We'll just—visit."

Somehow I managed not to laugh. "We'll see." I left his office and crossed campus briskly, reviewing my notes before calling Gadson. I felt giddy with the recognition of my own tenacity. Plus, I had a feeling this interview was going to be good. In my room I cleaned every scrap of clutter from the top of my desk. My laptop was in one of the desk drawers. "I did my best," Brett had told me when he handed it back. "I'd pitch it for you, but you seem kind of attached."

"I am attached," I'd confirmed, then waited while he scrounged in his pocket for the memory stick he'd promised me when he called to say he was done. He produced it, dangled it above my open palm like a key. "Everything's on there," he said, though he'd already told me this. "You didn't have a ton. Data-wise."

Somewhat used by now to his stream of unwanted opinions, I gave him the sixty dollars, cash, we'd agreed on for this transaction. He counted the bills, then pushed them into the same deep pocket. "If you need help down the line—especially picking out a new computer—you know who to call."

Whom to call, I thought. I said, "Thanks."

Then he said, "Is *Jo* for Johanna?"

"Josephina."

"Nice," he said, and gave me the same two-finger salute he'd given Wes in the computer store. "See you around," he said, taking a few steps backward before spinning on a heel.

He was right. It was all on the memory stick, in a single folder titled *jos stuff*. When I opened the folder, I realized how unlikely it was that he'd looked through my files. The titles were uniformly boring. *PoliSci Paper 1_first draft. PoliSci Paper 1_2nd draft.* All the drafts about Gary were the same: *Engl 326 draft 1. Draft 2. Draft 11. Engl 326 full draft.* The photos were in a little folder I'd titled only *GC*, and *that* folder was tucked in a media subfolder that included a lot of Art History slides. Everything was now in a safe place.

I had a notebook in front of me for this call. Gadson picked up on the second ring. He sounded a little groggy, though it was five o'clock and we were in the same time zone. In his occasional pauses I suspected he was rubbing his face. Even so, his words were precise and deliberate, instruments chosen from a tray. Within a minute of the start of our conversation I was sweating. I did somehow remember to ask him for permission to record the conversation before turning on the digital device I'd borrowed from Seamus. I held the recorder in the same hand I was using to hold my dorm phone. But I was also trying to take notes with my other hand in case the recording wasn't clear enough.

A dog was barking in the background, and my fingers on both hands were strained as he talked. He kept saying *frankly.* "Frankly," he said, "and it's taken me a while to be willing to say this, because of how— " He was still speaking as I wrote *a while to be willing to say this.* "Frankly, a dark streak."

"How so?" I asked, which I hoped sounded professional and crisp.

"You know that feeling you get about some people? Like, this person is different, and not in a good way." I tried to copy this exact point as he continued on. I thought I was listening to him and keeping up, but then a pause landed between us, and I realized he expected a response.

"Uh-huh," I said.

"Look, is this not a good time for you? We don't have to be

talking. I thought this was important to you. I'm the one putting everything on the line here."

"I'm sorry," I said. The problem was I couldn't take notes and think and talk and hold a recorder and a plastic phone receiver in my hand. Also, I was paranoid about something going wrong with the recording. I put down the pen. "Distraction on my end. It's over now."

"All right," he said reluctantly. "Frankly, I'm not convinced there's a ton to the story. It's pretty messed up if he was collecting body parts, but it's not like he went around murdering people, not that I know of. That would have been my business to know." He paused. "What newspaper did you say you work for again?"

"I'm a freelancer," I said, which was what Seamus had instructed me to say if anyone asked.

"Gotcha," said Gadson.

He sounded disappointed, so I babbled on: "I have contacts at national magazines." Afraid he'd press me on my contacts, I added, "Most importantly, I want this story. It matters."

"Does it?" he asked, his voice an odd mix of derision and wonder. "Okay, then. Here's what I know about Gary. I did have a weird feeling about him, but it was mostly a feeling, so I didn't make much of it. That's not my training, you know? Psychology or whatever? I'm a grunt who worked his way up to staff sergeant, that's all. Besides, there was his church background. We all knew his dad was a pastor."

"So you figured he was a good guy?" Immediately I regretted speaking. Seamus had told me not to ask leading questions.

"I guess," Gadson said slowly. I bit my lip to keep from prodding him. After a few seconds, he added, "Yeah. Because of his background, I think we all assumed he was trustworthy. Even though he didn't seem all that churchy."

"What does *churchy* mean to you?"

"Churchy guys don't laugh, but Gary didn't mind a joke. Usually."

The dog barked twice more, and I shifted my hands on the phone and the recording device. Outside, a wind rattled the dried oak leaves, but the sound didn't penetrate the glass. I'd learned to wait Seamus out. It was becoming easier to do in this in other conversations, too.

Gadson said, "Maybe there were things I shouldn't have ignored."

"Such as?"

"He became kind of a loner. Started going off sometimes. I would be like, 'Where the hell is Clemmens?' And no one could tell me. Or they were just like, 'I saw him headed that way.' Come to think of it . . . maybe that's when he, you know, collected those fingers."

"How often would you say he disappeared like that?"

"Once every few days? Something like that. And it was never when he was supposed to be somewhere important. So I thought, the guy needs some space. I guess I regret that now."

I was scanning my list of questions, trying to decide on the best follow-up, when Gadson continued: "People are always saying to 'trust your instincts.' Most of the time, I do. I have to, in this line of work. But it's hard to hold suspicions against your own guys. I mean, how can I do that? I have to trust them with my life. So I don't obsess over their character. Though maybe I should."

I waited, but Gadson didn't continue the thought.

"Did someone go through his things after he died?" I asked.

"I think I had Sauceman pack up his stuff."

"Did he find anything worth mentioning to you?" I couldn't help congratulating myself on this open-ended question.

"No," Gadson said. "I can try to put you in touch with him if you'd like."

"That'd be great."

Gadson told me he had to go then, which made my heart hammer because I had another hour's worth of questions for him. But he agreed to a follow-up, and then crooned, "Good girl." It took me a second to realize he was talking to the dog.

I WENT STRAIGHT TO JARRETT to transcribe the interview. If there was any trouble with the sound quality, his words might still be fresh enough for me to fill in the gaps. I plugged my headphones into the recorder, found that Gadson had come through perfectly. So had the dog, though the sound was now like a shovel on gravel.

My fingers skittered across the keys to keep up with the recording. I was again getting used to the larger format of the PC, though the size of the keyboard still strained my fingers. Once I was done, I scrolled through the interview. It was good stuff. It wasn't done yet, but I was going to get more. I was going to get more, and then send it to Seamus, and he was going to see that this was indeed good enough.

I exited Jarrett in the cold black of night. It was past seven, so I needed to hurry if I was going to get dinner. My knees still felt stiff because of the lab's annoying chair, but I pushed through the ache, strode briskly through the darkened campus. The occasional lamp cast weak circles of orange light on the snow.

"Jo?" I heard. "Jo!"

Lily and Helena were walking toward me on a path perpendicular to mine. I'd seen Lily twice since our breakfast. One of those times she was with Susan, who pressed me on where I *was* these days. But Lily simply murmured, "Jo's allowed to be busy." There was enough reproach in her voice to quiet Susan, but also just enough gentle teasing that Susan wasn't offended. I was losing track of the number of times I'd seen Lily's social graces rescue a situation.

"Where are you coming from?" Helena asked.

"Jarrett. My laptop finally bit the dust." Lily's expression melted in sympathy I didn't want, and I quickly added, "It's fine. It's easy to focus there."

"Did you get our email?" Lily asked.

"Yeah." I'd seen it come in before I called Gadson, but I didn't even open it. The subject was *Help w/ a PROTEST workshop next month?*

"I'm taking the lead on this one," Helena explained. "It's aimed particularly at the friends and families of survivors. I was wondering if you'd be interested in participating in the planning. I'd love for you to be a moderator, but we're happy to have you doing behind-the-scenes work too. Really, anything would help. We got funding to bring in a psychologist who specializes in trauma and family relationships."

"I did tell Helena that you've got a lot going on right now," Lily said with a hint of apology.

Helena said, "Lily wouldn't tell me anything other than that you're writing an article with Seamus." Then, "Did you know that my dad's family owns *THE YANK*? It's a culture magazine based in Boston." She said this like I might not have heard of *THE*

YANK. Like I hadn't seen it on grocery store magazine racks for years, flipped through its glossy pages in dentists' offices. It was a kind of upscale *People* that dabbled in politics and longer-form stories. The magazine's cover usually featured a portrait of whatever celebrity (typically one with ties to New England, given its regional interests) was featured for an "exclusive interview." The photo would be so big it would cover half or more of the magazine's block-letter title. Point being, I guessed, that *THE YANK* knew that you knew what it was.

Helena went on, "They hired a new editor to bring in longer investigative pieces. New England topics in, like, a *New Yorker* format. If you think what you're working on could fit, I'll talk to my dad."

"Seriously?"

"I could call him tonight. Try to catch him when he's having his late-night ice cream with Bailey's. He's always in a good mood then."

Lily grinned at Helena. "Your dad is hil-*air*-ious." Then she turned to me. "You'll like him, too," she said, and it dawned on me that Lily was the one who got Helena to bring this up.

"Oh. And," Helena said, snapping her fingers as she remembered something else. "They have a summer internship. Dad's always asking me to get someone smart I know to apply. He complains every year that they get some"—and here she cleared her throat so she could pitch her voice low and stentorian— "'*young man from Amherst who mistakes his own noisy opinions for intelligence.*'"

Lily laughed. "Your dad is so hard on the Amherst guys."

"He's an alum," Helena explained to me.

"Jo would be perfect for that internship," Lily said. "She was the best in our journalism class."

"Not true," I said, thinking of Lily's own project, which had prompted a review of maternity leave policies.

"By *far*," Lily said.

"So?" Helena asked. "Are you interested?" She was still being friendly, but there was the tiniest note of impatience in her voice. People with influence, I was remembering, prefer to share it with those who feel comfortable holding it.

"Sounds great," I said, hoping I sounded appreciative but not too eager.

"Cool. I'll put you in touch with Dad soon," Helena said. "And I'll send more info on the PROTEST workshop."

I didn't remember agreeing to help, though of course now I owed it to them. Helena and Lily continued on to wherever they were headed in the first place and I walked in the opposite direction just to give myself time to absorb this possibility. I wandered with purposeful aimlessness for three or four minutes, until I heard the clock chiming and realized I'd missed dinner.

GEORGIE

CHAPTER FOURTEEN

Thin, dry flakes turned thicker as I took the back roads from Pine Creek to our new place in Westbrook. It was going on eleven p.m. and the snow had been falling lightly since about seven. The highway would've been quicker, but I still preferred to drift home the slow way. I wasn't trying to delay my arrival so much as extend the anticipation. Sometimes the act of shaking off my big boots onto the little green mat Tara had put next to the door made me feel like I'd stepped into the exact life I didn't know I wanted.

I would've been home already except that I'd stopped to check in on Dad. I tried to see him at least every third day. I'd check the fridge for food, maybe bring some of the snacks he liked. He seemed to be doing okay, or at least not worse.

Tara and I had been in the new place for three weeks now, and I was two weeks into my new job as evening lead. Today was the first time, since the promotion, that I'd left work without feeling like an idiot. In fact, I'd figured out every single thing that came up. When I learned we were out of clean and dry towels because the laundry person hadn't changed the wash before they left, I switched the load myself, dividing it into four machines so it would dry faster, then sent Allie to the party closet for the beach towels we used for summer-themed events. When Henrietta escaped from the memory wing, I was the one who found her in the little-used rec room, using a highlighter to trace her hand on a piece of newsprint. I sat with her for a while, then, when I thought she was ready, led her back. She didn't even cry like she usually did.

Up through the day Tara and I had hefted our "new" used couch through the apartment door, I had felt a deep uncertainty about this whole thing. Was I really ready? But I was also tired of my own questions, and I managed to mostly keep my anxieties from Tara. A slight awkwardness was in the air as we hung the few posters Tara had brought out of storage, all from her travels. She kept asking me if this or that configuration looked good, and I kept not having helpful answers.

But now, with this slow and snow-swept night drive, I had time to congratulate myself for getting through that transition, and the one at work, the first few nights of which had left me sure Rita had picked the wrong person for the job. I didn't know where the incident reports were, I forgot to lock the back doors at seven, and I committed the cardinal sin of stepping away from the front desk—which was right by the front doors—when I was the only one there. I missed Rita, then, when she called at eight to see how things were going. She tried my cell phone next, which I answered even though I wasn't supposed to use my phone on the job. "Get your—or someone's—ass up front," she said. Then she told me I had to do a complete head count to make sure no one had left.

The next day, I told her, "Rita, I'm not sure—"

She silenced me with a stare. "Do not tell me you can't do this."

So I didn't. And now, I thought, she was right to stop me before I'd said those words.

Once home, I pulled into the spot beside Tara's little Subaru, saw through the ground-floor window the back of her head. She was on the couch. Probably reading, I thought. I imagined myself flopping next to her, maybe dropping my head in her lap while I told her about my day. The second I walked in the door, though, I knew that would not be the case. She sat stonily on the couch, staring at the wall, arms crossed. She didn't acknowledge my entrance.

"What's up?" I asked uneasily as I carefully pulled off my boots, aligned them just so on the mat. Even in the low light I could see her nostrils flare as she breathed. I sat next to her, then said, "You have to tell me what's going on."

"I don't have to do anything."

"Then *please* tell me what's going on?" It was strange to hear such pleading in my own voice.

We were frozen. Tara stared at me, and I sat like a car stuck in neutral, spilling fumes for no reason.

Then she started speaking, but lightly, as if explaining a mundane situation.

"I got a call," she said. "From your sister."

"Oh."

"So you already know."

"Know what? I mean—maybe—I honestly don't—can you just tell me?"

"All right." The dead calm in her voice sank me. "She's publishing a story about Gary and those photographs."

"Publishing—?"

She put a hand between us to stop me. "Publishing a story about my brother *in a nationally distributed magazine*."

I said, "Shit."

"She tried to lay the blame on her editor. Like, 'He's making me call you, I know this is tough for you . . .' She knows it's tough for me." Tara gave an awful laugh. "How sweet of her." Then she said, "Tell me the truth. Did you tell her about the photos?"

I nodded, miserably.

Tara's voice went back to light. "Because she tried to give you some deniability. She had all these general questions. 'Did you know about these photos?'"

"I had no idea she was going to—"

"To use them to make her big break? Georgie, if you didn't know that your sister has spent all of her life desperate for success, I have to wonder how much you know her at all."

"What did you tell her?" I said. I had to ask.

"That is completely my own business," she snapped. "Hey. You can't do that. Look at me."

I forced my eyes open. "I fucked up. I swear I didn't mean—"

"How did she get them? Did you steal them from me?"

"No!" I exclaimed.

Tara stared at me, then snapped her fingers. "That night you brought her over. And I was like, wow, she seems pretty cool. And then she disappeared into the house . . . When I came in and found her on her computer, what did she say? That she was working on a *paper*?"

"I know this looks really bad," I started.

"That's because it *is* bad."

I wanted to explain, but I already knew I couldn't. It would take too long to tell Tara how I got here. It would take, that is, about as long as my life was, because now it felt like one big series of circumstances mixed with mistakes. Tara couldn't know what it was like to have Jo as a sister—and to owe a sister like Jo what I owed her.

Tara said, "You know I want the truth out there. I've wanted it out there since the beginning. Whatever happened—needs justice.

But the people at *THE YANK* don't want justice. They want to sell magazines. And anyway, having *your* sister, who's never liked my family, write the story isn't justice. You know she called my parents, too?" She drew a ragged breath, and finally her voice lost some of its intensity. "Maybe I'm in denial," she said. "Thinking that the news about Gary could get out without it being so awful. I'm capable of a little self-reflection, you know. But even if I've been unreasonable, you have to understand how deeply you've betrayed me." Then she added, "One of us isn't spending the night here tonight. So am I leaving, or are you?"

I half wondered if I should fight or plead or reason. But the longer I sat there the more completely I knew that her disappointment was a wall without doors. I was the one who was leaving. I was the one with somewhere to go.

MY HEADLIGHTS SMASHED INTO THE flakes, huge and clumpy now, on the way home. They reflected the light of my idiocy back at me, made it hard to see anything else. My wipers labored to push the snow aside, and still I drove, listening to the white noise roar of the heater cranking out lukewarm air. I had really thought I was in the clear now. The fall semester was long gone. Jo was supposed to be on to different things. But what did I know of how my sister spent her time?

Actually, I did know how my sister spent her time. She worked.

In the morning, Dad found me at the table, hunched over toast I couldn't eat.

"Are you okay?" he asked, which was kind of a pointless question.

I didn't know where to start. I couldn't give him only part of the story. So I said, "I need to see Jo."

"Not now? In this?" He gestured at the window, the still-falling snow outside.

"I'll wait until it stops. Can I take your truck?" I didn't trust the tires on the Taurus.

He had so many questions for me. I could see them circling. Finally he asked, "Is she okay?"

"Jo?" I allowed myself a bitter laugh. "Jo is just fine."

He left, then came back with his keys. "Drive safe," he said.

FOR TWO HOURS I INCHED south on 95, leaning forward as if doing so would help me see through the walls of white the wind threw up. Midmorning things started to clear, and the cars ahead of me wore a pair of wide dark lines for my tires to follow. The traction gave me room to think. How would I say what I needed to say? *You're right, and I'm sorry, and can you* please *not go through with this?*

What did I think she was right about, and what was I sorry for? Everything, and everything. There had to be more I could say. Maybe, I thought, I should stop to figure out what that *more* was. I didn't stop. I kept thinking. Maybe we'd fight. Maybe, for once, I'd argue without backing down. I'd be patient but insistent. Compelling, not scary.

The sun was bright by the time I approached the Peabody campus. It took me a while to find parking, since most lots required a special permit and the ones that didn't were full. As I wove around campus, I saw heavy clumps of snow falling out of trees, landing soundlessly in the snow below. The spot I eventually found was questionable, two wheels high on a snowbank on the edge of downtown. I was hungry and hadn't brought food. I called Jo's dorm room from my cell but didn't get an answer. I knew she didn't have caller ID on that phone, but couldn't shake the feeling she was there and not picking up. I found her dorm, waited until a girl coming out of the laundry room on the ground floor saw me and let me in. Jo's door was closed, locked. I pressed my ear to it, heard nothing. I knocked anyway. Still nothing. I went to the library, didn't see her behind the desk.

By this point I was almost too hungry to think, so I walked to a café called Morning Glory near where I'd parked. I paid eight dollars for a macadamia nut cookie and a coffee, which I took to a high-top table near the front window. I was halfway through the cookie when I saw Jo's friend Lily approaching the café with another girl I'd met when I was last here. When Lily saw me, she brightened and pointed me out to the girl she was walking with. They came into the café, Lily exclaiming, "Georgie! What are you doing here?" When she wrapped me in a firm hug, my face was pressed against the silky mass of her dark hair. I needed more people like this, I thought. It had been too long since I was hugged by someone I wasn't sleeping with.

"Jo doesn't know I'm here," I told her.

"Are you surprising her?" Then, more alarmed, "It's not her birthday, is it?"

"I just need to talk to her."

I watched as a half-dozen thoughts flickered across Lily's expression. Then she announced, "We'll help you find her." She nodded at the girl next to her. "This is Helena, by the way."

"I think we met when you visited," Helena said.

"We were going to get drinks here," Lily said. "Can you wait for us to order? Or do you need us to come with you now?"

"I can wait," I said.

"Jo's been a little hard to keep track of recently," Lily said. "But we'll find her."

Helena slid out of her jacket. "We know she's been busy with her big article," she told me. "It's for the magazine my dad owns. But even *he* won't tell me much about it." There was an uncomfortable pause when I failed to respond one way or another. Lily brightly announced she was going to order and Helena hoisted herself onto the stool across from me. She was about my size, with the looks of a model. I guessed that came with your dad owning a magazine. I swept the crumbs from my cookie onto the floor as she asked, "How long are you staying?"

"Just dropping in to say hi."

"Not staying through the evening, then?"

"Probably not. Why?"

"There's this workshop by a group I volunteer for, PROTEST. Short for Peer Response to Every Sexual Trauma." She watched me try to get the spelling matched up in my head and chuckled. "The acronym is more of an approximation. Tonight's event will be led by a trauma specialist. We're going to feature some survivors on how they got support from their family and friends. What that looked like, I mean. Jo's been helping a little with the planning but, like we said, she's pretty busy with her article."

"Jo's been helping?" Surprise twisted my voice off-key.

"I wouldn't say Jo is *very* involved," Helena continued. "She's gotten a little more involved in the last couple months. She was at our Right to the Night event earlier this year." She paused, kept preparing to say something, then trying for a different angle. "I am aware that these themes have touched your family."

I was blinking at her, trying to process, when she volunteered, "I wouldn't refer to it at all if I didn't . . . if my life hadn't been affected too." Now she seemed to read my baffled expression as something else—disappointment, even anger—because she hurried on, "Never mind. Just something Jo said once. I'm sorry. You barely know me. It wasn't right for me to bring it up."

Lily was coming back to the table now, holding two paper cups brimming with foam. She moved gracefully around a toddler who wasn't watching where he was going. Not a drop spilled.

Helena was looking at me miserably. "I'm sorry for saying anything," she said, distressed. "I don't know why I did."

I wasn't upset with her, though. "Honestly, I'm glad if Jo told you."

Lily set the drinks down carefully, listening without looking at us.

Then I said, "Jo needed to tell someone. I sure wasn't going to talk about it."

Lowering herself onto the third stool, Lily patted her hair, sipped her latte, and remembered to pull two napkins from her pocket, one of which she placed next to Helena. "Are you talking about what I think you're talking about?" she asked.

"I know I shouldn't have brought it up," Helena said. "But Georgie didn't mind."

"I don't mind at all," I repeated. I couldn't understand her concern. "If Jo told you, then it can be in the open without me doing the telling."

Helena was nodding vigorously. "That's important. That you see it as your sister standing by you. She really does want to support you, though she might not always know how. That's true for a lot of family and friends. I'm sure if you looked back over the years you could find ways she was trying to help."

"Yeah," I said slowly. And then, "What exactly did she tell you?"

"Oh." Helena looked at Lily, who looked back at her with an expression that said, *This is your problem.* "To put it precisely." Now Helena studied her lap as if to find the words there. A coffee grinder roared, and the toddler started shrieking. Then she said, quietly but audibly, "That you were sexually assaulted by a friend of the family." She paused. "That this has been—between you two, affecting your relationship. That it's been hard." Another pause. "Do I have that right?"

The chaos of the café crashed on all sides of us. For five seconds I was very still.

"Well," I said, finally. "I would tell it a little differently. But sure, let's call it right." I drained my coffee and set the cup down too hard. Why on earth would Jo twist the story that way? But the answer landed right in front of me, a cartoon anvil missing me by a hair: *Because she had to say something. And this was the safest thing to say.*

I didn't even consider telling them the true version. This was Jo's world, these were Jo's friends. I didn't want to be the reason they learned about her lie.

Now it seems I should have set the record straight. Maybe we could've helped her avoid what followed.

Neither Lily nor Helena could figure out what to say next, so I volunteered, "At least you know why the article is so important to her." I saw they didn't, so I added, "Same guy."

Lily clapped a hand over her mouth.

"No," Helena said.

"This isn't going to—endanger anyone, is it?" Lily asked. "Once he finds out he's being written about like this?"

My laugh sounded like a croak. "She's not in danger," I said. "I promise."

Helena slid her phone, smooth as a river stone, out of her pocket, flipped it partway open to light up the time. "I have to go meet someone about this workshop. Lily has my number and can call me if you need me. It's so great to see you again, Georgie," she added, with enough earnestness that I knew she was still trying to make up for her mistake.

After Helena was gone, Lily asked quietly, "Can you tell me why you're really here?" And then, "It's okay if you can't be specific. But I've been a little worried about her. She's putting so much into this article and—I know it's great for her, but—I have my concerns."

"It's a family thing," I said. "Jo's fine."

"That's good to hear. But I'm sorry about the family stress." Lily's decisive energy made clear she was willing to move on. "Have you checked her dorm yet?"

I nodded. "And the library."

"I'll take you to Jarrett," she said. "Her computer died, and that's where she writes. If she's not there, we'll come up with other ideas."

I wiped the rest of my crumbs from the table while Lily got a lid for her to-go cup. We walked out into the blinding light of sun on snow.

Jarrett Hall was made of gray stone, and with its small windows and columns, it looked like a mix between a prison and a city hall. But it was too small to be either. Lily swiped us in, then pointed down a narrow, carpeted hall. "The computer lab is the last door on the right. There's a window, so you'll be able to see if she's in there. If she is, just give me a nod, and I'll take off. If you need me later, you can call." She pressed a scrap of paper into my hand. I didn't know at what point in the last half hour she'd decided to write down the number for me, but I was glad to have it.

The hallway, which had a low ceiling and dark blue carpet, was quiet as a library. The door to the lab was made of the same safety glass as the doors at Pine Creek. Through the web of wires I saw my sister sitting at a corner computer. Her back was to me and she was perched on a padded office chair, her chin resting on a folded knee and her opposite ankle tucked under her. I could tell she was biting a nail because of the way she kept jerking her head.

I looked back at Lily, who was still holding her student ID and politely giving herself something to do by spinning it between her middle finger and thumb. She nodded at me now, as if to say, *Go in.* I nodded back, realizing that if she weren't standing right there I might not.

This was the role a mother was supposed to play. A mother was supposed to be there to say, *Give it a try. I'll be here if you need me.*

I entered slowly. The room's ventilation system was so loud Jo didn't even hear me. Black desktops lined every wall, but she was the only one in there. I wasn't trying to creep up on her—I just wasn't ready to announce myself. I got close enough to read the words on the screen. The cursor was blinking at the end of *Ethics reports rarely yield a court-martial.* Jo moved her hands from the keyboard to a notebook, started flipping through pages.

I cleared my throat. Jo gave a gasp and scrambled to her feet. The complicated position of her legs made getting up hard to do.

She had a hand to her chest, presumably to calm a pounding heart. "What on *earth*, Georgie!" She was trying to block the computer screen with her body.

"This is what you're going to wreck my relationship with Tara for?" I said.

She gave me an *Isn't this rich?* grin. "You're the one who told me about the photos and said I should write about them."

"Not in a national magazine! I didn't tell you to steal photos from my girlfriend!" I tried to remind myself I had not driven down here to immediately launch into my accusations. I had intended to ask for mercy, but I no longer wanted mercy. I wanted to be right. I wanted Jo to fix this.

"Yes, Georgie. *Please* lecture me on doing the right thing."

"I didn't do anything!"

Somehow I knew that Jo had me exactly where she wanted me. "Exactly so. You didn't do anything. I called you in desperation—I called the *one* person I needed—and you wanted nothing to do with me. You were disgusted with me and you thought I deserved—"

"That's not true!" I was shouting. A girl came into the lab just then, looked at both of us, and backed out.

"Don't rewrite history," Jo hissed.

I was stunned by what Jo believed. Mentally I zipped through the years since then. Jo disappearing off to college, seeming to want little more than occasional stiff phone calls. Jo's intense focus, which seemed always somewhere other than where I was. I knew I'd messed up that night she called me from the motel, but hadn't we moved on from that? Didn't I pick her up at the gas station, hadn't I tried to be there for her ever since? Couldn't we just agree that both of us had made mistakes without needing to score the entire thing?

Hadn't I been doing my best? Taking care of Dad so Jo could go off and chase her dreams? Not asking Jo for a thing?

And the story she told herself was that I'd never done anything to help her. My focus shifted and I saw my sister all over again, but this time—almost against my own will—as a small, fierce, cornered thing. A creature using aggression to hide its woundedness. Which came from Gary, partly. And also Mom. And Dad. And me.

If only she would soften toward me. If she shifted her shoulders, relaxed her mouth by one degree, took one step in my direction, I would gather her to myself.

As if she was reading my thoughts, she said, "No. You don't get to play the good guy."

I felt a crushing weariness. "I'm sorry."

"Why do you have to say it like that?"

"Like what?"

"You don't sound very sorry."

"Because I've said it a hundred times already!"

Now Jo did take a step toward me, but in a way that made me want to take a step back. "No," she told me quietly. "You've never said it. Not once."

She was too icy, too precise, too sure. I dropped into one of the computer chairs. "I feel like I did," I said. "I feel like that's all I've been saying for years."

She spun her own chair around to face mine, sat carefully. There was the smallest generosity in her posture. She wasn't forgiving me, but she wasn't throwing me out, either. She looked at her fingernails, their ragged edges where she'd bitten them to the quick. "Well, you never did. I should have warned you that I was going to call Tara."

"Yeah. You should've."

"You did tell me you weren't sure you wanted to be with her."

"I'm never sure of *anything*," I said. "Obviously." Still, the phrase *be with her* made me feel like I'd been pushed to the edge of a cliff, and I was briefly overtaken by a kind of emotional vertigo. The empty space below me was life without Tara. How could I have never accurately taken the measure of how far I had to fall without her?

"What do you want me to do?" I whispered.

My sister was still studying her nails carefully, preparing her answer.

Please, I thought, a prayer, maybe the most honest one I'd said in my life.

She looked at me with those sharp, sure eyes. "I want you to leave," she said. "So I can finish this and get it sent out. But I don't want you to—" She looked away now, inhaled a sip of air. "I don't want you to leave me alone forever. I want you to read it when it comes out. I want you to tell Tara that I'm sorry." She looked back at me. "I think that's it."

I stood, then hesitated, hoping for more. There wasn't more. Now she was the one waiting for me to go and I was the one who needed her. But I would do what she asked. So I left. When I got back to the truck, I found a parking ticket pinned by a wiper, bobbing in the breeze. I texted Lily: *things are fine, I'm headed back, thx again.*

drive safe, she replied.

I traced the edges of my phone with the pads of my thumbs, then tapped out, *keep an eye on her?*

Her response came back so fast it was like she knew I would ask before I sent the request: *you know i will.*

CHAPTER FIFTEEN

JO

The day after Helena first suggested to me that I could try to publish my story in *THE YANK*, she sent me an email.

> Hey jo! my dad wants to talk to you. he says to call him tonight around eight. don't let him intimidate you. he's a total softy, but he also wants people to stand up for themselves. don't worry and good luck!! xx H

What, I wondered, did it mean to be a softy who wanted people to stand up for themselves? Was I supposed to be fierce or witty? Demanding or quietly firm? If I wasn't supposed to worry, why did I need luck?

He picked up on the first ring. "You must be Jo from Peabody," he said. He sounded like a man with a cavernous chest. Like my dad sounded in his best moods. Or maybe like my dad would've sounded if his life had been totally different.

"Hi, Mr. Murphy."

"Don't 'Mr. Murphy' me. It's Murph. Everyone calls me Murph—the gardener, the interns, my wife. If they could talk, my dogs would call me Murph." Clearly he'd been using these lines for years. I heard a delicate clinking and remembered Helena's comment about ice cream and Bailey's. "Now, don't panic, Jo, but I'm going to give you thirty seconds for the elevator pitch. Try me."

I was ready for this. Seamus had made all of us write a pitch and then revise it endlessly. When people in class had complained that he cared more about how we wrote our pitches than our articles, he'd said, "No pitch, no article, hmm?" And then, "If you want to make money, play the game."

When I was finished, I closed my eyes, felt something tighten around my heart. I waited. *Clink-clink. Clatter.*

"My goodness, Jo," he said. "Not to say I wasn't planning to take you seriously, but . . . I wasn't planning to take you seriously. This . . . this is something. Is it true you've been working with that Matthews fellow? Sean?"

"Seamus."

"Seamus. Right. Same thing. I can say that because I'm Irish."

When I said nothing, not sure if I was supposed to find this funny or not, he muttered, "Tough crowd," and then, before I could respond, "What's your schedule like tomorrow?"

"It's—" I almost said *totally open*, but thought better. "I'm somewhat flexible," I said.

"Give me a number. Aaron will call you between, let's say, nine and eleven."

I gave him my number.

"All right, Jo from Peabody. No promises, now, but let's just say I'd love it if I could be the one to launch your career. If you write half as well as you prepare for phone interviews with magazine owners while you're still an undergraduate, then you write well indeed. Helena was raving about you, and she'd tell me the truth if you were a dud."

"Thank you," I said.

"Don't thank me—thank *her*," he said. "I'm just doing what's good for my business. You take care, Jo from Peabody," he said, and hung up.

After breakfast the next morning I stationed myself at my desk. I didn't want to leave even to use the bathroom. Aaron Bartson didn't call until 10:42, and my bladder was tight by the time my plastic dorm phone emitted its shrill ring. Aaron's voice was neither loud nor deep, but his clipped speech made my heart hammer.

"I already had a feature planned for the May issue," he said. "But I've been given clear instructions to see what you've got." A pause. "Hello?"

I'd missed the prompt. "Hi. I'm here—"

A small, exasperated sigh. "What've you got?"

I gave him the pitch, a poorer version of what I'd given Murph.

"Hmm." A silence. "You've got a draft?"

"Yes."

"Send it over?"

"Sure. I—" Suddenly I needed to qualify my work. It was a draft, but written by *me*. There must be something wrong with it. My inexperience had to stain every sentence. But he was already giving me an email address, which I scrambled to write down. We hung up. I emailed him the draft, then hurried to the bathroom. On my walk back to my room, I heard my phone ringing again.

"Good news first," he said. "You've got quite a story. If I decide to take it, I can offer you a dollar fifty per word. We'll aim for about five thousand words total." Over seven thousand dollars. That was more than I could make all summer doing just about anything at this point. Aaron was pressing on. "Bad news now. No way can I take it in this form. You need to do a big revision. First, have you even tried to interview the family?"

"No, but they're really not going to—"

"Make it official. Ask them for a comment. You're a professional now."

"Okay." My reluctance was quickly clobbered by the thought of seven thousand five hundred dollars. My name, my words, in *THE YANK*.

"Second. You're leaning a lot on Gadson. I know the point is that everyone else is hiding something, but you need to cover your bases. Confront the other guys on the squad with this information."

"Okay." I wanted to ask what *confront* meant to Aaron Bartson. Did Facebook messages count?

"Third. Army. You've got to ask around about the investigation there. Fourth. Context. You're assuming a lot of knowledge about how the Iraq war has played out. Don't do that, especially for American readers, most of whom can't distinguish between the Iraq war and the war in Afghanistan anyway. You're writing to people who are dumb, but think they're smart. Those are the people who read *THE YANK*. You may never, ever quote me on that." I couldn't tell if this was supposed to be a shared joke. "Fifth. You use the construction 'not only . . . but also' way too much. How soon can you have a new draft?"

I was about to start another semester. I imagined how quickly I could possibly do everything he was describing, and said, "Two weeks?"

He gave a dry laugh. "How about Tuesday?"

Five days. "Okay."

"Murph said you're working with Seamus Matthews?"

"Yes."

"Good guy. He can help you," he said. "I've got a few more notes for you."

"Hold on." I realized I needed to write down what he'd already told me before I started anything else. He sighed; I scribbled. "I'm ready," I said, then wrote furiously as he rattled off additional feedback. Expand the hook, make it a slow burn. More time on scenes even if I had to "kind of imagine them." More quotations; don't rush the ending.

"If you need help, let me know," he said.

"Thanks," I said, though I could tell he didn't want me to ask.

"There's no contract yet, unfortunately," he said. "Just impress me with this revision."

"Got it."

"Excellent. We're all excited about this. Talk soon." He hung up.

AFTER MY CALL WITH AARON BARTSON, I spent the day in Jarrett, writing another round of messages to all the guys who had previously evaded my questions. With each new message I sent, I felt even more like a world-weary reporter, cynical about everything except their own ability to see a story through. Seamus emailed me with a casual *would love to hang out before I leave town if you've got time*. He was leaving the next morning. I didn't respond, partly because I wanted to let Seamus drift away without further comment, and partly because something about this second round of questions I'd sent out had brought a steady trickle of responses. Why, I wondered, had I previously given up so easily? I had weakly taken their *no comment* responses as the end of the story. Maybe it was the newfound confidence in my tone, or maybe time had eroded their resistance. Within only six hours I had written messages from Russell Duquette, Luke Sauceman, and Nick Lanzi. Duquette and Lanzi offered phone conversations. Sauceman wrote, *if ur talking to Dillon id beware, him and Gary were pretty tight.*

This flurry of rcsponses confirmed the strength of my story. I got more details about the day the boy came at them with a grenade, which was really unfortunate, they all said, it really sucks to have to shoot a kid. It was Gary's idea to take the photos. The guys said that Gadson turned his back and told them, "It's not my business what Clemmens does with his camera," which aligned with what Gadson had told me ("It was stupid of me to let him take photos. I know that's disrespectful. I own that. But I had a lot on my mind"). When Gary lingered at the scene afterward, they let him do it. *We all thought gary needed space*, Duquette wrote. *He seemed to be going through some stuff.*

The responses consumed me with everything they did and didn't say. I was already revising the piece, working in these quotations, drafting follow-up questions for phone interviews. The constant, steady light in the Jarrett computer lab confused my sense of time. I felt like I was living in one everlasting moment, and also like maybe a week had passed. I'd brought a bag of granola into the lab, and I periodically looked around before pouring some straight from the bag into my mouth, so as to not leave crumbs.

I knew I had to contact the Army and, worse, the Clemmenses. I would do it the next day, from my dorm. Each time I started drafting a script or even an outline for conversation, I got too overwhelmed to continue. I wasn't worried about whether Mark or Miriam thought I was a nice person, though I did not look forward to disappointing Tara. What I feared was feeling stupid, incompetent, or small. I was afraid of doing something ridiculous like bursting into tears.

By the end of the day I knew I needed someone to convince me that I could manage these conversations. Seamus let me in wordlessly. There was a pile of suitcases and duffel bags by the door, but otherwise the apartment was untouched. I had known his office was borrowed, that the majority of those books and wall hangings were not his, but somehow I had not put together that the same was true of his apartment. Those dishes, the love seat where we'd made out. None of it belonged to him. Who was he, really? What kinds of plates would he choose for himself? Had I also been borrowed, a piece of his Peabody experience from which he'd clean every trace of himself on the way out? I actually liked the idea of living on for him as a pleasant and temporary memory, nothing that had time to tarnish or break.

I said, "I got a call from Aaron Bartson. At *THE YANK*."

His eyebrows went up. "And?"

"He wants to publish the story."

"Incredible!" He gave me what felt like a firm, friendly, firmly friendly hug. He released me, but only so he could shake my shoulders. "That is wonderful."

"He wants me to revise."

"Of course he does. You'll do great. Tell me everything he said." He motioned me to one of the stools at the kitchen's small island. I could feel him taking on the wise mentor role. As if a college dean were watching this interaction, studying it for impropriety. He poured each of us a glass of chocolate milk.

"Either we drink this or I'm pouring it down the drain," he

said. The packaging had cartoon animals on it. Seamus thought it was funny that he sometimes bought food marketed for children.

I told him everything I remembered of Aaron's requests. He nodded as if he'd expected all of this. He had a few drops of chocolate milk in his short mustache, about which I said nothing.

"He wants me to call Gary's family."

"That's essential in a story like this."

"You didn't tell me to do it," I said.

"I didn't want to ask you to put anything on the line unless you had more than a visiting professor with some ideas about where your story could go."

"You should've given me the heads-up," I said.

"I did." He shrugged. "I tried to, anyway."

"You did not!" I meant to sound teasing, but anxiety bent my voice.

"I knew it would upset you," he said. Then he softened. "It's tricky to be writing your first piece about people you have a history with. Ideally you would've started with something less personal."

"I'm not scared of them."

"Obviously you are, a little. But that's okay. It would be weird if you weren't." The line of chocolate milk had spread. Did I have one, too? I wiped my lips. He looked past me, then met my eyes. "I owe you an apology."

My heart dropped. I could tell, from his sudden gravity, this wasn't about the article. "Don't," I said.

"I do," he said. My resistance only increased his resolve. "I was really surprised to learn how young you are." I rolled my eyes, but before I could interrupt, he put up a hand. "But I realized that I'd never bothered to figure out your age because I didn't want to have to think about it. And that wasn't responsible. So I'm sorry."

It took me a few moments to process my disappointment. Something I had liked about Seamus was how he cared, but wasn't too careful. Gary had been the other way around. I didn't want Seamus to be careful now, didn't want him to try to correct something before he left. I didn't want guilt to color his memory of me.

"I want us to stay friends," he said. "I think you're going to have a real career. Maybe down the line . . ." He didn't finish the thought. "I'm trying to consider the future. Whatever that looks like."

"No," I said. "You're trying to protect yourself." My words had found their mark. His woundedness made him look pouty, which made me glad I had to go. "I have a ton of work to do," I reminded him.

"All right," he said. He walked me to the door. Before he opened it, he turned to me. "Let the record reflect that I wanted to do right by you."

I didn't know how much of me felt bad for how desperate he seemed and how much of me just wanted to be able to leave. I said, "I know. Thanks." We exchanged a quick hug, and I was back in the February cold, hurrying to my room. My accusation that his apology was self-protective drifted through my thoughts without landing. How much did I mean it? He had mentioned the future. Was he that serious about me, and if so did his seriousness change my feelings? I slowed, wondering if I should go back. But my feet kept carrying me forward. At this point, any end was good enough for me.

GETTING REACTIONS FROM THE CLEMMENSES the next morning didn't take long. First I called Mark and Miriam. They weren't home, so I left a message. I'd thought I would need to ask Georgie for Tara's number, but I found it on the Bear Pond Caretakers website.

"Nice to hear from you," she said. "I was just wondering when you'd be back in town. Georgie and I have a place closer to Curtisville. You should come visit."

This piece of information felt like landing on a wobbly rock in a stream crossing. There was no time to think about my next move. I had to make it fast.

"I'm calling for a—" I thought about apologizing, or qualifying, or trying to ease us into the subject, then remembered something Seamus had said in class: *Your subjects, your sources, they're not your friends. They actually trust you less if you worry too much about what they think*. "I'm writing an article about Gary. Evidence of war crimes has surfaced."

A long pause. "Tell me about this evidence."

"I have photographs of body parts, for example, that he seems to have collected."

Even more coldly, "Tell me about how you got those photos."

"I can't divulge my sources." I was relieved to be on the phone because I knew I was flushed. "I'm calling for two reasons—first, to let you know that the article is underway. Second, to see if you have any comments."

"You're publishing this?"

"Yes. In *THE YANK*."

She punished me with a long silence, and then she hung up.

Mark called me back about half an hour later. Instead of hello, he said, "You have got to be kidding me." I heard a woman's voice, presumably Miriam's, in the background. "Just a minute," he told her. His breathing grew labored, and I guessed he was carrying the phone upstairs. "Does your dad know you're doing this?" he asked.

"My dad has nothing to do with it," I said.

"You know he was in the hospital the other week?"

This did give me pause. How little I knew of Georgie and Dad. "Are you saying you have no comment?" I asked.

I could still hear him breathing, less from exertion than anger. I could feel him deciding whether, or how, to deal with me. "My son," he said, "was a good man."

GEORGIE CAME TO CAMPUS AND left again. I didn't have energy to waste thinking about what this had done to her and Tara. I did all the interviews I could. I got all the official *no comments* from people who weren't going to talk to me anyway. I worked through all my revisions, often finding solutions in the margins of my efforts, in the margins of my time. I spent a whole day obsessing over a four-hundred-word passage in the middle of the article. Then, my blood sugar so low I'd stopped feeling hungry, I went to dinner, where the right string of sentences occurred to me. I scribbled them in the only notebook I had on me, dribbling my minestrone soup on the page as I did. It was all effort, and waiting, and occasional insight, and fear. Nothing worked the way I'd planned, but my general impulse was right: Spend enough hours bent over a keyboard and something good has to appear. I left Jarrett only for meals and for a couple hours of sleep each night. I missed my first week of classes, first to finish the revision and then because four hours after I'd emailed it to Aaron I came down with a fever and spent the next two days in bed. Lily brought me Gatorade and nighttime cold medicine, then helped me sign into my email on her laptop so I could see if Aaron had written back. He had:

> Fine work, Jo. We'll be proud to publish your first piece. Contract info coming soon, plus a first round of edits. Will also put you in touch with fact-checking dept. Sit tight for now—have a drink! You earned it. AB

Lily screamed and danced in my room. I laughed and fell into a coughing fit. Usually just half a dose of over-the-counter cold medicine was all I needed, but I took a full dose this time, then slept for eleven hours. When I woke, I was sure that the email, and Lily's reaction, had been a dream. I needed to get to a school computer to see. When I opened the door, I yelped at the big thing flying toward my face. It was a piece of construction paper, which someone had taped to the doorframe with a length of floss. It fluttered and spun in front of me while my heart returned to something resembling a normal rate. CONGRATS JOURNALIST!!!! it said, the JO underlined three times. I suspected Morgan.

Lily had done the work of spreading my news places I wouldn't have thought to alert, like the Public Affairs Office at Peabody. An intern from the office called. She'd been in Seamus's class with me and was now charged with writing a press release about my article. I adopted that apologetic tone again. I knew it was my only choice going forward. "I'm really lucky," I told her. "It's good timing." What I meant, naturally, was *I earned it*. All those afternoons and evenings drinking my nutrients in Jarrett. All the penny-pinching and every pain in my neck. I had told myself that all my work was for a reason long past the point when I believed there actually was one anymore. And look at me now.

Over the next weeks, my life at Peabody changed entirely without really changing at all. I kept the same hours, did more or less the same things. Two factors in particular, though, made the same old things feel new. First, I bought myself a white MacBook. I hadn't been paid yet by *THE YANK*, but I had just enough money in my savings, and I was confident about the check coming in. The speed and grace of my new laptop made me feel like I was cruising down a scenic highway with no traffic in sight.

Second, I moved to the fourteen-meals-a-week plan. This further ran down my savings, but I also immediately liked the results. Adding lunch in a dining hall left me with an additional facet to my meager social life. Typically someone would see me, pat the empty spot next to them. At first it was because people knew about the article and wanted to ask me about it. I half expected them to quickly decide I wasn't so interesting after all. But one conversation had a way of leading to another, each interaction a harvest, and a seed.

I'm not saying I was the most famous girl on campus. The thing about a school like Peabody is that at almost any time somebody's worth talking about. The volleyball team was headed to the national championships. A senior art student was going to have a solo show in Boston. Now I was good at something, too. Even with the demands of my new classes, I'd started another piece, this one about teenagers who were prescribed OxyContin after injuries or surgeries. I'd heard a few awful stories from girls at Peabody, about cousins, neighbors, friends. I knew other journalists were writing about Oxy, but the teenager angle seemed overlooked.

"That could be really effective," Seamus told me. He'd emailed me to set up the call, but now that we were on the phone I sensed his interest was elsewhere. "Especially once you establish yourself with this first piece. Identity does matter for journalism, and if you're writing about this as a young person—but doing professional-grade work—you're bound to sell it." He asked if I had any interest in visiting New York. We agreed that my spring break would be a good time, but spring break came and went without further discussion. I stayed on campus, working at the library and reading about OxyContin. I knew, on some level, I was doing this to channel my anxiety about Dad without having to think too specifically about his case. Something would have to be done about Dad, eventually. I planned to figure it out over the summer. Till then, Georgie would have to deal with it. We weren't talking at this point, but I knew she'd keep an eye on Dad.

Then it was the last week of March and the magazine was out. I was featured on the Peabody website and in the local paper. A crew from Channel 7 in Portland drove down to interview me; a dean volunteered his office for the interview. Aaron said he was submitting my work for a national award. Morgan told me she'd overheard one of the English faculty saying it was the best article she'd read in a while. "You're famous," Lily told me proudly. I got used to having messages on my dorm phone. I even got a vaguely threatening letter in my school mailbox. The letter seemed more quizzically unhinged than dangerous, but Morgan, who was with me when I read it, made me report it to the police. Reporting it made my story interesting all over again, and my classmates kept offering to walk me places.

Ten days after the piece came out, I had a voicemail from Justin Kramer. He identified himself as a staff writer for *The Atlantic*, said he wanted to talk to me about the story. He sounded so upbeat and friendly that I felt sure he was going to offer me something—an internship, maybe even a job. Which goes to show how clueless I was. A staff writer shows this much interest in you only if *you're* the story.

He spent the first few minutes of our conversation complimenting passages in the article that he thought worked well. Then he asked about my research. I still burn with shame when I remember how happy I was to talk about it. How thin the veneer of my self-deprecation was, how easily he must have seen the contours of my pride underneath. I thought we were talking shop. I'd never heard of Justin Kramer before, but I googled him on my MacBook while we talked, and now his headshot was staring at me. He wasn't conventionally handsome, but I could tell from his photo that he didn't care to be anyway. Looking at this photo made me see how hungry for affirmation Seamus had been. I'd probably do better to have Justin as a mentor than Seamus. So when Justin first started giving me advice, I took it in stride. Maybe it was a bit of a risk to rely so much on Gadson's testimony, he said. Maybe I should have found someone who wasn't on Gary's squad to give me some perspective.

"The thing is, Josephina, I've been rereporting your article, and finding some pretty significant issues with it." Then he said, "But I didn't tell you that yet, so don't worry. Nothing you've said is on the record. You can go on the record whenever you'd like, though." A pause. "Maybe you're not ready to do that yet?"

The first person I called was Seamus. "I know Justin," he interjected, only three sentences into my explanation. "Good guy."

"Wait. No." I hated how he was mirroring my own dumb enthusiasm. I raced to the punch line.

"Oh," he said. And then, "*Oh.*"

"Say something else."

"It's not uncommon for a piece to be rereported. It's usually not great, but it doesn't have to be terrible. Maybe he finds a few slipups. Maybe he noses around for a couple weeks and decides that what he's coming up with isn't worth the full treatment."

"The full treatment being?"

"Some sort of article of his own."

"In *The Atlantic*."

"We're not sure it's coming to that. He said—you said—you didn't talk to anyone outside his squad?"

"I talked to the people Aaron told me to talk to."

"Maybe that was a mistake."

"Seamus—!"

"The best thing to do now is wait and not panic." He paused. "Even if it gets a little hairy, it won't be that way forever. Sometimes something that seems bad in the short run actually helps. Like, your article might end up being read by thousands more people than would've seen it in the first place."

"Because maybe it was wrong!"

"Is that what you think?"

This brought me up short. "No," I said. "I could have gotten parts wrong, but it's not all wrong."

"Then you don't have much to worry about. You did good work. Even if your story gets tweaked, that fact doesn't change."

Seamus called me four hours later. Somehow I hadn't moved from my desk.

"Kramer called me," he said.

"And?"

"It's not good."

MY STORY GOT MORE THAN TWEAKED. It got pulverized, in an online-only piece called "Getting It Right," published two weeks after mine. Justin Kramer's version was shorter than the original article by about half, but it felt twice as long because each sentence landed like a blow. Somehow he'd even tracked down Brett, who did indeed notice the photos in the process of transferring the data off my old laptop, connected them with the journalism proposal I'd mentioned to him at the dining hall. He attested that the photos had been uploaded in late November. Tara confirmed that's when I visited with Georgie. *The only logical conclusion*, Kramer wrote, *is that Prescott stole the photographs.* He wrote that my article represented *the kind of anti–Iraq War thinking that has become so reflexive, especially among the young and highly educated, that no nuance or complexity is allowed, and the first plausible culprit is named without a moment's hesitation. Obviously*, he went on, *crimes of war* were *committed here. But that doesn't mean the wrong person should be blamed, or blamed too soon.*

Kramer's article suggested Gadson might have egged the squad on to civilian killings. Gary might have participated, but also could have been trying to collect evidence against Gadson. Hence the photographs. Dillon Washington had told Kramer everything he knew. Dillon Washington who wouldn't talk to me.

There is a risk in correcting the record, Kramer wrote, *because perhaps what most people will end up remembering is how a young journalist got it wrong, not how a corrupt staff sergeant corrupted most of his squad and scared the rest into silence. Journalists are called to serve the truth. The profession must be protected against the whims of popular opinion. And it certainly must be protected against the kind of deprofessionalization that happens when untrained journalists take on complex topics.* There were a few sentences where he qualified his criticism of me.

Maybe I had meant well, though given my public disdain for the church run by Gary's father, some animus on my part had to be considered. Kramer held *THE YANK* responsible for publishing me, instead of *leaving this rookie investigation where it should've stayed—in a college classroom.* In Kramer's view, Aaron Bartson should stick to what he knew, which was *Boston-area socialites and their offspring.* Pat Murphy, he went on, *seems to still be unsure, himself, of the direction of* THE YANK. *Rigorous print journalism may be dying, but that's no reason to strangle it with a grab for the sensational.* Kramer even sniped at Seamus, *who has been known in the past to take shortcuts generously referred to as "problematic," and whom I was, unfortunately, not all that surprised to learn was involved, though I was surprised that Peabody College would make such a questionable hire in the first place.*

Even that wasn't the end of it. A day later, the *New York Times* ran a short piece summarizing my article, the stir it raised, and Kramer's corrections. They plucked a photo of me from Facebook, one of the few I'd posted. I'd taken it myself, positioning Dad's camera on my dresser at home, setting the timer, getting the dappled light coming through the leaves outside my window. It was supposed to approximate an author photo, my expression piercing, my thoughts on weighty matters. Behind me were my closet doors, blank enough that you were supposed to fill in a nicer house, a nicer life, than the one I had.

I'd missed the call from the *Times* reporter because Lily had made me swear, on my MacBook, that I wouldn't check email or messages for twenty-four hours while this storm "blew over."

Prescott did not return a call requesting comment, the article said.

I'd also missed at least six calls from Georgie. I didn't listen to any of her messages all the way through, but the system wouldn't let me delete them until they'd started playing. So I kept hearing her say *Hey Jo* in increasingly desperate tones.

A TAP AT MY DOOR interrupted the next tidal wave of shame.

"I know you're in there," said Lily, her voice through the door about as muffled as my hunger.

Then, "Please let me in."

Then, more loudly, "I haven't seen you in two days. If you don't open the door right now, I'm going to the campus police."

I opened the door. Lily's eyes darted over me, then past me. Though there was no noticeable shift in her expression, I could tell she was smelling the room. It must smell bad. I hadn't realized. I couldn't smell what I was living in.

I hated how elements of every life are knowable to other people in a way that they're not to the person actually living it.

When Lily looked at me again, she said, softly, "I'm really sorry."

"It's my own fault," I said.

Now she frowned. "I wouldn't say that's—"

"I know you're trying to be supportive." Actually, I hadn't spent much time yet thinking about how, or to what degree, I was guilty. Mostly I'd been riding swells of dread, each new one lifting me to an awful, dizzying height and then rolling me over. Now that I had someone in front of me, though, I felt I had to say something more than *This is awful*. Insisting on my own guilt actually felt productive. "I got carried away. I didn't think I was writing lies, but I also needed what I wrote to be true."

"Because he's the guy who assaulted your sister."

Had I told her this? It didn't matter. I nodded.

"It was a good article," she said.

"It wasn't good if it was wrong."

"I disagree."

"Why does it matter?" I asked. Each ungenerous thought I'd ever had about Lily came rushing in. How she wasn't as smart as she wanted to be, how she thought she knew everything about "survivors," how she pretended she was a totally normal, relatable person while also being so effortlessly pretty, loving mangoes and merino wool and leather-bound notebooks.

"Because I care about you," she said.

I said, "The financial aid office called."

"Nothing's happening to your aid, is it?"

I told her how, two days before, I'd been summoned by a woman with glasses on a beaded chain. She'd pointed to the scholarship description: *Recipients of this award will be held to high ethical standards, reflecting those of Maud T. Browning; any recipients deemed to have fallen short of these standards will no longer be eligible for scholarship funds.* Before even giving me a chance to defend myself, she took her glasses off, laid them on her small, flat chest, and said, "We did get a call from Edgar Browning this morning."

"He can't do that!" Lily exclaimed now.

"He can. In good news, Peabody is not considering kicking me out, 'not at this time,' anyway."

"There shouldn't be a question of whether you can stay! What about Seamus? He gets to sail off into the sunset?"

"The article wasn't that nice to him," I pointed out.

"That's all he gets? A slap in an article? While you get all this?

Just because you're inexperienced and—?"

"I screwed up," I said.

"Jo, you should be able to screw up."

"Not everyone," I said, too pointedly, "gets to screw up and come out the other side so easily."

She frowned at me. I knew I was being shitty. I also felt an anger with Lily that I knew was too irrational to name aloud: She still didn't know what I'd never told her about my past. More than that, I'd misled her on purpose.

"I'm the one Gary—" I said, and paused. On one hand, I didn't know how to finish the sentence. On the other, I didn't need to finish it anyway. I said, "So."

Outside my window, every twig on the oak tree was studded with tiny knots. I remembered the brown leaves that had persisted through Christmas. Now a new cycle was beginning. The way the tree carried on made me feel a weariness I was sure would never subside. The world went about its business. It didn't care if a life was being dismantled.

Finally, Lily said, "I get why you didn't want to tell me, but it hurts that you lied."

"There was nothing you could do," I told her.

She frowned. "I've spent years educating myself on what can be done. Maybe you, or another survivor, doesn't *want* to do anything. But you can't tell me there's *nothing* I could do." She paused. "Do you think I cofounded PROTEST because I wanted to put it on my résumé?" Then, quietly, "Maybe that is what you think."

I closed my eyes. Yes, this was the sort of thing I had occasionally thought.

"You need to figure something out here," she said, her voice almost a whisper. I braced myself for whatever unkind thing she'd been holding in about me. *You think you're better than everybody else.* Or *I was only trying to be friends with you because clearly you had none.* Though my nerves were already tender, I found myself wanting this new pain. Wanting proof that we were never really friends.

But what she said was "You're not as alone as you think you are."

After she left, I spent a few minutes thinking about how someone can leave without leaving you. Lily was mad at me, but she wasn't done with me, either. She wasn't going to quit. This not-quitting a person was what I'd wanted from Mom. For a while, I'd told myself that Mom was involved from afar. I convinced myself that every distracted phone call was proof of how much she cared. How at some point she was going to step back into my life.

Putting that hope away had taken a long time. Maybe that hope had warped me more than I knew.

How, I wondered, did you fix a self so broken? I rummaged on the shelves of my mind and found only junk answers. Then I thought, *Maybe you don't.*

I picked up the phone.

"Jo," my sister said. I didn't say anything. Georgie knew better than to say *Hello?* or *Are you there?* What connected us was so vital and so damaged. The two Fridas flashed in my mind. "Can I come get you?" she asked.

I was nodding, not speaking.

"I'm coming," she said. "I'm coming right now."

CHAPTER SIXTEEN

GEORGIE

People think that living at a senior center means you read a lot. But I didn't see much reading at Pine Creek. I did see lots of napping with books in laps. I saw residents spend forty minutes choosing a book or two from the Pine Creek "library," filling out a borrowing card, and then using the book as a coaster for a month. I also saw plenty of magazine subscriptions sent by kids and grandkids who felt guilty about not visiting. These subscriptions had an awkward way of auto-renewing even after the person they'd been purchased for had died. They usually ended up in the break room, in a repurposed Depends box. That's how I found Jo's article.

I was at work early. I was there early a lot now, because it was better than being home with Dad. Dad didn't know about the article yet. Even Mark hadn't told him. I worried this meant Mark had cut him off without saying so.

It was not a good stretch. All Dad knew about me was that things between me and Tara hadn't worked out, but he seemed only vaguely sympathetic. What mattered most to him were his regular drives to New Hampshire, which I didn't know how to stop. Anyway, I took on every extra shift I could. At least Rita liked how prompt I was.

The magazine was so glossy it felt greased. I sat with it in front of my rusty locker. Jenna Bush was on the cover. Below that, yellow text read *JENNA COUNTING DOWN THE DAYS! EXCLUSIVE MAID OF HONOR INTERVIEW!* After that, in white, was *THE TROPHY HUNTER: A PREACHER'S SON AND CRIMES OF WAR.*

Kristina, one of the new hires, bustled in. She'd worked as a CNA at a Boston ICU and wanted all of us to know that this was peanuts compared to her old job. She moved like someone who wants you out of the way because they're carrying too much, but who also wants you to stop and admire their accomplishment. I smelled her spearmint gum as she leaned over my shoulder to study the cover.

"If they were getting married in Kennebunkport instead of Texas, my friend would've been mixing drinks at the wedding. He knows all their orders."

"Huh," I said.

"*One* of the Bushes always asks for an ice cube in her white wine," Kristina said, then gave a dramatic pause. When I said nothing, she clarified, exasperated, "It's low class!" Then she added, "But that's people for you. We're not so different after all." She traced a purple-painted fingertip down the cover of the magazine. She tapped *THE TROPHY HUNTER*. "I heard about this on the radio. That guy was from around here, wasn't he?"

"We have a . . . mutual connection," I said. "I thought they might want to read this."

Kristina cackled. "That's how it is around here. Everybody knows everybody. Stuff always gets out in the end."

Did it? I wondered. I wasn't so sure. Thinking that secrets always got out just because you heard something surprising once in a while seemed like a giant underestimation of how much happened in other people's lives. There was too much to ever, ever know.

I had fifteen minutes before my shift. I took the magazine out to the car, laid it against the steering wheel. The article started on a two-page spread with the pictures splashed across the top half. I tried not to look at them again. The title was in block letters styled to look like they'd been sandblasted. My eyes lingered on my sister's name in neat caps. Then I started to read.

> In the beginning was Word of Life church, and Word of Life church was true to God, and Word of Life church spoke for God.

I recognized right away how she'd rewritten the first words of the Gospel of John. I felt a drop of awe—how clever, how sure this opening.

> The church sits on Route 9 in Curtisville, Maine, just a quarter mile east of the high school. It was started by Pastor Mark Clemmens in 1995. Clemmens's enthusiasm for conservative theology—women were barred from any position that might give them authority over men; same-sex relationships were a sin—might have been a death knell for Word of Life if not for how appealing he managed to make his restrictive theology sound and how skilled he was at "growing the church."
>
> The plant-related metaphors, so common in contemporary Christian language, are particularly fitting in the case of Word of Life, because the building in which the church is still housed used to be a garden center. Those early services were held in a high-ceilinged room that still smelled like dirt.

JO'S VOICE WAS SO FAMILIAR it seemed to drill straight into my brain, like she was right here reading me the piece. Yet even if it was familiar, the voice had also been transformed, so that it had a power and authority even I, as someone who thought I knew the extent of her skills, couldn't have anticipated.

Tara now doubted that her brother was as guilty as the pictures made him seem. She thought Jo had gotten the story wrong. Reading this, though, I was sure Jo had it right. Didn't she? How could she *sound* so right and not also *be* right?

> Pastor Mark flogged his new congregation with enthusiasm. Membership rose by forty percent in his first two years. He embodied the confidence that came with great faith and was so self-assured it could be hard to think for yourself if you stood too close. After all, he was not only a handsome, imposing man and a skilled orator. He also had a beautiful wife and children who were remarkable, each in their own way. Second-born Tara was so devoted to her faith that, when asked in a first-grade Sunday school meeting what she hoped to be when she grew up, she responded, "A martyr." Her older brother Gary was different. He wasn't quite what you might call troubled, because his delinquencies never landed him police citations or school suspensions, but to know him was to understand that he was quite comfortable exploring boundaries, and pushing past them when it suited him. For a senior prank he orchestrated the rearrangement of the room of teacher Eliza Marsh, who was open about her clinical OCD. But Gary oversaw more than the rearrangement of desks and chairs—he superglued them to the floor. Marsh made it halfway through first period before she had to leave. The

general consensus was that Gary had crossed a line. But no one could stay mad at him for long. He had an air of humility when he admitted a wrong, even if the air was so practiced you had to wonder how deep his regret actually went. Besides, he himself then got to lead a spontaneous, popular event at the high school that evening in which he and his teammates from the varsity basketball team ate pizza and blasted Eminem while they pried every last metal foot from the linoleum. The next morning, Gary showed up with a big bunch of roses for Marsh, who burst into tears when he gave them to her.

Gary's extraordinary athletic abilities must be mentioned in the context of the trouble in which he regularly found himself—and that was how people phrased it, that Gary found himself in trouble rather than went looking for it. He was a small-town star privileged with all the normal small-town star treatment—little boys staring hungrily at him at the pizza shop, people he barely knew calling "Great game!" out their window as he walked along a street. When he went to the University of Maine on an athletic scholarship, everyone saw him as another Cindy Blodgett in the making—all the more exciting because this Cindy Blodgett would be male.

But after two seasons with the Bears, Gary announced he was leaving school and enlisting in the Army. He was killed in an IED blast last September.

As of early January, the sign outside the high school still read R. I. PEACE PVT G CLEMMONS IN OUR HEARTS FOR-EVER [sic]. The heads of a few winter-worn teddy bears were still visible at the base of the sign, where the snow was thin.

The story almost anyone from Curtisville would tell about Gary is simple: a tremendously talented young man from a good family, a brave patriot, an awful but heroic death. People remember his peccadillos with nostalgic ease and treasure all the other memories they can muster—Gary arriving late, always, to church, coming down the center aisle with a surefire grin in the middle of announcements; Gary bending to bop a five-year-old on the head, maybe offer the little guy a piggyback or a toss in the air, which you tried to smile through even if your child sailed too high for comfort.

All of this remembering could easily provide a lasting, soft-focus look at Gary and his charmed life were it not for the photographs that surfaced—

I'D STOPPED BREATHING. When I moved the magazine to the seat next to me, I felt a stiffness that made me feel like I hadn't budged in hours, rather than minutes. I knew I owed it to Jo to read the whole piece. But I didn't have to read it in one sitting, did I? Besides, my shift was starting soon.

My heart leapt when my phone rang. Every day I hoped for a call from Tara. But it was Rita, wanting to know if I was at work yet so we could talk about a staff training.

"I'm in the parking lot," I said. "I'll be right in."

THE NEXT DAY WAS SUNDAY, but Dad didn't go to church. He rarely went anymore. I spent part of the day wondering if Dad could be spared hearing about the article forever. I imagined draping some protective cover over him, then realized that was what the drugs were doing, which made me feel a relief I then felt terrible about.

But that evening Dad started shouting at me from the living room. I hurried out of my room, thinking he was hurt, but found him leaning forward on the couch, squinting at the TV as if he couldn't see it. A newscaster with bright lipstick was saying, ". . . article in the magazine *THE YANK* has shocked a local community . . ."

Dad's face was glossed with sweat. His T-shirt clung to his back. Pointing the remote at the TV, he held the volume button. Bright green bars filled the bottom of the screen.

"It's too loud!" I called, but he couldn't hear me.

". . . son of Mark and Miriam Clemmens, and a local basketball star, has been accused of committing war crimes." A shot of Mark Clemmens saying, "Off church property. Go. No media. No media."

"Before we continue the story," said the lipsticked newscaster, "we would like to warn our viewers of the explicit content we will be showing in the next few minutes."

Now Jo was on the screen, sitting in a big wooden chair upholstered with a print of looping vines and flowers. Next to her was a fireplace, above that an oil painting of a field and mountains. She wore a little black microphone clipped to the collar of a plain black shirt. She looked like she was wearing makeup. She looked older than I'd ever seen her before.

". . . journalist and Peabody College student Jo Prescott sat down with Channel 7 News to discuss her explosive story."

Off-screen, a voice said, "Tell us about where this story came from."

Jo had already mastered the permissive smile of someone

famous or important—someone who knows that their presence alone is worth other people's time and money. "Well," she started, and seemed to think. "I did grow up in that community, and actually had some ties to Gary's family. Which gave my story some pretty essential texture, I think, because it's partly about the awful things that happened in Iraq and partly about a culture that might have bred this kind of thinking."

"Are you blaming the church for this violence?"

"Not directly—and that's not what the article says either. It's more of a factor, a sub-question to the question of what led Gary to do these things."

"And what is your answer? What led him to do this?"

Two of the photographs flashed on-screen—the boy in the dirt, the finger in the bag.

"None of us will ever really know," Jo said. "But I think part of it was being brought up in a community that considered him exceptional and that, despite all its talk of sin and 'fallenness,' never could accept those qualities from its own."

Dad's head was in his hands. I took the remote, turned the TV off.

"She can't do this. She left us already, and now she's trying to ruin me from afar."

"I don't think she wants to ruin you," I said. "It's Gary she wrote about."

"What does she know about war? Does she think the other guys wouldn't do twice as bad to our own?" Now he looked at me, his mouth melted in a frown. "What did I do wrong?"

"You didn't do anything wrong."

"I never was good enough for her. All I did was try to be good enough for her." A bead of sweat was now visible at his temple. "I need to call Mark." He stood with effort, then tipped, grabbed the coffee table for balance.

I didn't bother trying to stop him. I went back to my room so I didn't have to listen. I ended up far enough away to miss the words, but I couldn't escape the tone—pleading, apologetic. It sounded, by the end, like he had gotten the absolution he hoped for, because when the conversation ended he sighed, then sobbed, then shook out some pills to ease the pain.

THE NEXT DAY, HE SAID he was going to get a copy of the magazine. I admitted I had one. He gave me a long look that asked what else I hadn't told him. I offered to let him read it. He took it to the kitchen table, sat before it with an air of formality, as if it were a textbook. He read so slowly, so quietly, I wondered sometimes if he was reading at all. But then he would turn a page. When he was done he pushed it away from him the way you might push away a dinner plate after eating too much. He stood up, looked out at our driveway. The bushes didn't have buds yet. They were just a mess of twigs. He asked, "What do you think of all this?"

I realized now how much I had hoped to never need to choose between Dad and Jo. I could only say what I thought.

"The evidence against Gary is pretty strong."

"I mean about this whole thing. Do you really think that the"—he picked up the magazine, searched its pages—"that the 'church built a community in which the sins of men, because they led to repentance, were constantly overlooked, excused, even condoned'? Is that what you think Mark is about? Is that why you think I followed him to Maine to support the church? So I could *sin*?"

"No," I said, but I was only answering Dad's last question. That line in the article had made me realize Jo had named something I had noticed without being able to identify—like when someone says *I smell smoke*, and then you can, too.

But I didn't think Dad was like this.

"How is it," he asked, "that Jo could lose her mother to self-interest and then spend the rest of her life blaming *men*?"

I didn't know what to say to this. I believed Jo was right in her assessment about how the church viewed men, but Dad had a point too.

TARA TEXTED ME, FINALLY, ABOUT ten days later: *have you been in touch with jo?*

no, I wrote. *why?*

you might want to watch the news tonight, she replied.

how are you? I asked. And then, *im sorry*. But she didn't respond.

Dad watched the news most nights, so he wasn't going to miss it, whatever it was, and I wasn't going to try to keep him from it. By now I'd given up the idea that I could control any of this. It was unfolding out of my reach.

Admitting how much I didn't control had, paradoxically, helped me take a few steps of my own. I had opened a savings account, set up an automatic deposit. I looked for another apartment, started calculating a monthly budget based on my income. Having done this with Tara made me ready to do it myself. I didn't like thinking about what it would mean for Dad once I left again. I also knew it would be easier to do the second time around, which made me think of Mom.

That day there was a spring snow, heavy and thick. It stuck to the rims of things, fence tops and the lips of gutters, before melting in a warm sun. I had the day off work, and I spent it mostly in bed, reading a dark mystery set in Ireland and eating stale Town House crackers. Rita had suggested it to me, then lent me her copy. I liked reading even the bleakest mysteries, which promised answers no matter how chaotic the story got. I skimmed the final chapters before joining Dad for the news.

The newscaster's lipstick was more purple this time. She said there had been *new revelations* about the Gary Clemmens story. Channel 7 had sat down with the Clemmens family to discuss.

Dad scooted to the front of the couch. He was sweaty again.

Tara was the first of the Clemmenses to get a close-up. Her hair was neater than usual. This fact alone made her look about five years older. She was wearing what we used to jokingly refer to as her "dress T-shirt" because it wasn't from a road race or volunteer event. Looking at her hurt. I knew the skin at the back of her neck. I knew the contours of her skull. I knew how the edges of her ears got cold, how she licked her lips when she was trying to figure out what to say.

But all of that knowledge counted for nothing.

"I reported the photographs I found," she was explaining. "For a while things were moving slowly with the Army, to the point that I even wondered whether they'd move at all."

"Did you consider any other measures?" the off-screen interviewer asked.

"Yes. But I didn't want to jump to conclusions," she said. "Easy as that might have been."

There was a cut to a picture of Jo's article in print. A male, his voice stiff with the excitement of someone who has bad news about somebody else, said, "This disturbing story about an Army specialist collecting the body parts of Iraqis has been rereported by Justin Kramer in *The Atlantic*. Kramer's story pointed to staff sergeant Thomas Gadson, as well as some of the other members of his squad, who according to Kramer may have been involved in some targeted killings as well as the collection of body parts. It's unclear what exactly Clemmens's role was, but Kramer leaves open the possibility that Clemmens may have been collecting evidence against Gadson. The Army has begun a formal investigation into both Clemmens and Gadson. Its representatives declined to comment for this story."

The camera returned to the Clemmens family—what was left off it. Pastor Mark and Miriam sat on a couch in the Word of Life parlor. Tara was in an armchair next to them. Mark had his big hand wrapped around Miriam's smaller one.

"My understanding is that you know, personally, the author of this article?" the interviewer asked.

Mark held his eyes closed for one second, as if being forced to shift his weight onto a painful limb. "This young lady, I—" The way he avoided saying her name made him seem like he was being generous. "I would like to believe she meant well."

"You would *like* to believe she meant well, but . . ."

"It's unfortunate, isn't it." Mark allowed a moment in which it seemed he wanted to let the subject go, but then his voice got a notch louder, like he was continuing a conversation in a noisy room. "If she had any problem with us, with our family, or our belief system, she could have simply told us. We would have received her in love. This public attack, though, feels targeted. As Christians we expect to suffer for our faith, but that doesn't mean the suffering doesn't pain us deeply."

Tara slowly crossed her arms. I could tell she felt reluctant, or at least conflicted, about the interview. The corners of her eyes were gathered in concern.

"You were friends with the person who wrote the story," the interviewer prompted Tara.

"We knew each other growing up," Tara said. "I don't mean we were never friends. I just don't want this to be a narrative of some huge betrayal."

"But it still hurts?" asked the interviewer.

"Of course it hurts. My brother's body came home in parts. This felt like a further violence—"

I could tell she said more, but the interview had been edited, spliced with other footage of Miriam folding bulletins, photographs of Gary as a kid and star basketball player and in his fatigues. Now there was a shot of Mark standing beside the thermometer that showed progress on the gym fundraiser. "Since his son's death, Mark Clemmens has devoted himself to building the Garrett Joshua Clemmens Memorial Gymnasium. At first it seemed the project might be derailed by the story in *THE YANK*, but ever since the focus of the story has shifted, Clemmens has fielded dozens of calls."

Mark now: "It's been difficult to keep up with the influx of interest. Veterans and Christians across the country have reached out, wanting to help me honor Gary's memory. It's been incredible, actually. We're very moved by it." He smiled at Miriam. "Most people assumed the gymnasium goal might be too ambitious. Now I see that maybe it wasn't ambitious enough."

The lipsticked newscaster returned to end the segment. Dad jabbed the remote at the TV and the screen cut to black before she got four words in.

"This is not good for Jo, is it," he said. In the silence I could hear the faint ticking of the clock he'd stared at for, possibly, hundreds of hours. "You sure you don't want to contact your sister?"

"You could call her," I said.

"She trusts you."

I snorted. "I wouldn't say that."

"She trusts you more than she trusts me."

"She ruined things between me and Tara." As I said it, I knew I didn't believe it. I ruined things between me and Tara. Still, I wanted to feel like I deserved the option, at least, of leaving my sister to deal with any mistakes she made. Couldn't there be a few moments where I got to weigh my choice before inevitably, obediently choosing not to desert her? "I'll reach out," I said. And I did. I called and left a voicemail I already guessed she wouldn't listen to. I sent at least four emails over the next day and a half. I'd started by reaching out only because Dad made me promise, but now my worry grew with every passing hour. Dad was worried, too, but his worry was only going to increase mine, so I told him I'd made brief contact and Jo said things were tough but all right. Then I called Lily, who told me Jo was in her room—Lily kept stopping by and listening.

"Should I come get her?" I asked.

Lily hesitated. "I'm not sure what's best. She definitely wants space. I know she has food in her room." Then, directly, "Do you think she would hurt herself?"

"No," I said quickly. I thought of that night she'd marched into the cold. But hadn't she made it through? Hadn't she called me for help? "I don't think so," I said, more carefully this time.

"I'm going to reach out to the counseling office just in case,"

Lily said.

"You've done a lot for us," I said.

"Your sister is special," Lily replied.

"I know," I said, with more feeling than I could have expected.

That afternoon, Dad claimed he would rake the lawn. Last fall's leaves lay wet and plastered to the grass. I paused getting ready for work to watch his efforts slow, then stop. He leaned the rake against the front stoop, came inside. My phone dinged, a text from Tara: *that news segment didn't do justice to what i said.*

I wrote, *i know. i could tell.* I hoped she would understand all I meant by this—that I saw her, felt her, knew her, missed her. That even if I still wasn't sure we were supposed to be together in some cosmic way, the way I'd messed up did feel cosmic. That I loved her. My fingers hovered over the number pad as I searched for another phrase for her. Before I could start tapping it out, my screen lit up.

"Jo," I said. Though she didn't respond, I knew she was there. I thought about asking, *Are you okay?* but I already knew the answer, and she knew I knew it. I thought about the failure at the heart of every relationship that mattered to me. Was accepting failure part of loving someone, or did loving someone mean trying, always, to overcome it? Why had it taken me so long to understand that this was the question that mattered?

"Can I come get you?" I asked. But I didn't want it to be a question. So I turned it into a statement and walked out to the car, still wearing my scrubs.

JO

CHAPTER SEVENTEEN

Between my call to Georgie and the moment she came into my room, I'd made my decision. I was leaving Peabody for good. Maybe in a few months or years I would think this was foolish. But I also knew I couldn't be here anymore. And after every surprise I'd been handed, I wanted to hand one out in return.

I was right to guess that Georgie wouldn't try to stop me. We took what I didn't need to the thrift store. What I didn't need was about half of what I owned. The donation pickup wasn't open yet, so we left my plastic set of drawers, wobbly shoe rack, clothes I'd never felt comfortable in, books I'd never read again, and mini fridge under the sign that said NO DUMPING. Everything I was keeping took us only three loads to bring down to the Taurus. I couldn't help feeling like all of campus was watching me pack up. I imagined hundreds of eyes peering down at me, pitying me, maybe even thinking I deserved what I got. I didn't know, and didn't want to know.

We barely talked for the four-hour drive. My body seemed to get heavier as the car rolled east and then north as I got closer to the home I'd fled. The heaviness wasn't peaceful, or relieving, but it was also different from the dread that had swamped my senses for days. Maybe this was what people meant by being at rock bottom. Maybe rock bottom meant feeling, finally, the simple, unavoidable gravity of my own existence.

Obviously, the heaviness was also just exhaustion.

As Georgie and I approached the bridge into Maine, she moved the car into the right lane. I peered all the way down into the Piscataqua River, iron gray but glossed with light.

"We used to call this the dinosaur bridge," Georgie reminded me, and a memory occurred to me, plain as a word I'd long stopped trying to recall: Dad driving us to Maine. Georgie asleep, again, in the back seat, her face slack in rest, her bottom lip hanging wetly open. The atlas spread across my lap. The humped bridge looming in the gathering dark, the spots of light reflected on the river below. Soon after we slid down the far side of the bridge, our headlights landed on a sign welcoming us to Maine: THE WAY LIFE SHOULD BE.

"We're here," Dad said.

"Where was the border?" I asked.

"We just went over it."

"But *where*?"

"I think it was on the bridge."

His answer wasn't good enough for me. I clicked on the interior light, lifted the atlas to my face. Up close, the line of the border was blunt and inexact.

"Maybe the whole bridge is the border?" Dad offered. And then, "Can you turn that light off?" I was glad to turn it off because now I was crying. Tears surprised me, because even at eight years old I hardly ever cried. I hadn't cried the first time Mom left us, back in Michigan, or when she called to say she wasn't going to be back in two weeks after all. I didn't cry when she came back for a few months only to leave again. Though I didn't know it yet, I wouldn't cry when Dad got hurt, or when I realized I was nothing to Gary but a container for something he wanted. I wouldn't cry when I was sure I'd been rejected from every college I wanted to attend. I wouldn't even cry when I was nationally embarrassed, when what was supposed to be a gateway to a profession I wanted was bolted in my face because of my own mistakes.

But I did cry, that long-ago night as we drove deeper into Maine, because I'd always imagined the dividing line between places as thin and exact, a hairline crack marking a profound and unassailable change. Now all borderlines seemed blurred.

"What's wrong?" Dad asked, finally noticing, and I wailed, "There was supposed to be a difference!" I needed a clearer geography. I was already living in a world with inscrutable boundaries. Did I or did I not, for example, have a mother?

"What?" Georgie asked, now. I realized I had muttered the words *I didn't know* under my breath.

"Nothing."

The silence was strained with all that Georgie wanted to know that I didn't know how to explain.

I said, "Are you and Tara—?"

"We broke up."

"I'm sorry."

Georgie shrugged. "It was probably going to happen anyway."

I didn't know what to say to this. Even if she was being honest, we couldn't deny that I was the one who had ended the first good relationship she'd had.

"I'm moving on," she said. But for the first time in as long as I'd known her, Georgie didn't sound comfortable drifting on to the next thing. She sounded sad and weary.

Georgie parked carefully behind Dad's truck. It looked like someone had made a poor effort at starting to rake the lawn. A corner patch was mostly cleared; the rest was thickly blanketed with brown, dusty leaves. Our collective failure would be gathered into this small house. I didn't know if I could stand it. I also didn't know why I'd ever expected anything else. You couldn't escape the past. That was the lesson of every novel I'd read, every history paper I'd written. Somehow I'd thought it didn't apply to me.

Each of us took a duffel. I grunted with effort as I maneuvered through the enclosed porch, with its mountains of shoes and years-old newspapers still rubber-banded. Georgie threw her weight against the door to pop it open. I saw Dad's feet first. They were levered up on the couch footrest, splayed open in sleep. When I turned the corner, my first thought was he looked dead. He was too still, too gray in the face. But when I approached, I saw the slight swelling in his chest.

"Why is he like this?" I asked, more loudly than necessary. I wanted to wake him up. Maybe then he would prove to me it wasn't as bad as it looked.

"It's his meds." Georgie's voice was quieter. "He needs a nap in the afternoons."

We were rousing him. He glanced at me, confused, then struggled out of his resting position. "Thank God you're home," he said, hugging me. When was the last time he'd hugged me? I forced myself to return the hug, briefly, then slithered out of his grasp. "I've been worried about you," he said.

Have you? I wanted to ask. *From your spot on the couch?* "I'm fine," I said.

"Georgie and I are here for you," he said. "We're family. We're going to support you." It seemed like what he thought he was supposed to say.

"Right now," I said, honestly, "I am hoping to be left alone."

• • •

NEITHER DAD NOR GEORGIE BOTHERED me for two days straight. I floated in and out of my bedroom, made sandwiches with ingredients I'd bought myself and which neither of them touched. I didn't open my laptop, didn't read emails, didn't look at the news. I reread books from the series I'd loved when I was younger: *Narnia*, *Redwall*, *A Wrinkle in Time*. The books had remained as I'd left them under my bed, lined up in order, hundreds of pages telling me to be brave and true and right, and not a single page about how to fix a mistake I'd sensed all along I was making and still suspected I'd make again if given the chance. Occasionally I walked down the street until I could see the cars flashing by on Route 9. I watched this movement like it was a river, then turned home, where I could feel the house absorbing me like I was one more messy pile.

Dad and Georgie had occasional conversations. Georgie would ask Dad if he wanted some cheese and crackers, or Dad would say, "Georgie, c'mere, see this," and then I'd hear them chuckling or agreeing softly about something. All Dad did when he saw me was ask how I was doing. He never had to ask Georgie that. He already knew.

There were brief periods when I was convinced it would all blow over, which was what Seamus had promised me, again, the last time I talked to him. There were still more periods when I saw that calm as artificial. I should be figuring out what I was doing next, but I couldn't face the question. In fact, that question was surprisingly easy to avoid. I'd once found a biology test of

Georgie's with a red *F* at the top. She'd answered less than half the questions.

"These are multiple choice," I'd said. "Why didn't you guess?"

"I didn't want to guess," she said, shrugging. It made no sense to me at the time. Now I saw how ignoring a question might be less painful than looking at everything you didn't know.

My third day home, I took out my laptop. Old windows, including from before Kramer's article, leapt to the screen. I began closing them out. But among them I found a Word document of notes toward what I had hoped would be my next piece. The one on teens and Oxy. Somehow I'd already lost track of how much work I'd done. I had ten single-spaced pages of quotations, links to news stories online. I remembered I had downloaded some journal articles from the Peabody library, and I found them in another folder on my desktop. It was comforting to see my old self at work, laying a foundation, ferreting out the most interesting details and angles. I put my fingers to the keyboard. I had no real hope of publishing this. But this was what I did, wasn't it? Wasn't it what I wanted to do?

An hour, maybe two had passed when I heard a tapping at my door. Georgie. "I'm going to the store," she said. "Anything I can get for you?"

"No thanks," I said.

She lingered cautiously. I missed Lily, how she would show up at my door, engage me in a subject serious or silly. How at first I might regret the interruption, but then, after she'd left, I found I was thinking more clearly.

"Want to come in?" I asked, and she did, sitting carefully on my bed. "I know it's dumb to be working on this," I said, gesturing at the document on my screen, "but I started this other article before . . ." I didn't need to finish the thought. I said, "It's about OxyContin dependency. A lot of teens get a prescription for even routine surgeries. Some of them end up addicted." I paused. "And some of them end up dead."

Georgie's eyebrows went up. "Whoa."

"I know."

"I bet you'd write a good article. Maybe—"

I shook my head, and she let it drop. Then, after glancing back through my open door, Georgie gently closed it.

"I'm well aware Dad is—that Dad has a serious issue with it now." Her voice had dropped to a near-whisper. "He's been doctor shopping. He drives over state lines. I don't know what to do."

"God," I said. It was worse than I'd thought.

"I should have told you sooner. He started getting extra pills around the time I moved out. But I didn't want to have to stay with Dad and worry about him."

I could see, now, the layers of her worry. I saw, even, her effort. It wasn't obvious like mine, it didn't result in accomplishments, but it was there. A real dedication. A willingness to be with someone, rather than just do something.

"You've been handling a lot," I said. "I . . ." Was I ready to apologize for this? Why not, though? "I'm sorry I haven't been here. I don't want you to blame yourself. The drug can do awful things. I know that now." I gestured at my research. "It's not your fault he's taking so much."

Something twitched in Georgie's expression. I took it for a flicker of deep feeling, possibly relief.

"Thanks," said Georgie. Then, "I don't expect you to stay here forever. You've got to move on. Dad and I will—" She let out a slow exhale that puffed her cheeks. "We'll figure it out."

I felt a swell of gratitude for her. She was right that I needed to leave. Staying would suffocate me. I would start by looking at local apartment listings.

"I wouldn't go far," I said. "I want to help out more." I paused. "And I can start doing some research. Dad would probably listen to me."

"More than he'd listen to me," Georgie said. Then, closing her eyes, "I would really, really appreciate that."

I knew now that I would leave the house as soon as I could. But there was one thing I had to do before I went. Something only I was capable of.

"Garbage bags," I told her. "That's what you can get me. The big black ones, like the kind they put in bins at the school cafeteria."

She nodded. She knew why I asked. The bags she brought me were thick as shower curtains. While she was at the nursing home the next day, I began. I would make the house livable again, even pleasant, before moving on. It was a penance I didn't mind. Dad came out of his room when he heard me shaking out a garbage bag so big I could probably use it as a parachute. He watched silently as I started in on a pile of magazines, VHS movies, and CD-ROMs. The main themes of what I found were Christian living, dog training, and pain management. I threw it all away. Within fifteen minutes I was seeing floorboards that hadn't been exposed in years. I glanced at Dad. He'd sat, was still watching me with an inscrutable expression. *Stop me if you want*, I thought. I dropped a stack of *Chicken Soup for the Soul* books into the bag. Not so much as a blink.

The next time I looked over, he was asleep. I worked through the rest of the living room, filling four bags and dragging them to the curb before walking into Dad's room. I gathered up the shirts that draped a shape I was pretty sure was a chair. I dropped the shirts down the basement stairs. A laundry pile. They needed to be washed. Everything needed to be washed. I filled another garbage bag with clothing I deemed too stained and worn to wear. Under his bed were four boxes of empty or mostly empty Kleenex, an inch of dust and dog hair, and two indistinguishable lumps that would require me to crawl through the dust to uncover, which even in my single-minded state I wasn't willing to do. On his bedside table were four glasses of water, two half-empty Poland Spring bottles, a stack of paperbacks, and two remotes for the small TV on the dresser. The bedside table had a drawer that was open two inches. In the drawer I saw orange pill bottles. So many bottles, all but two empty. Proof of what Georgie had told me. Some filled at a CVS in Westbrook, some at a Rite Aid in New Hampshire. One pill bottle had no label. I didn't know if this was concerning or not. I was tossing the empties when my eyes fell on one of the labels: *MARLENE WOODS*, it said. *OXYCODONE 40MG. NO REFILLS.*

This was odd, and possibly very troubling. Was he buying on the street? Part of me didn't want to know, but then again I wouldn't be able to stop a situation I didn't understand. I pocketed the bottle.

Three more bags were at the curb by the time the sun started to set. Dad lumbered up to me on my way to the shower and said, "I shouldn't have let it get this bad." I said, "No problem," and kept going. I wished he hadn't said anything. I wanted him to go back to denial. Denial was easier than both of us surveying the scope of his negligence.

While he settled in front of an NBA game, I went to his computer. He didn't have Wi-Fi and it was awkward to get my laptop connected to the yellow DSL cord that delivered his pokey internet service.

It took me less than a minute to locate Marlene Woods's obituary. She passed away peacefully at Pine Creek Senior Living Center. Family members by her side. I took out the pill bottle again. It was dated November, well before Georgie moved in with Tara. But well after she'd started working at Pine Creek.

In the next room over, the announcers started shouting, the crowd roared. "Can I borrow your truck?" I called. No response. I looked up directions to Pine Creek, then plucked Dad's keys from the wall beside the refrigerator. I needed a few minutes to adjust the seat so I could see over the hood. The truck was on the old side, nothing fancy, but it had a big engine. I drove fast.

Whether I would confront Georgie in front of anyone else I had not yet decided. But I would confront her, both with the evidence of what she'd done and with her lie to me, hours before. I couldn't believe *she'd* made *me* feel like I was receiving undeserved grace.

I was driving too fast now. I slowed so I wouldn't miss my turn.

The sliding glass doors parted easily for me, and I stood in a large foyer tinted pink by the setting sun. The man behind the front desk said, "Can I help you?" I recognized Georgie's work clothes on him.

"I'm looking for my sister, Georgie. She works here."

"Georgie's sister!" He brightened. "She'll probably be in the dining area, helping with the end of dinner. That way," he said, pointing. Then, as I walked down the hall, he called after me, "Nice to meet you!"

I'd expected Pine Creek to feel more depressing, just a waiting room for death. But it wasn't dreadful. From the dining area, there was a round of laughter. I found three old women sitting together.

"How can we help you?" one of them asked me. She had a white collared shirt under a flower-printed sweatshirt and a splotch of pink blush on either cheek.

"I'm looking for Georgie," I said.

"You're not her sister, are you?" another woman asked. This one wore large glasses and had a cluster of bristly white hairs under her chin.

The guess surprised me. People almost never claimed we looked alike unless they already knew we were related.

"She's told us about you," the woman with glasses and the tiny beard said. "You go to Peabody, don't you? She's so proud." A sick ache in my chest now, cavernous. "I always tell her, 'Be proud of yourself, too, Georgie. You don't have to go to Peabody to be someone important.' Don't I say that, Mary Jane?"

The third woman, petite and with a short, neat haircut, spoke now. "Your sister is really special. So caring and protective of us. But I bet you know that already. I bet she took good care of you, too."

I couldn't stay in this place where Georgie was so dependable and upright. I couldn't bear knowing that they told me the truth about who she was to them. I fled.

THE DIRECTIONS TO PINE CREEK had been too simple to write down. But now, distraught, I couldn't perform them in reverse.

When I first realized I'd made a wrong turn, I thought it would take five minutes to get back on track. Five minutes turned to fifteen. I found a road I thought was headed in the right direction, but ten more minutes passed and I still wasn't recognizing much. The light was fading faster now.

I passed a few houses, a shop that might be closed for the evening or, given its decrepit look, closed for good. I saw lights farther down the road. There seemed to be a clump of businesses up ahead. I pulled into the first parking lot I could.

It was the motel. Same row of windowless red doors facing a crummy parking lot. Same little office with the chipped black shutters. There was a light on inside. I could even see a figure behind the desk.

In a series of jerks bordering on reckless, I got the truck turned around. Just down the street was a tiny strip mall. One of those businesses had a lighted red sign: LIQUOR. So this was where Gary got it. Next to that, a grocery store that seemed to be open. It was the only place I could imagine entering.

The store had the quiet feel businesses do shortly before they close. Scraps of music overhead; in the distance, the clattering of baking pans. Of the three checkout lanes, only one had a cashier, a boy who looked fifteen. When I asked him for directions back to Curtisville, he said, "Where?"

"Curtisville," I said, impatiently. It wasn't *that* far away.

A woman was now in line behind me. Dark brown hair, slightly wavy, with a bit of gray at the temples. Dressed for comfort, not for show. In her cart were oranges, eggs, two loaves of bread. A teenager about the boy's age skipped toward us carrying a package of cookies. She had long, flat hair, wore slider sandals and a sweatshirt that said HORNETS JV SOCCER. The woman's face broke into a smile. Whether she was going to say no or yes to the cookies, she delighted in her daughter. She delighted in watching her do anything at all, even skip through a grocery store on a Tuesday night.

Then the woman turned to me. "I'll help you," she said.

In the parking lot she tried to give me directions. Her daughter stood there eating a cookie and watching me with big, innocent eyes. Sensing that I was computing nothing she was telling me, the woman reconsidered. "Follow me," she told me. "I'm going that way. I'll pull over at an intersection and turn my flashers on. Take a right. That's 237."

I'm sure I wouldn't have got home without her, swamped as I was in a grief so thick that her red taillights were all I could see. I didn't cry, though. It wasn't a grief like that. This was, maybe, the grief of finally knowing all that had been taken from me. What I should have had, and what I'd never now have. Grief at all the broken choices that dogged my every step.

I still couldn't believe how foolish Georgie had been, and then I wondered why I was surprised that she would be so foolish. Had she thought about what would happen if she were found out?

Angry as I was, I didn't want my sister to go to jail. Partly because of the problems that would cause for me, but more so because even I didn't think she deserved it.

What on earth, though, would teach her to *think*?

In front of me, the woman slowed, pulled over as promised. Her flashers a clear signal. I made the necessary right.

CHAPTER EIGHTEEN

GEORGIE

I know Jo's cleaning frenzy was on a Tuesday, because Wednesday morning was trash pickup, and I watched as men tossed the huge, glossy bags into the back of the compactor. I'd spent years thinking that, among all that junk, were important things that needed to be saved. As the truck roared away, though, I couldn't think of a single thing in the mess that truly mattered.

I was surprised I hadn't seen my sister yet. Usually she was already knocking around, getting up for snacks between stints at her computer. I drifted into the bathroom to shower. The rooms where Jo had done the most work gave me a new-haircut feeling—light, breezy, a few degrees cooler than I was used to.

Before I stepped into the shower, I pulled a crumpled gift bag from under the sink, filled it with empty shampoo and conditioner bottles, dried-out mascara tubes, nubby blue eyeliners, body glitter I bought in seventh grade. I was seeing things I hadn't really seen in years. Toilet paper tubes with one white square still glued to the cardboard. Small black combs threaded with hair. Rusty nail clippers, crinkled tubes of toothpaste, a stack of crossword books we used to keep by the toilet. Even while I showered I found a few things to get rid of. A graying loofah, two razors whose rubber grips were lined with mold, a rusted can of Barbasol.

I wasn't exactly doing this for Jo, but I expected her to appreciate it, so after my shower I walked into the living room, dropped the bag in the middle of the carpet. Jo was sitting cross-legged on the couch, tapping on her new laptop. She moved her eyes to me.

"The house looks nicer," I said.

"Thanks." Her eyes went back to the screen. "Getting ready for work?"

"Rita asked me to come in early." I liked how much inside information Rita was starting to reveal to me—family dramas, concerns about staffing and regulators, new protocols, inspection results. She shared all this with me like an equal, which, when I pointed this out, she said I practically was.

Jo nodded in a way that made me realize she wasn't really registering my answer. After our conversation a few days before, I thought we were on different footing now. Then again, I knew she had reasons for being hard to live with. So I pushed aside my disappointment and finished getting ready for work. I was surprised when she followed me to my car.

"What are you doing?" I asked, but she didn't say anything. I closed the door, buckled, saw the pill bottle on the dash.

I dropped my forehead onto the steering wheel, closed my eyes.

Jo got into the passenger seat. "It's interesting what you're not saying right now. You're not saying 'There's a good explanation.' Like, the bottle was empty and your earring broke and you needed to keep the pieces together. Or, I don't know, you found out Pine Creek doesn't recycle, and you wanted to save the planet and—"

Jo was still talking, but I couldn't hear much above the roar of how seriously I'd fucked up. Why had Dad hung on to the bottle? But also, why on earth would I think he would take care to dispose of them? Of all the junk in the house, how had Jo homed in on this?

"Are you listening?" she asked.

"Yes." My forehead was still against the steering wheel.

"What did I just say?"

"I have no idea."

"Look at me," she said. I looked. She was so much like Mom—so fierce when she was sure of herself, so fearful when she wasn't.

Now, she was fierce. I wondered briefly if it would help to tell her how extraordinary she seemed to me when she was like this.

She said, "Here's what you are going to do."

RITA'S OFFICE WAS NARROW, WITH a low ceiling. Behind her was a large window. Bits of light caught on her beaded earrings.

"Have a seat," she said, pushing a slim binder across her desk. The cover read *2008 North American Eldercare Conference*. In the front pocket was a registration sheet. "Pine Creek sends me every year," she said. "I was thinking that you should go this time. You'd learn a lot. I'd want you to do a short presentation for the staff when you get back. I already got approval from admin. Pine Creek would pay for your travel, lodging, and conference fees."

I could tell she'd been excited to surprise me with this. I closed the binder carefully, as if it were an ancient, crumbling document.

"You're not interested?" Rita asked crisply. "Or the dates don't work?"

I shook my head.

"Spit it out," she said.

"I'm quitting." I knew Rita would want me to use the real word for what I was doing, instead of softening it with a term like *leaving* or *moving on*. I said, "I can do my last two weeks or whatever."

Rita crossed her arms. "You're telling me this now."

"Something came up."

"Did someone die?"

"No."

"Is someone you love sick?"

"No."

"Are *you* sick?"

"No."

"Do you have a fantastic new job opportunity?"

Not trusting my voice anymore, I only shook my head.

Rita drew the binder back across the desk, stacked it on the other side of her computer, well out of my reach.

"People come and go a lot in this job," she said, though it was clear from her tone that she was not saying this to make me feel better. "But that means I'm always looking for who I can count on. Who's reliable? Who's got that combination of a good head on their shoulders and a good heart? Who sees this as more than a job, but doesn't get so attached that they wear themselves and everyone else out? I don't find those people often. You were only the second in my career. The first one manages an inpatient hospice center now. I was sure you'd do as well or better." She let this sink in. "And also," she said, "You have to think about what it looks like for you to be leaving so suddenly. Am I supposed to give you a good reference if I get a call in a few weeks from someone who's thinking about hiring you?" She paused. "Does any of this change your mind?" she asked.

"No," I whispered.

"Speak up," she barked.

"No," I said. "I'm sorry."

"All right, then." She turned to her computer to pull up the week's schedule. I saw a tremor in her hand. She was that mad. "I'm going to find a sub for you today. Come back tomorrow to sign your exit paperwork. I'll leave it at the front desk."

"If you need me to stay, I'm happy to—"

"Nope." She shook her head. "I'll figure it out."

When I lingered, she said, "Get out of here, Georgie. I have work to do."

I CROSSED THE TAR-PATCHED PARKING LOT, lowered myself into the car. A bright sun illuminated the dust on the dash. I wiped it off with a palm, then clapped my hands in the open air outside the car. The dust floated sideways and down, like ash.

I realized I was waiting for something. Maybe Rita would guess why I was leaving and she'd charge out the doors pointing an accusing finger at me. Or I'd get the confidence—or the recklessness—to go in there and tell her what had been happening right under her nose. Maybe she'd grant me some kind of immunity if I told her about Lee.

The automatic doors didn't budge, though, and neither did I. Afternoon droned around me, cars slid up and down the road. A kitchen worker came out with a bag of trash she heaved into the dumpster.

Jo had demanded only that I quit. She wasn't going to tell anyone. She said she didn't want me at Pine Creek anymore, because she was worried I'd take more and get caught, or give more to Dad. She reminded me that if I was found out, there would be jail time. And that would ruin Dad for good. I told her I had taken pills only a couple times, that I wasn't giving Dad anything now.

"You weren't buying them?" she asked.

"No!" I said, and then I caught myself. Her eyes bugged. "Just once!" I cried. She heard me with the suspicion of someone who's heard it all before. She seemed to think *I* was dependent on the pills, and she was right. They had reached out their tentacles and captured me, too.

The day was warm, and I drove with all my windows down. I tried to tell myself this was what I deserved. That I was, in fact, getting off easy. Air poured over me like a thick, fast river, swamping my senses. Maybe that's why I didn't feel my rage building.

When I turned into our driveway, I saw Jo loading one of her bags into the back of Dad's truck. Her glance in my direction said everything I needed to know. She was making her escape before I returned.

I parked the car. My hands jumped as if in response to a detonation somewhere deep in my body. When she came out of the house again, carrying her backpack in one arm and a bag of linens in the other, I stalked toward her. She put her things on the pavement, eyed me warily. I said, "You spent years nagging me about getting a real job and making a life for myself. Then, when I did exactly that, you had to ruin it because you're the only one around here who's allowed to have a good life."

Her eyes flashed. She was up for the fight. "You ruined it for yourself. I wanted you to apply to college. I wanted you to have a better life. And you wanted to sit around."

I realized this wasn't the argument I wanted to have anyway. "You don't know who you are unless you're superior to me," I said. "So you went around telling everyone at Peabody about, oh, your poor struggling sister who was raped. They're your friends and you can't even tell them the truth."

Her expression looked like a parody of joy. "I can't tell the truth? You're the one who's been stealing—"

"It wasn't like that!" I shouted.

"Of course an exception should be made for you," she continued. "Because it's you, Georgie, the perfect daughter everyone loves. You've never had to actually do the right thing as long as it seemed to everyone else that you were."

Her contempt was tidal, wiping me off the firm ground of who I was, of who I had always needed to be.

She stepped back, as if to get a better look at the sorry person I was. I got back into my car. I still can't say whether it was more anger at her or hatred of myself that decided my next move. I revved the engine in a way that made Jo retreat a few steps. But Jo didn't need to be worried about her own safety. It was her backpack—with her precious plastic MacBook in it—I aimed for. It felt too slight as I first drove over it, so I reversed for good measure. Jo cried out as if she'd been hit, then dropped to her knees to extract the fractured thing, hug it pitifully to her chest. She was rocking. Dad was stumbling out the side door. "What is going on?" he shouted at me, but the question was pointless with the broken computer in Jo's lap, me in the driver's seat of a car.

Watching my sister's unfettered grief, I tried to suppress the first pangs of regret. I left. My windows were still down. I imagined that the air pouring over me could wear away every selfish part of me. In time I could become a smooth kernel of goodness.

But I would have to live centuries for that to work. My life was too short for all my destructive edges to be worn away.

How long had I confused being calm with being good, being steady with being right? I'd lived as if the worst sin were anxiety, when most of the harm I'd done had come from insisting that I was at peace. I'd seen getting Dad pills as a short and even innocent error, rather than the grievous and dangerous wrong it was. I'd judged Jo for being uptight, even as I'd known, somewhere deep down, that I might have been part of her fear. I'd thought she was shallow for wanting recognition—but that's what I'd wanted, too, only in a different form.

I was driving toward Tara's. This was the final wild hope. That I could show up at Tara's door, sorry enough, desperate enough that she would help me.

And maybe she even would. I knew, somehow, that she would pity me. But it was too much to ask. I needed to bear my mistakes on my own.

I pulled onto the gravel at the side of the road, ran my hands repeatedly around the rim of the steering wheel, as if I could coax the car into being something other than the weapon I had used to destroy the last nice thing Jo had in this world.

I had nowhere to go except back home.

NATURALLY, JO AND DAD WERE gone when I returned. A cloud cover rolled in. I lay in bed for a while, then went to Jo's room. It looked like it had before she'd come home—neat, clean, sparse. I stood there until I could feel my presence disturbing the space she took such care to maintain. I heard Dad come in. He kept heaving sighs. I went out to see him.

"I screwed up," I said.

He opened and closed his hands, as if to say, *Well, yeah.*

"Where did she go?" I asked.

"She asked me not to tell you."

"Are you serious? I'm not going to go over there and—"

"I know," he said. He sank onto the couch. "You two used to be close. And then, right around my accident, that stopped."

I tried deflection. "You were hurt."

"I knew there was something else going on."

"Why didn't you say anything?"

He shrugged. "I didn't want to interfere."

But Dad, I thought, you should have interfered. It was your job to find out what was happening. Maybe you wouldn't have gotten something out of Jo, but you would have gotten something out of me. The essence of it, at least. Maybe you would have been able to put some pieces together—Jo's sudden aversion to church, the general direction of her quiet fury.

What might have been, had Dad involved himself, unspooled in my mind so neatly it was as if I'd lived it in another dimension. I could imagine the awful awkward conversation with her. How Jo could have found a way to say it without saying it. Then I imagined what would have been excruciating family counseling that still, somehow, had a healing effect. I imagined Dad confronting Pastor Mark. Confronting Gary.

I wanted to say something more to Dad, but he'd decided to heave himself upright. He needed some pills. I could tell when he was headed for them.

In his wake I reconsidered, imagined a different series of events. I imagined Jo letting on, but not quite spelling it out. I imagined the way Dad might rush to defend Gary, or worry whether Pastor Mark knew—or, if he knew, what he thought of it. I imagined Dad insisting that Gary and Jo get married, just as he had married Mom.

But how could that have worked? Jo had just turned fourteen.

Jo had just turned *fourteen.*

The fact of her age wasn't new to me, but the meaning of it was. I felt sick. Night filtered slowly into the room. I could hear the television in Dad's room. He might be awake. Why not tell him everything? I was tired of secrets. It was time it all came out.

In his dim room, I snapped off the TV. I said, "There's something you should know." I turned around. Even in the shadow, Dad's gaze was so flat I couldn't read it at first—Anger? Disappointment? Despair? I said, "I'm sorry I didn't tell you this before. Something bad did happen to Jo, but it involved Gary, and we never told you about it." I stepped closer. "Dad?" I raced for the switch, and the overhead light flooded the room. He was grayish and still. I put a hand on his chest. It wasn't moving. Or was it moving? Slightly? I felt for his pulse—finally, a faint heartbeat.

I couldn't say how long I spent shaking him and shouting—probably no more than five or seven seconds, but that scrap of time is still stuck somehow to the present, so that some part of me will always be there in that room, afraid it's too late.

There were two paramedics, a guy and a girl. They ignored me as they bent over him. One pulled down the side of his sweatpants to give him an injection. They didn't wait for it to work, just started carrying him out. I helped them lift his body.

He needed another dose of naloxone on the way to the hospital. If I had called even a few minutes later he might have been gone. But I didn't know that yet. By the time I saw him again, in the ER, he was shivering and groaning. Withdrawal, I was told.

And even in that moment, I wanted to say, *He's not an addict.*

"I'm here," I told him, but he didn't seem to hear me, and

instead bent over the bed to puke in a bucket. Later, when I walked down the hall to do paperwork, I saw another overdose come in. I recognized him—Kyle Wooter. He'd been a few years ahead of me in school. I heard one of the techs say, "One more and it will be a hat trick for today."

I knew not to be offended by this—I knew, from working at Pine Creek, that dark humor is the only way to talk about things that you can't actually mourn because you have a job to do.

Back in the room, I found Dad staring at the wall. He'd finally gotten some methadone to help with the withdrawal.

"I don't want Jo to know about this," he said.

"That's fine." I agreed before I'd even thought about it. Of course Jo should know about it. She was the best suited among the three of us to figure out what to do next.

"It wasn't a—I wasn't trying to—it was accidental," Dad said. But then he turned away from me.

"It's okay," I said, though we both knew that nothing was.

The doctors told me they'd keep him there for up to two days. That was hospital policy. After that I'd need a plan. But for a plan I needed my sister, and I didn't know where she was.

JO

CHAPTER NINETEEN

I signed for my new apartment online just hours after I decided what I was going to make Georgie do. After she left for work, I'd disappear. I knew it was cowardly. I even started wondering if I really needed to make her do this. If she refused, I had no recourse. She had to know that. Up until the moment she disappeared around the wall of trees in the road's wide bend, I expected her to stop, throw the car in reverse, come screeching back to call my bluff: "What are you going to do if I refuse to quit? Send me to prison?"

Of course I wasn't. She was a good person. At least, she had a kind of innocent belief that all you had to do was make the right decisions and everything would work out for you. That was how Dad had been, too, stoutly giving up more than he ever should have, because he believed someone else's story about what was right.

It was pathetic, wasn't it? But then I asked myself what might have become of us if Dad hadn't remained devoted to Mom, and then to us. I had partly blamed Dad for driving Mom away. But Mom left us as much as she left him.

And maybe Dad hadn't simply done what Mark told him to do. Maybe all these years he had given Mark credit for telling him to do what he would have done anyway.

I knew I was justified in telling Georgie she had to quit her job.

But the sorrowful way she accepted my terms somehow meant that maybe she shouldn't have to. Maybe I'd pushed her too far.

Then I reminded myself how serious her crimes were. Her *crimes*. My errors were, technically, professional. I hadn't knowingly written lies in my article. Taking those photos was a civil offense, but nothing compared to trafficking in federally controlled substances. Where was the justice in my life being destroyed, and hers being left intact?

So, while she was off quitting her job like I had decided she was supposed to, I told myself this was right. She herself thought it was right. I planned to give us a few days or weeks. Then we'd start figuring things out. Like what to do about us. And what to do about Dad. First, though, I had to move out. I didn't realize, until Georgie left, how badly I wanted to be gone before she came back. I asked Dad for a ride to Coswell Island. I only said I was moving out. He didn't ask questions. My mistake was in underestimating how much he was going to slow me down. Did I have enough in the way of furnishings? Kitchenware? I accepted an extra power strip, table lamp, and saucepan, just because it was easier than saying no. When Dad disappeared into his room, I was glad to get him out of the way, even if it meant more loading up for me.

While I was pumping up the tires on my old bike, he came out with a box of things he wanted me to have. You'd think I was moving four states away, not twenty minutes. He started showing me what was in there: my fourth-grade Student of the Year award, a yarn mat I'd woven in middle school, a baby book Mom had kept for me and Georgie. "She didn't end up writing much in it," he said, taking it out and opening to a blank page decorated faintly with teddy bears. "But in case you want to see—"

"Thanks." I took the book from him, dropped it back into the box. I couldn't stand this right now. Plus, I didn't have time.

We almost made it. I was coming out with my last load when I saw a flashing through the trees twenty yards down Henry Street. Georgie, in the silver wagon. Her rage somehow as clear to me as the reality of the tires turning onto our driveway.

ON OUR WAY TO THE island, Dad asked if I was all right.

"I'm fine," I said. My backpack was at my feet, the broken laptop back in its sleeve. I already knew I wouldn't be able to touch it again for a while.

"I didn't raise her like that."

"I know." This was true. Georgie and I had our fights when we were younger, but they'd never been so destructive. She'd never been cruel.

Neither, though, had I.

When I didn't respond, he said, "Are you all right?"

"You already asked me," I said. "It was a bad argument. It's just a computer."

"I know you're fine," he said. "But are you *all right*?"

This I could not answer. At least he didn't try to talk it out, didn't try to force some Dad-and-daughter heart-to-heart. I wondered if the silence that accompanied us on the rest of the drive was the right moment to say it: *Dad, are* you *all right?* Or maybe, *Dad, you can get help*. I had by this point started a list of clinics, treatment centers, though they were on the laptop. I'd even started researching his options for bankruptcy. But now, in his presence, I faltered. What if I said the wrong thing? What if talking only made everything worse?

Was this why Georgie avoided the subject with Dad? Or why she'd never tried to talk to me about what happened with Gary?

But I didn't want to think about that. So the next moment kept being the moment in which I spoke, and then we were arriving at the rental, and I was busy trying to keep Dad from carrying anything too heavy for him, and then I was hugging him, and then he was gone.

"I want to have done right by you," Dad said.

I couldn't look at him. "You did," I said. I wasn't sure that I meant it, but I wanted to mean it, which was maybe the same thing.

COSWELL ISLAND WAS ABOUT A mile in circumference and dotted with mostly modest houses, though every once in a while there was a brand-new structure or a gleaming addition too large for the plot it sat on. My furnished studio was in the daylight basement of one of the smaller, older houses. The entrance was a sliding glass door, hung with a heavy curtain for privacy. Inside was a wicker love seat, a tiny kitchen area with a toaster oven and microwave, a boxy TV with a VHS/DVD player built in, and a curtained-off corner for a bed. Down a nub of a hallway was a closet, a bathroom barely larger than the closet, and a door leading to the upstairs. On the door was a handwritten note: *Emergency use only.*

It didn't take long to unpack. Clothes in the small dresser, a few books by the window, sheets on the bed. I would need to bike to the local Shaw's for food. If I left soon I could get back before dark.

The last thing I put away was the box of keepsakes Dad had given me. I was trying to lift it onto the highest shelf in the closet when the bottom gave way, and I leapt back to avoid the falling trophies. The glass broke on my Student of the Year award. I was shoving it all back in the box when I saw a silver disc. *Good Guys ep 1–4*, it read in Sharpie handwriting I'd recognize anywhere. On the back of the jewel case was a sticky note: *Thought you and the girls would like a copy!*

Instead of going to the store, I sat and watched all four episodes on the old TV. I had seen the first two episodes when they aired almost seven years before. Watching it again, I recognized little. At the center of the show were four male friends, each styled to be different from the others in a way that masked their essential sameness. Tony was dark-haired and muscular, Jimmy was tall and clumsy, Jake was round and fast-talking, and Carl was small and liked to fight. All four were being divorced by their wives: Tony for kissing his high school girlfriend at a bachelor party; Carl for being emotionally unavailable; Jake for losing his fourth job in a row; Jimmy for being a general slob.

The premise was that while the guys had made mistakes they weren't adequately sorry for, they were likable and funny in a way that made you want to forgive them. So the whole premise was actually, as the title made clear, that the guys were good.

Part of me wanted to write a paper destroying the show, and part of me wanted to write Mom and ask, rhetorically, if she was proud of this.

I was so confused. I'd spent years mentioning the show to people because I'd thought it was at least okay. I'd thought it was a neat thing that Mom did. Now I saw that it wasn't.

It was too late to bike to Shaw's, so I ate the only food I had, a frozen burrito Dad had insisted on giving me. The toaster oven took forever, and I gave up on waiting while there were still ice crystals in the middle. I made the bed and tried to sleep, but my thoughts were a jumble of scenes from the shows, and the sound that came from my backpack beneath the tire of Georgie's car, and how Dad was so worried, and how Mom used to tuck the same lock of my hair behind my ear, over and over, while she told me about her big dreams.

She had made her dreams mine to the point that I had been willing to smother parts of my grief over her leaving.

The effort had been worthless.

I HALF EXPECTED NOT TO receive my payment from *THE YANK*, but it landed in my checking account shortly after I moved in. I had enough to buy a used Camry. I could live for another couple months on what was left over, but I couldn't let myself sit around and watch my account dwindle. I applied to be a substitute teacher. I'd heard once that it was an easy way to get decent pay. There were only a couple weeks left in the school year, but the administrator I talked to assured me they had a shortage. All I had to do was fill out an online form and do a background check.

I thought the background check would take at least a week, but three days after I signed off on it I got a call at five-thirty in the morning. It was the first call I'd received on the basement landline; the phone jangled so violently I startled upright, confused and panicking.

They wanted me to fill in for a math teacher at my old high school.

I wore a cardigan over my cherry-print blouse. I hoped I looked older and stern, but I wasn't halfway through attendance during first-period algebra when a guy in the back row called, "How old are you, anyway?"

"Old enough," I said, without looking up from my printout. "Kelsey Farringer?"

"She's not a day over twenty-four," he stage-whispered to the guy next to him. General laughter. I kept my expression even. If only I were going on twenty-four.

"Kelsey Farringer?" I repeated.

"She's right there," he said. "Kelsey! Hey, Kelsey!"

A girl on the window side of the room lurched upright. She'd been hunched over a sketch pad, her long hair hanging like a barrier between her and the rest of the class. "Here," she said apologetically.

"What are you drawing, Kelsey?" the guy asked. "She's an *artist*," he said. He was talking toward me, but for the sake of everyone. I registered, now, his size. He was one of those high schoolers who made a standard desk look like it was designed for a first-grader.

I saw it immediately: Gary's moves recycled through him.

Weirder still to realize that Gary's moves were recycled from someone else's.

He was the last one on my attendance sheet. I readied myself to parry whatever stunt he wanted to pull. Then my eyes fell on the name: *Travis Wojciechowski*. He was grinning at me.

"Travis . . ." I said.

"It's *Whujahousekey*," he said, so quickly I still couldn't catch it. "Now you try."

"No thanks." I made a check next to his name.

"That's disrespecting my culture. I'm going to tell the principal."

Why were they like this? The cool guys? Why was everything an opportunity to remind you that they were strong and you were weak? Why did nothing work against them except a collected clarity I'd never had? Why did Kelsey Farringer seem more equipped to handle life than I did? I stared at him, anger red in my cheeks. Someone said, "Oooh, she's mad at you." He smiled. He had me right where he wanted me.

I walked to the principal's office.

"I have to go," I said.

"What?" The assistant was the same woman who had sat at this desk when I was a high school student. She had a pleasant round face, wore earrings that matched her necklace. A plastic placard, styled to look like wood, had her name engraved on it: Ms. ROSLYN.

"Sorry," I said. "I can't do this." I was shaking a little.

"Is it Travis?" she asked. She lowered her voice. "Honey, he's just a little shit."

I couldn't help laughing. I looked at her then, really saw her, a woman most people wouldn't call pretty, a woman whose clothes even I could tell were out of touch. A woman whose big smile hid the knowledge in her eyes. Maybe I was inventing our connection, but I half believed we were thinking the same thing: *Travis might not be just a little shit. He might be worse. But what could we do about that?*

"Here," she said, getting to her feet. "I'll walk you back." She produced a flowery sign that read, *BACK IN FIVE . . . OR MAYBE NEVER!*

I could only follow dumbly. As we walked into the room, she said, loudly, "And since you asked about detention slips, I'll show you where Mr. Bixby keeps them."

"I didn't do anything!" Travis said. "She wouldn't even say my name!"

"Here's how you fill them out," Ms. Roslyn told me, waving me over. As we pretended to look at the yellow stack of detention slips, she whispered, "You can do this."

THE NEXT WEEK, I WENT to the public library to browse their books and check my email. I had a message from Lily. She'd be at her family's island house for the second week of June and wanted me to come visit. I made a brief attempt to read pity into her email, but the tone wouldn't stick. Besides, I wanted to see her.

I took the ferry over on a blustery day. I always forgot how much colder the air was over the water, even in the bay. I started on the upper deck, then retreated to a lower floor, to get the same view but through scratched windows. Lily met me at the dock, gave me a big hug, insisted on pulling my suitcase all the way to the house, about half a mile away. Somehow we managed to talk animatedly without touching on the subjects of Peabody, my article, or my current situation.

I unpacked my things in the guest room, which had an old braided rug on a painted wood floor and a bed whose frame emitted a mighty squeal when I sat on it. Lily introduced me to her parents. Mrs. Neils had a tidy bob and gold-rimmed glasses, and Mr. Neils had a light brown beard flecked with gray. I could see Lily's future in the kind-looking lines around their eyes.

"I hope you like japchae," Mr. Neils said.

"With beef bulgogi," Mrs. Neils added.

"Tina makes the best," Mr. Neils told me.

They looked at me with hopeful expectation. I hesitated, feeling incurably provincial. Then I smiled. "I like everything," I said.

Mrs. Neils laughed. "Right answer," she said, and shooed me

out to the porch with a glass of lemonade. I sat on a weather-worn Adirondack, listened to the crash and pause of the waves fifty feet away, closed my eyes against the late-day sun, warm but not hot. I felt comfortable for the first time in weeks. I liked the mismatched old interior of the house and their no-nonsense kindness.

Once Lily was done with her dinner duties, she joined me on the porch.

"We don't own this house," Lily said. I wasn't looking at her, but somehow knew she had also closed her eyes against the sun. "It belonged to my great-aunt. My dad's cousins let us stay here for free for a week each summer." Her comment was gently pointed.

"I wasn't fair to you," I told her. I needed to state the simple truth.

She nodded. "True. But you were also more of a friend than you know."

"I hope so," I said. Could it be that, despite how wrapped up I'd been in my own story the last few months, I'd managed to be there for her in ways I simply wasn't recognizing? *Please*, I thought, my heart lurching a little, the feeling strangely familiar. Then I remembered my earliest instances of prayer: earnest, simple, almost wordless.

I didn't know to whom I might be praying. But, right now, I didn't need to.

We listened to four wave crashes. I told her how my old Spanish teacher, Señor Ortega, had laid out a plan for me. He said I should finish my degree at Southern Maine and then stay there for a master's in teaching. I could even get provisionally hired as a teacher while working on the master's part-time, as he had.

"So that's what you'll do?" Lily asked.

"I actually like substitute teaching, so I think I'd like regular teaching, too." I thought of the regular lunches I had with the assistant, Ms. Roslyn. How her stories about the students—their alcoholic parents or brothers in jail, the horrible divorces they'd witnessed—had somehow told me how to be with them. I couldn't hate anyone whose saddest secrets I knew.

"You'd be a good teacher," Lily said. "I never wanted to say it because I knew you hated when Edgar told you that. But you were always a big help to us on our papers."

"Thanks," I said, pleased. Then, "I'd rather hear it from you than from him."

"Ha," she said.

Señor Ortega didn't think I'd keep teaching for long. "Teach for a while. In ten years, go get a PhD, change careers, or whatever." I could see him work to reframe the point. "I mean, thirty is still young. The decision you make now is about where you start, not where you end."

Lily and I had opened our eyes. We watched a black-and-yellow ferry churn toward one of the neighboring islands. Gulls wheeled and dove over a lobster boat. I could feel myself breathing. This wasn't box breathing. It was involuntary, slow and deep, continuous as the water folding itself over at the edge of the ocean. It was the sun, I thought. No, the rest. Then I thought, no, it's the company. I closed my eyes to feel the shape and texture of this friendship, a container holding both of us exactly as we were.

CHAPTER TWENTY

GEORGIE

The breaking-ground ceremony for the gym was scheduled for Gary's birthday. Pastor Mark had all the money he'd hoped for and more. He'd even been featured on a national morning news segment. He'd quoted Romans 8:28. *In all things God works for the good of those who love him.*

I hoped Jo hadn't seen it, but I hadn't wanted to ask. Every third day now she took Dad to the methadone clinic. I'd wave to her from the window and she'd wave to me from her car. About once a week we talked on the phone—about Dad, and how his treatment was going, and what options he had.

Dad seemed to be doing well, but the fact worried both of us.

Two weeks after this protocol began, she let herself into the house. I found her looking around quietly. I had continued her work. The house wasn't spotless, but it was different. I was deciding what belonged on which shelf, finally making all those decisions about what we didn't need.

"It looks nice," she said.

"I'm not done."

"I know."

I wanted to tell her that I'd done much of this cleaning at night, when I couldn't sleep for fear that Dad had gotten more pills, that he had a hidden stash, that he'd take too many again, that I'd wake up to find him dead. I wanted to tell her, too, how now that Dad was steadier, the gravity of what I'd done had become a black hole of regret. It wasn't wrong in the criminal sense only. I'd been foolish. I'd been selfish. If he'd died of an overdose, I would've been partly to blame.

I'd heard that Lee had moved to Connecticut. I didn't know if that meant someone was onto him or whether he was simply taking his business elsewhere. It was not out of the question that the police would show up on my driveway at some point. I could only hope that by the time Lee was caught, he'd have forgotten I ever bought anything from him, or it somehow wouldn't matter anymore.

A few nights before, I'd written Jo an apology partly about the laptop and partly about everything else, then rewritten it to take out everything that sounded too close to an excuse. I had the letter in my room now, and wanted to give it to her, but also wondered if it would be self-serving to do so.

"Jo—" I started.

She waved me away. "I know."

I wasn't sure what she meant by this, but now Dad was coming into the room. He eyed us warily.

"Ready?" Jo asked him.

He nodded and followed her out to the car. I saw her wait for him to buckle himself, saw her adjust the vents just so. I wondered if she wasn't going to leave us after all—not to say that I thought she would live nearby forever. But I wasn't sure anymore that she would, like Mom, pick up almost every trace of herself as she went.

DAD AND I TRIED TO make the best of a dreary Fourth of July situation by grilling hot dogs in the backyard. Hulk lay on the back patio with his chin on his paws. When I rolled a tennis ball across the lawn, he looked at me like I had to be kidding.

Dad had gotten through the first ninety days of methadone and was on an every-other-day schedule. He was already talking about weaning himself off, which neither Jo nor I were ready for. Right now he was listening to us, but I could tell his resolve was building, and I dreaded having to face him when he was sure. He was going to his twelve-step meetings. He had made some friends there. One of them went to a different church, which Dad had visited with her. He said they weren't dating, but I still wondered.

I was bagging groceries at the Yarmouth Shaw's, but I'd recently landed an interview for a job as a home aide in Freeport. The job was three fourteen-hour shifts a week. Dad, who had not pressed me for details when I said I'd left Pine Creek, talked like everything was going to work out, but there was something too stiff and habitual about the conversations to be convincing. The truth was that neither of us knew if any of it was going to work.

Dad was distributing buns onto the grill for toasting when I heard a car engine shut off. Something about how the door slammed told me who it was. I jogged around the side of the house, cursed the sticky latch on the fence, tried to get to her before she changed her mind. She was wearing a thin sweater, blue with colored flecks. Her cutoff shorts trailed six-inch white threads to her knees.

When I was close enough, I saw that there was something a little wild in her expression, like she'd just come out of a deep woods.

"I met up with Jo," she said. "I barely know why I agreed to talk to her. I guess I thought maybe I could prove to her how bad she'd made this whole thing for us." She looked at my feet, then up at me. "She told me what my brother did to her."

Something in my chest sank. It wasn't bad news, but it wasn't good news, either. Tara had a hand in her hair, was tugging a clump of it as if it were attached to thoughts she was trying to produce. "Why didn't you tell me? Did you not trust me? Did you not think it was pertinent?"

I didn't tell her because Jo didn't want me to. Because Tara would want to make it right and couldn't. Because Tara didn't know that being Jo's sister was like hearing little whispers for help from behind a door slammed and bolted in your face.

"I couldn't," I said. "I tried to talk to her about it once and she shut me down."

"You tried to talk to her *once*?" Tara's look put a crack in my confidence. The crack spread, branched.

"Did you come all the way here," I asked, wearily, "to tell me I'm a bad sister?"

"No. I am. Obviously." She turned toward her car, and I was afraid she was going to get in. But she leaned against the hood. "I needed to tell you that I know. I get it now. Why she decided the story had to be told that way."

"I think she likes you," I said. "Respects you, I mean."

"She said as much," Tara said. Then, reading me perfectly, "I'm not best friends with your sister now. We're not going to start hanging out without you."

She knew I wanted to go back. I wanted to be in the trailer when Tara returned from turning off someone's water on a subzero night. I wanted to hang wet socks above the woodstove, I wanted to swim a six-pack of beer out to the middle of the pond. Wanted to claim her mouth, wanted her to push her nose into the warmth of my neck.

Somewhere in the distance were two muted pops. Fireworks were illegal in Maine, but people drove to New Hampshire to buy them.

"I miss you," I said.

"We're not getting back together."

"I'm not trying to—" I said, but we both knew I was. She was looking at me as if I were an old shirt or piece of jewelry she was lingering over before putting back in a drawer. I reached for something to say, to hold her here. "Are there any more updates about the investigation?"

"It seems everyone's working on it now. Maybe someone will get to the bottom of it. Gadson was almost definitely the one who took the body parts." She seemed relieved to share. "Now the question is how many others knew about it, and whether Gary took photos to incriminate Gadson or whether he was taking photos for his own reasons, maybe because he thought it was cool or maybe because he wanted to be able to blackmail Gadson later. I'd like to believe Gary meant to do the right thing, but I can't say that for sure. Maybe no one ever will." She shrugged. "Time might tell, though I don't know how many people will still be paying attention if it ever does. My parents still think he was a hero."

Another *pop pop pop*, and I heard Hulk whining. He was following Dad, who'd come around the house to see who was here.

"Food's ready," he told me. And, "Hi, Tara." Then, a little awkwardly, "You're welcome to stay."

She shook her head. "No thanks." Dad nodded and turned back toward the yard.

"One last thing," Tara said. "I've had a chance to think. I was relying on you in a way that wasn't good for me. That's not your fault, but it does mean you won't be seeing me for a while." She shook her head to keep me from saying anything more. "You want this relationship most when you're not in it. I think you'll be okay."

A FEW DAYS LATER I was eating one of the leftover hot dogs—Dad had made far too many—when the phone rang. I leapt to get it. I was trying to intercept calls from the collection agencies while we sorted out the bankruptcy.

"Georgie? Is that you?"

My heart stumbled. "Mom?"

"Hi, honey. How are you?"

My eyes bugged at the inanity of the question. "Fine," I said. I didn't ask how she was. I didn't care.

"I'm trying to track down your sister," she offered into my silence. "I saw some news about her that made me want to reach out." Then, stiffly, "I do try to follow how you two are doing."

But the news about Jo was months old. Had Mom only just found out? Or had she simply waited this long to call?

"I'm trying to offer her some support," she said. I liked sensing that she had become wary of me. "I called the Peabody offices, but they couldn't help me. They cited some privacy thing."

I didn't confirm this.

Mom sighed. "I'm aware that you and I have plenty to talk about as well."

Did we? I didn't think so.

"Can you tell me anything at all about how I can contact her?" she asked. Her neat, can-do facade was crumbling. But I found I didn't want her to beg, not out of pity for her but because I didn't want to deal with it.

"I'll take your phone number," I said. "If you want."

"Sure," she said. I wrote it on a cereal box tab because I couldn't find paper fast enough.

"I gotta go," I said.

"Then I won't keep you. Love you, Georgie. Bye."

I shook my head at the phone. *Love you, Georgie?* She didn't love me. Still, I hated the way the phrase snagged in my mind. *Love you, Georgie.*

"Who was that?" Dad asked me.

"Jo," I said. "She's just checking in."

I liked that he believed me—that he saw Jo calling to check in as a normal thing. Because by that point it kind of was.

THE NEXT MORNING I DROVE to Coswell Island with the cardboard in the breast pocket of my shirt. Maybe she wouldn't want me showing up at her home. Maybe I should give it to her at the door, or slip it into her mailbox. We were still capable of wounding each other. Maybe that was reason to keep our distance for a while longer. Indefinitely, even.

But we had kept our distance for years, and look where that got us.

Besides, I really thought Jo would want me to bring her this news in person.

AS I DROVE ACROSS THE bridge to the island, I saw kids playing on the beach below. I remembered how, when Mom visited us in Maine before leaving for good, Dad had rented a house on Higgins Beach for a couple nights. He was trying to prove to Mom that we could be a family. But Mom spent most of the time reading novels on the couch and phoning her friends in California, and Jo started doing that thing where she was clinging to Mom while trying not to look like she was clinging to Mom.

The second day, I found my sister doing a jigsaw puzzle in the living room, ten feet from where Mom was scribbling on a manuscript.

"Come outside," I told her. "Let's play."

"I don't want to," she said, without looking up.

"We can build a moat," I offered.

"You *dig* a moat," Jo said. "And no."

Something roused Mom. She looked up at us with those sharp eyes that brooked no disagreement. "Go with your sister, Jo. Have some fun."

Jo paused like she might resist, but instead said, "There's only one shovel."

"You can have it," I pleaded. "I'll use my hands."

She followed me, blinking, into the sun.

The moat game is simple. It's not even a game, because there's no chance at winning. Still, most kids who visit an ocean beach try it eventually. You dig a trough in front of the oncoming tide. The idea is that if you dig deep and wide and fast enough, you can stop the water coming up the beach. Part of you knows it's impossible and part of you is sure you can do it. Maybe because of the *work* element, Jo was absorbed from the second her shovel hit sand. I matched my effort to hers, first heaving sand with both of my hands and then running back to the house for a Tupperware still lined with watermelon juice and seeds. I scooped chunks of wet sand, threw them blindly behind my head, where they landed with a heavy splat.

Our moat must have been three feet deep when the first wave nudged a tongue of foam down its damp, cool wall. We doubled our efforts, shouting and shrieking and bailing, until we were swamped. We ran up the beach laughing, collapsed in a sandy heap on the couch. Mom had gone somewhere else, but we didn't need her anyway.

I liked thinking about that afternoon we spent hurrying to prevent the inevitable. On some level we knew we'd fail, but each of us kept going anyway, because the other hadn't given up.

We returned to the beach at sunset. The tide was out again, and we walked slowly on the smooth sand where we'd played. No sign of our struggle remained.

ACKNOWLEDGMENTS

The history of *Good Guys* is full of good people.

My haphazard obsession with writing was guided by brilliant teachers including Jim Shepard, Karen Russell, Peter Ho Davies, and Michael Byers. Thank you all.

Over quite a few years of writing and rewriting, friends and family read and responded to drafts and excerpts. Thank you, Ali Shapiro, Maya West, Inez Tan, Katherine Jamieson, Jean Arthur, Debby Greene, Brooke Carnwath, Carter Walker, Mari Anzicek, Linda Misener, Ruth Misener, Andrew McPherson, Julie McNamara, Amy Leach, and Jennifer Acker. Special thanks to Megan Sweeney, for your many insightful questions as the story found its footing.

Thank you, Claire Luby and Daniel Grant, for lending me your home. Thank you, Sarah Drummond, for the vision of belonging. Thank you, Carl Bromley, for that coffee. Thank you, Esther Kim, for the home stretch help.

My agent, Lauren Wendelken, championed this book and provided invaluable feedback along the way. My editor, Michelle Capone, brought tremendous skill to this project and understood so well—often better than I did—the heart of the novel. Thank you, thank you. Thank you, Mike Lindgren, Katrina Weidknecht, Pia Mulleady, Jay Pabarue, and Hanna Lafferty.

Thank you to my parents, Chris and Linda Misener—for your bottomless love, for reading to me, for encouraging me to find my own way. Thank you to my all-star siblings, Ruth Misener and

John Misener, for decades of care and companionship. Thank you to my MIL and FIL, Gail Anderson and Daniel Elsass, for believing in me so thoroughly and for welcoming me into your family.

Thank you to my husband and most valued reader, Kirke Elsass, for giving me so much time to write while you were working on a dissertation. You are the truest friend a heart could hope for. And thank you, Linden and Kira, for raising your mama and letting your mama raise you. You bring me more joy than you will ever, ever know.

MINDY MISENER grew up in Maine. She is a graduate of Williams College and the University of Michigan's Helen Zell Writers' Program. Her prose has appeared in *Image*, *The Missouri Review*, *The Common*, *The Christian Century*, and other outlets. Currently a student at Yale Divinity School, she is on track to be ordained in the UCC.